FRAUD:
WHY DID THEY DO
IT?

Bill Duff

First Published 2008 by Appin Press, an imprint of Countyvise Ltd.,
14 Appin Road, Birkenhead, Wirral CH41 9HH.

British Library Cataloguing in Publication Data.
A catalogue record for this book is available from the British Library.

ISBN 978 1 906205 20 1

ACKNOWLEDGEMENTS

The Institute of Counter Fraud Specialists (ICFS) and the Counter Fraud and Security Management Service (CFSMS) from both of which I was able to obtain research into fraud cases during my employment as a Fraud Specialist.

Robert Holland, Property Sales, La Manga, who provided me with background into property purchases in Spain.

Walk Andalucia, whose walking holidays gave me the thoughts for the introduction of the two main characters.

1

David Parish is a Fraud Consultant within both the Public Sector and Private Sector, where he investigates fraud on behalf of the Health Service, Local Authorities, Pension Schemes and the Benefits Agencies. He also acts as a Consultant Fraud Expert for Insurance Companies across Europe and has a strong relationship with the police both in the United Kingdom and Europe. The police, who will often contact David for advice, gave him the nickname Mr Fraud which now follows him throughout the legal establishment.

David Parish's prowess as a Fraud Consultant has earned him great respect and demand in an area where criminal activity is now seen as highly productive, for both teams of gangsters and individuals, who think they have found an easy way to make money. His tenacity and investigative skills have led him to many parts of the world in the search for fraudsters. The end result is often the incarceration of many who have tried but failed to escape the clutches of David Parish. There is no freedom for fraudsters.

Paul and Anita Chambers left their Basingstoke home and rushed with their three year old daughter, Susannah, to get the bus, and make sure that they caught the 7.17 a.m. South West train from Basingstoke Station.

When they arrived at Waterloo at eight o'clock, the rush hour was in full swing with people dashing in all directions, they had to hang on to Susannah hard as she nearly got knocked over by the crowds. They walked quickly downstairs to the Tube station and caught the tube train for the six stops to Euston. It was then only a short walk, and it was only a quarter to nine when they entered the Children's Ear, Nose and Throat Ward, in Euston General Hospital, London. Susannah was having specialist treatment to her ears, and had been referred to Mr Ali at Euston General Hospital. It was the third time they had made this awful journey, but this, they were hopeful, would be their last, at least it was the first time that they had all managed to get their three seats together on the train.

They were due to see the consultant later today, and any further treatment should then be able to be completed in Basingstoke. They bought a couple of steaming hot coffees from the vending machine and looked for somewhere to sit down and relax after their hectic journey. In the waiting area, they sat next to another couple who also had a young daughter. They appeared to be similar ages to Paul and Anita who were twenty eight and twenty seven years old respectively. The two young girls started playing together with the dolls and toys while they waited for the Doctor.

Anita said to the lady. "It is nice to see the children play together, Susannah has been having problems with her ears and is now having grommets inserted. What's your daughter in for?"

The other lady replied "Alice is going to have a throat operation, there's a problem with her adenoids so she will be in for a good week or more. Oh, I'm Zoe, this is my partner Rik".

"I'm Anita. That's my husband Paul and our daughter, Susannah, she's three".

The girls continued with their game and Paul finally got chatting to Rik

"Did you have far to travel?"

"No, we live local and we only have to walk a short distance.

How about you, do you live nearby?"

"No such luck, we live in Basingstoke, the journey takes a couple of hours and we end up having to get the bus, train and tube"

Zoe commented "That must be costly if you are making the journey on a regular basis"

Anita sighed and replied "It is expensive, and neither of us are working, we both lost our jobs three months ago when the local food services factory closed in October. But we get benefits and are allowed to reclaim all the costs of the journeys from the hospital. We just have to make a note of all the fares and then go to the cash office near the front of the hospital to complete the travel expenses claim form. Its two pounds fifty each for the bus fares, thirty one pounds each for the train from Basingstoke to Waterloo and then five pounds ten each for the day pass on the tube. This daily tube ticket is quite good and covers all the zones we require. We've worked it out that the total cost for each journey is seventy seven pounds twenty but, fortunately, we've only had to make the journey three times. The cash office just asked if we were on benefits and then asked us to fill in the form and gave us the seventy seven pounds twenty. They didn't appear to do any checking, just seemed to accept our word, good job were honest, hey! You're lucky that you live so close, we had to make the return journey home one day and then return later to collect Susannah, but we were lucky that time, the cash office did pay us the seventy seven pounds for both of our journeys, and we don't have to pay for Susannah as she is under five."

The nurse came in to the waiting area and called "Susannah, time for you to come and see the Doctor"

Both Paul and Anita got to their feet and having finished their coffees, placed the empty plastic containers in the waste bin, and followed the nurse with Susannah.

Anita quickly turned to Zoe and Rik saying "It was nice to

have met you; we hope Alice gets better soon"
Zoe and Rik smiled and nodded goodbye.
Alice shouted "Bye Susannah"

Zoe Ferguson sat back quietly thinking, both she and her partner Rik Jeffreys were also receiving benefits and her mother also lived near Basingstoke. Their financial position was not too bad at the moment as she didn't work and so could claim all the appropriate benefits, and as Rik did not work officially, he could also claim various benefits. He raised extra money as he was involved in some minor criminal activities including the drugs scene, and did have a police record, but whilst he was an occasional user of drugs, he was not an addict. Some extra money would always be useful, Zoe thought, I must have a chat to Rik when we get home.

The nurse interrupted Zoe's thoughts when she entered and called "Alice, your turn now. Would you like to bring your Mum and Dad in with you as well?"

They all walked along with the nurse and sat in the treatment room awaiting the consultant, Mr Ali, who was the specialist for the Children's Ear, Nose and Throat Department.

Joan Anderson, the receptionist said "Could we just check all our records and contact details please, while you're waiting"

Zoe looked at the information and calmly told Joan "Oh, we have changed address and now live with my mother in Basingstoke" and quickly wrote the new address and her mobile phone number on the form.

Rik was slightly taken back but did not say anything, he already knew that Zoe was up to something and probably had some ideas for claiming travel expenses from what he had overheard before. Both he and Zoe suddenly looked at Alice, dreading what she might suddenly say, but Alice was still playing with her doll and had not heard the conversation. Alice might have prevented Zoe's plans before she had even started. Children being children!

4

They settled Alice into the hospital ward where she was soon mixing with the other children. They had also found out from one of the nurses that Susannah had been discharged and had already left with her parents.

They both gave Alice a hug and Zoe spoke "We are just popping home, we'll be back to see you soon, bye-bye darling"

Alice smiled and waved good-bye playing happily with her new friends. They walked along the hospital corridors which were busy with trolleys carrying patients and people rushing in and out of the different wards. Nurses were chatting about what they had done and where they had been the previous evening, whilst completing their daily tasks.

Zoe and Rik walked to the front of the hospital calling at the cash office on the way. They rang the buzzer and a lady opened the window.

"Can I help you?"

Zoe spoke quietly and asked "Can we have a form for claiming travel expenses, please?"

The lady, Julie Travis, informed Zoe "You have to be claiming certain benefits before you are able to make any travel claims you know."

"Yes, we know about that and have checked that we are entitled to claim our travel expenses from Basingstoke"

The lady gave Zoe the form who acknowledged "Thank you, we will be back later and I will return the completed form then."

They walked along the street and turned into Tottenham Court Road and popped into Tesco to get some shopping before crossing the road by the Gentleman's Club. They could see the big BT Tower overshadowing the road on the right hand side with University Street on the left which leads to University College London; a couple of groups of students had obviously

5

picked up some lunch and were chattering as they walked towards the University.

The weather was quite good and Zoe was now feeling quite cheerful thinking about the plans that she had in mind. The shops were looking quite busy with the brighter weather putting smiles on the faces of the shoppers and the people just out for a gentle stroll. They then passed the NHS Health Authority offices, where a neighbour was just entering, before they then crossed Capper Street, going into Starbucks Coffee on the corner. It had been a while since they had eaten, so a couple of classic cappuccinos and a double chocolate muffin each were well appreciated.

As they left the coffee bar, they passed Lloyds TSB on the right where Zoe used to have her bank account; she had not used it for a couple of years now. The old fashioned but lovely Memorial Church, was a bit further down on the right, Zoe was trying to think what looked different to it today, and nearly managed to knock over the lady selling the Big Issue magazine, she was so engrossed in her thoughts. Apologising, they moved quickly on, trying to avoid the people pouring out of Goode Street Tube Station, just across the road before the Marks & Spencers Food Shop.

They then turned into the side street where they rented a two bedroom flat above a shop. The walk from the hospital had taken them less than a quarter of an hour.

As they entered the flat, Rik said to Zoe "You were quick off the mark about fiddling the travel expenses, not a bad idea for you. You know when you were talking to the lady at the cash office window, I saw Keith Simpson's girlfriend sitting in the back, the one with blonde hair in a pony tail, she was on the phone. Think her name's Linda Barrett and I'm pretty sure that she's in charge of the cash office itself. Don't know what she thinks about Keith getting and using drugs, which he buys from Tony Jones. If Keith doesn't watch out he'll blow that job as a motor mechanic and that won't do us any good, as we need him to help us sort the cars for some of our business ventures"

Later that afternoon, Zoe and Rik left the flat to return to the Euston General Hospital in order to visit Susannah. They turned right at Tottenham Court Road and walked in the opposite direction that they had taken in the morning, they again passed the same lady still selling the Big Issue Magazines. As they entered the hospital, Zoe went straight to the cash office, rang the buzzer and the window was opened by a blonde lady with a pony tail, which Zoe assumed was Linda Barrett.

The staff badge confirmed her thoughts and she handed the travel expenses claim form that they had completed at home, to Linda, together with the evidence of the benefits that they were both receiving. Zoe received £142.20 for two journeys, which covered £124 for the train journey from Basingstoke to Waterloo, £10 bus fares and the £10.20 for the day tickets for the tube travel. No evidence of the journeys was requested and Zoe placed the money in her purse with a smile.

She spoke to Linda "Our daughter Susannah will be in for a couple of weeks and we will be making the journey a couple of times each day. May I have some more forms for me to fill in each day?"

Linda handed Zoe a supply of the travel claim forms. Rik had waited around the corner, as he did not want Linda to see him in case she recognised him. He had been in the garage a few times where Keith worked and had seen Linda when she had called in on Keith.

Zoe continued to present the travel expenses forms to the cash office, claiming for two or three journeys per day. It was nearly always Linda who would normally complete the paperwork and make the payment. By the time Susannah was discharged from the hospital after fourteen days, which was longer than expected, with Susannah getting an infection, Zoe had claimed over £2100. They had made several copies of the travel expenses claim forms but Susannah was now out of hospital. Zoe then had another thought, would the cash office know that Susannah had left? She decided she would call back tomorrow or the day after and try presenting another travel expense form; after all, it was only a fifteen minute walk from their home. So the next day, Zoe left the flat, turned into Tottenham Court Road and walked to Euston General Hospital and made her way to the cash office. She claimed for three return journeys from Basingstoke for both Rik and herself and received £211.40 before making her way back home. The whole trip had taken half an hour and worth over £200. Not a bad little trip thought Zoe.

A little while afterwards, following an idea from Zoe, Rik went to see Keith Simpson in the garage where he worked, arriving just before Keith finished for the day. All the other mechanics were removing their dirty overalls and collecting coats to head home. He overheard two of the younger lads arranging a night out, clearly on the look out for a nice couple of girls from the conversation that was going on.

Rik approached Keith saying,

"Fancy a pint after work? I've got an idea on how we can both make some extra money. See you in the George and Dragon in ten minutes?"

"Yep, get me a pint of lager in"

Rik went into the George and Dragon, ordered the drinks and sat in a corner waiting for Keith to arrive. He nodded his head to a couple of locals and two of the mechanics who had called for a quick drink before making their way home. In this hot weather, the drinks were soon demolished.

Keith arrived within five minutes and sat down at the table in the corner with Rik, "What is this idea of yours, Rik?"

Keith sat back, enjoying his pint while Rik explained Zoe's plan in full detail.

"Right, now, you know that you are allowed to claim travel expenses when you visit a child in hospital and when Susannah was in Euston General, we claimed travel expenses"

Keith interrupted "You only live near the other end of Tottenham Court Road, you'll not get much for that short distance"

"Hear me out" said Rik "We give Zoe's mothers address in Basingstoke and pretended that we both made the return journey two or three times a day, which works out at over two hundred quid a day. Long term, that's roughly fifteen hundred pounds per week and even though Susannah is not in hospital now, we have still continued to claim. This can't last long and somebody is bound to get suspicious. Now, we saw your girlfriend Linda there, and we know she's in charge of the Cash Office, so we thought, let's get Linda to turn a blind eye"

Keith was startled "Hey, no chance. Linda is straight, she won't get involved"

"I am not asking her to be involved, just pretend she didn't notice anything wrong if Zoe is calling with the travel claim forms. If we all go along with this idea, the money can be divided three ways, a third for you, a third for me and the final third for Zoe, as she will be doing all the work. That is five hundred quid per week for you Keith, not bad for doing nothing, what do you think?"

Keith got to his feet, grinning broadly and downing his pint before he left saying.

"Leave it with me, I'll try to talk to Linda tonight"

Linda arrived home at their flat in Hackney, slightly later than normal as she had been shopping at the supermarket after leaving work. Keith had telephoned Linda telling her not to bother thinking about the food, saying he would prepare the evening meal, which, in itself, made Linda suspicious as Keith would not normally make the meal unless he was after something. Linda glanced at the recipe page open on the side in the kitchen, knowing that if Keith cooked, he would always use a proper recipe.

Moroccan baked chicken with chickpeas and rice; it smelled lovely and looked really delicious, thought Linda, wondering what he was up to and thinking, that is even before a word has been spoken. Suspiciously, a rather nice bottle of Australian Cabernet Sauvignon had been opened to go with the meal.

"And how was your day?" asked Keith.

"It was fine, but never mind all the pleasantries. What is all this in aid of Keith? What are you up to?"

"It's just a little treat" Keith smiled.

Linda then went upstairs to get changed. She came down, ten minutes later, and Keith handed Linda a glass of the red wine. He was using the special wine glasses, a Christmas present to Keith from Linda's mother.

"I thought you had no money" commented Linda.

"That's what I want to talk to you about, but sit down and enjoy the meal"

They sat down and enjoyed the meal; the Moroccan chicken was one of Linda's favourites. Chicken thighs on the bone were used to retain the flavour and were accompanied by chick peas, lemon slices, yellow peppers, onions and pitted black and green olives, along with the basmati rice which was all cooked in the one pot with a variety of spices making it rather special. The meal was finished and the bottle of Cabernet emptied before Keith started to talk about his conversation with Rik.

"Do you know a lady called Zoe Ferguson?"

Linda thought for a few seconds before saying "There's a lady of that name who has a child in our hospital, she lives in Basingstoke and travels in with her partner to see their daughter. She claims travel expenses at the cash office. They actually make the journey quite a lot but are able to claim because they receive benefits. They've claimed several hundreds of pounds"

Keith smiled "Would you believe that they live off Tottenham Court Road and their daughter left hospital a couple of weeks ago. This scam is worth about fifteen hundred pounds per week to them, but they'll let me into the scam and give me five hundred pounds per week. It'll help sort our money problems out"

Linda said angrily "That is despicable, I'm going to report them, you only want the money to buy drugs, I know you're a user"

"That's not true, I thought we may be able to move from this flat and get a nicer place to live. We might even be able to consider starting a family. You don't have to do anything, just pretend not to notice anything unusual about Zoe Ferguson's travel claims, they're already committing a fraud and you obviously didn't know about it, did you?"

Hesitantly, Linda said "No, I honestly thought that they lived in Basingstoke, I had no idea their daughter had left hospital"

The fraud continued for a further two and a half years with both Zoe, and occasionally Rik, calling at the cash office when they knew that they would be attended to by Linda, who worked full-time and was often on her own. They thought this may help avoid any suspicions by the other two ladies, Julie Travis and Michelle Doyle, who both worked part-time in the cash office.

The cost of the fraud was now in the region of £300,000 and Linda was starting to get extremely concerned, as the financial benefits were evident in their life style these days. They had not moved out of their two bedroom flat yet, but they did have a better car and their social life was more extravagant, although she did feel that Keith was getting more into drugs, his behaviour at times was quite irrational. The contents of their flat also showed their increased wealth and although they had considered moving, Linda thought people may wonder how they could afford it.

There relationship was going through a bad patch at the

moment, mainly due to Keith's increasing reliance on drugs. So, deciding that a holiday might help matters, they arranged to stay at a five star luxury hotel at Marbella on the Costa del Sol in Spain and that was when things started to go wrong.

A little old lady, Cyridwen Roberts, aged eighty five years had been in the hospital to have a knee replacement and called at the cash office to claim her taxi fee of £3.50, which she preferred rather than waiting to be collected by the ambulance, which was often late and she hated waiting around. The consultant had insisted that an ambulance was used for a couple of weeks, but she was now much more mobile and able to use crutches quite comfortably. The new knee was getting much better but now the other knee was starting to create some problems, she would have to mention this to the physiotherapist again. She was also due to see the consultant afterwards so thought she would let him know as well.

She stood behind Zoe Ferguson who was talking to the new lady in the cash office, Tracy Dickinson, and heard her say that the travel expenses were for the journeys she and her partner had taken from their home in Basingstoke to Euston General Hospital.

The elderly lady had recognised Zoe who lived about fifty yards from her flat and when Zoe left with the cash, she informed Tracy Dickinson

"The lady in front of me, Zoe Ferguson, doesn't live in Basingstoke, her daughter, Susannah plays with her friend, Lucy, who lives next door to me. I know she was in this hospital, but that was about two or three years ago, the little girl next door told me all about it then"

Tracy Dickinson was undecided what course of action to take about the information from Cyridwen Roberts. She had only worked in the hospital cash office for a matter of weeks and would normally have mentioned it to Linda, but she was on holiday in Spain. Tracy did not really understand what Zoe

Ferguson was up to, but thought it sounded very serious, so she examined the hospital policies and procedures to check who it should be reported to.

She was sure it would be somebody in the Finance Department and decided to report the conversation with Cyridwen Roberts to the Director of Finance at the hospital, Stuart Bradley, who, once some idea of the size of the fraud had been established by his staff in the Finance Department, looked up the appropriate documentation relating to fraud within the Health Service and found the telephone number that he required. He then decided that he should be contacting the well known and highly respected Public Sector Fraud Consultant, David Parish.

2

The telephone call from Stuart Bradley to David Parish came when David was in Manchester investigating a pension fraud on behalf of the Local Authority and the North West Transport Authority.

David had listened to Stuart Bradley explaining the detailed situation with respect to the travel expenses fraud at the London hospital. He had then informed Stuart of his involvement in a pension fraud but hastily arranged a meeting two days later, and in the interim, David promised that he would contact a Local Fraud Specialist, Peter Daley, who was based in London. This was quickly arranged, with Peter calling to see Stuart at Euston General later that day, Peter would then be able to undertake some preliminary research prior to David's arrival.

David is forty four years of age, never married, but has had a longstanding on and off relationship for the past seven years with a Spanish lady, Alisa Garcia who is a senior officer in the Guardia Civil based in the Andalucia region of Spain. Alisa now has an apartment in Seville but did live with David for three years in a villa on the Costa del Sol. At that time, David was employed by U.K. Insurance Companies investigating fraudsters who were active in both Spain and the United Kingdom. These investigations, would, however, involve visits to many European countries and occasionally the United States. His foreign exploits have earned him the name of Senor Fraudo.

14

He lives in Liverpool, but the nature of his work entails much travelling and living out of a suitcase, he also has a cottage in the Lake District, which is often used as a base for his passion of walking and trekking, although his love of Spain sees him stepping forth, when time allows, through the many walking regions of Andalucia and Murcia. Walking was also the favourite pastime of Alisa Garcia and she had often joined David on his treks through Andalucia.

The pension fraud involves a brother and sister who were receiving pension monies on behalf of their mother and father, the only problem was that both parents had died over ten years ago and they failed to advise the relevant Pension Scheme Administrators that both their parents were now deceased.

The brother, Carl Sutherland had been authorised to withdraw funds from his parent's joint bank account when they were still alive and he had continued to use this facility since the death of his parents. He had never informed the bank that his mother and father had died and the bank account was continued to be used by Carl to receive the pensions and make the necessary withdrawals.

Each year the two Authorities would send the appropriate form requesting confirmation that the two pensioners, Francis and Mary Sutherland, were still alive and eligible for the pension. Carl and his sister, Rita, would then complete the documentation, forging signatures and returning it to the respective Pension Schemes.

They were caught out by modern technology with the introduction of a data matching exercise that involved all Local Authorities, Pension Scheme Authorities, Health Authorities and Benefits Agencies. One of the many data checks made as part of this exercise was to compare the names of people receiving pensions with the information held by the General Register Office, which registers births, marriages and deaths. This was an exercise that started in 2007 and the details provided by the General Register Office confirmed Francis Sutherland had died in 1995 and Mary Sutherland in 1997.

Once the Pension Schemes were aware of the information, they stopped the pensions whilst they continued with additional research and to obtain more detailed documentation. Francis Sutherland had worked for North West Transport Authority and Mary Sutherland for the Local Authority. They were, surprised, however, when they received telephone calls from Carl Sutherland asking why the pension payments had been stopped. Both Pension Scheme Administrators advised Carl that they had received details of the deaths of Francis & Mary Sutherland to which Carl had informed them that they were mistaken and both parents were alive and well, and were sitting at the table eating breakfast.

David had been asked to investigate the comments from Carl Sutherland and the information that had been provided to the Pension Scheme Administrators. He had obtained the death certificates from the General Register Office and made discreet enquiries with ex-work colleagues of both parents as well as neighbours. He had also met with that a Manchester based Fraud Specialist, Brian Lewis, who would be used to assist him in the investigation. It was soon evident that Carl and Rita's parents were deceased and this was a fraud instigated by Carl & Rita Sutherland over a period of many years.

The pension for Francis Sutherland was £8500 per year and that of Mary Sutherland £6200 per year, it was fairly obvious to David Parish that this fraud was worth about £160,000 but he would soon obtain an accurate figure from the two Pension Schemes.

David had obtained Carl Sutherland's telephone number and decided that this would be his initial contact. He picked up his phone and pressed the buttons.

"Hello"

"Oh Hello, is that Carl Sutherland?"

"Yes, who's that?"

"My name is David Parish; I am a Fraud Consultant for the Local Authority, North West Transport and the Pension Schemes. I understand both Pension Authorities contacted you regarding your parent's pensions and you stated that your parents were still alive"

"Yes"

"I have copies of the death certificates of both your parents. Your father died in nineteen, ninety five and your mother in nineteen, ninety seven and you signed both certificates as the informant when reporting their deaths to the Registrar. I think that you shouldn't say any more at this stage Carl but I'd like to see you next week, when you should be accompanied by a solicitor"

"I don't really understand, you're not the police but you say you a fraud investigator?"

"That's correct. The choice is yours Carl, you and Rita either speak to me and a colleague, Brian Lewis, or the Police will be informed and they would then call and arrest you both"

"I work as a butcher in a supermarket and my day off is a Monday. Is Monday okay?"

"Yes, I do have your address and your sister's address. I'll write to you confirming the date, time and venue and I will leave it to you both to arrange for a solicitor to be present. Do you have a solicitor?"

"Yes, Mark Weston from AGK Solicitors"

"It'll be better if you contact him and let him know that we have agreed to meet next Monday. I'll give you my phone number, have you got a pen?"

"Yes"

"My mobile number is zero, four, nine, seven, four, three, six, eight, three, two, one"

"Thanks"

Half an hour later, David's mobile phone rang.

"Hello, David Parish"

"Hello David. This is Mark Weston; I understand that you have just spoken to Carl Sutherland?"

"Yes, I have. You're very quick off the mark"

"I just thought that I'd like to catch the famous Mr Fraud, whilst I can. Will you send me a copy of the letters that you are sending to Carl and his sister?"

"Sure, I'll send them off today"

"I presume that you'll be giving me some type of disclosures before the interview?"

"But, of course, I'll give you a disclosure pack when I see you next Monday. We'll call you in prior to the interview to give you the pack so that you'll be able to discuss it with your client"

"Thanks, I'll look forward to seeing you in person then"

In view of the urgency of the London meeting, Brian Lewis was completing most of the paperwork for these meetings prior to the interviews with the Sutherlands next Monday. David had sent him an email with all the appropriate attachments, following their meeting, yesterday afternoon, in Manchester, when Brian had also taken copies of the other documents that he would require. Brian would now be able to transfer the attachments to his computer and printout the appropriate paperwork. He would also be able to get the background information which would help him prepare for the interviews.

3

It was Wednesday morning as David caught the 6.27 a.m. Virgin Express from Liverpool, Lime Street to London Euston, which was due to arrive just before 9 a.m. It would then be only the short walk to the General Hospital where a quick meeting would be held with Stuart Bradley before he caught up with Peter Daley to get a fuller picture of the fraud. David had worked with Peter a couple of times and knew he would be making a thorough investigation. No doubt, he would be waiting with a list and full details of the suspects.

David actually enjoyed these train journeys to Euston, he carried his laptop and would be able complete some work on the pension fraud on the journey down. The other alternative form of travel would have been to fly from Liverpool's John Lennon Airport, to London City Airport. The flight would have left at 6.45 a.m. arriving in London at 7.45 a.m. but the locality of the Hospital from Euston Station made the train journey preferable in this case.

He got onto the second class coach and found his seat and placed his luggage bag on the rack above his seat in preparation for the journey to London, he then placed his laptop case on the seat next to him, which, hopefully, would not be used. David preferred second class at this time of the morning, as first class contained mainly the business sector with the non stop mobile phone dialling tones with loud telephone conversations taking place during the early morning journey, so it was much more peaceful in second class. His morning improved as an extremely

19

attractive young lady sat opposite him and placed what appeared to be a modelling portfolio on the table.

"Good morning" David said

"Good morning," was the reply along with a lovely smile.

When the announcement came that the shop was open, David got out of his seat and walked to the next carriage, taking his laptop with him. The self-service shops on the virgin trains were better than the old buffet cars and he collected his usual, Premium Bacon Roll and placed it on the counter before asking the assistant for.

"A Large Americano, please"

She filled the large coffee container and handed it to David.

"That'll be four pounds forty nine please"

David handed over a £5 note and collected the change.

"Thank you"

This would keep him going until he arrived in London and he made the short trip back to his seat in the next carriage. The beautiful young lady opposite was on her mobile phone and David, using his investigative background and being rather nosy, discovered that she was going for an interview for a job at one of these glamour magazines and the portfolio contained the photographs that they required as part of the interview. Hope she gets the job thought David.

He finished eating the bacon roll and drinking the coffee before he opened the laptop case, got out the laptop and plugged it into the socket at the side of the table. Once the laptop had come to life, he brought up his notes on the pension fraud.

David was kept busy on the laptop and made some notes and questions to be asked when he met up with Peter Daley later that morning. He then took out his memory stick, which he placed in the laptop and transferred the information that he may require, before removing the memory stick. He would now be able place the memory stick into one of the hospital computers in London and let them print out the documents. He then closed down his laptop computer and placed it back in the case.

It was now 8.30 a.m. and the train was due to arrive in Euston Station in less than half an hour. His young lady traveller was looking in her make up mirror, checking her makeup and hair and making sure everything was in place. David thought to himself, no improvements are necessary, if only he was twenty years younger.

The train slowly pulled into the station and all the passengers started to collect their belongings and put on their coats, it was a little breezy but quite pleasant weather in London in April.

"Good-bye, do have a nice day" he said to his lovely female travelling companion.

"Thank you, fingers crossed, I'm having an interview with a top modelling magazine"

"I'm sure you'll get the job"

"I hope so"

The train coaches soon emptied with everybody rushing to their differing locations from the crowded station into the tube downstairs or the busy London streets.

David's meeting with Stuart Bradley was booked for 10 am so David was a little early. Rather than go straight to the Hospital, he decided to have a quick coffee at the Train Station so had a choice of places to get a drink. He stopped at the first on the left and ordered coffee.

He finished the coffee and it was now 9.35 a.m., he took the short walk to Euston General Hospital, crossing a couple of roads before entering the front of the Hospital. He then made his way to the Executive's Offices for his meeting with Stuart. He had met Stuart once before, when David had made a presentation on fraud to a national meeting attended by Directors of Finance from many different hospitals. David Parish entered the offices which were on the first floor and approached three ladies, busy working at their desks, who were obviously Personal Assistants to the Directors. He was unsure who was Stuart Bradley's Personal Assistant and spoke in the direction of all three ladies.

"Good morning, I have an appointment with Stuart Bradley, my name is David Parish"

"He is expecting you, I'll tell him that you're here" said the lady on the right and smiled as she picked up the phone. The name on her identity badge was Louise Elliot.

"Hello Stuart, David Parish has arrived, I'll bring him through"

David followed Louise and entered the office of Stuart Bradley, where he walked over to Stuart and shook hands.

"Good morning Stuart, nice to see you again. Well perhaps not in these circumstances"

"I couldn't agree more, would you like a drink?"

"Coffee please, milk and no sugar"

"Cup of tea for me please Louise" Louise left the office and closed the door.

They both sat down, Stuart turned to David asking.

"How up to date are you? I know that I gave you some details when we spoke on the telephone a couple of days ago. A member of my staff, Simon Gardner, has been working closely with your colleague, Peter Daley, who is in an interview room downstairs next to the cash office. They have all the travel claim forms and itemised listings of the individual entries, we're now looking at a fraud which may be in excess of three hundred thousand pounds"

"So I've heard, I've been in regular contact with Peter and spoke to him at home this last night; I'll go downstairs to join him when I leave here. Peter has mentioned the names of Zoe Ferguson and Rik Jeffreys and we will contact them to arrange a meeting. I'll be informing them that we will be wishing to interview them separately and the interviews will be taped under caution, and they should be accompanied by a legal representative. I did, however, also ask Peter to examine a large sample of the travel expenses claim forms, in order to see which staff member had authorised the claims. The name of Linda Barrett always appears. This scam has been going on for more than two years, with several claims being made each week. Linda works full time and there are a couple of other ladies who work part-time, Peter and Simon Gardner think that most of the claims investigated to date have been paid when Linda Barrett was in the cash office on her own. I think that we'll need to speak to Linda, but I believe that she's in Spain on holiday and that she is due back in work tomorrow"

"Yes, Simon Gardner has updated me on the findings, I've arranged for a member of Human Resources to be available tomorrow morning, when I will suspend her from duties, pending your investigation into the travel claim expenses"

Their conversation was interrupted when Louise brought in the tea and coffee.

"That's fine, Stuart, I'll go downstairs in a minute to examine what Peter has uncovered and get back to you later today. I did make some enquiries with the police, Linda Barrett is clear with no previous convictions, but her partner, Keith Simpson is known to the police, he was found guilty of driving a getaway car in a robbery several years ago and served twelve months in prison. He is also known to frequent the drugs scene but, so far, only as a user, that will cost him money, and as he's only a motor mechanic, the pay will not be that great. They have recently purchased a nice car and tend to a bit extravagant, and this holiday to Spain is in Marbella, not the cheapest of places"

"I see that you've been doing your homework, David. I've known Linda Barrett since I arrived here two years ago and have always found her quite pleasant. I do find it strange, though, that this hasn't been picked up, you have to be suspicious. We are, naturally, looking at our systems in the cash office, to prevent this type of thing happening again. No doubt, our Internal Auditors will be taking a close look; I'll be informing them to have a look in due course"

"Before I go Stuart, I need some documents printing out, I have a memory stick containing the information, is there a desktop computer downstairs that I can use to get them printed?"

"Give it to me David, I'll do it here, there is no printer in the room downstairs, it is in the cash office, its better that I do it here"

Stuart placed the memory stick in his desktop computer and printed the documents out for David. He then gave the paperwork to David who placed it in his briefcase.

"Thanks Stuart, if we need a couple of rooms to arrange taped interviews and a holding room, is it possible here?"

"Sure, let me know and I'll arrange it"

"Thanks, I'll speak to you later"

David then left the office and the Executive's Department and made his way downstairs to meet up with Peter Daley in the room by the Cash Office. He passed the corridor leading from the entrance of the hospital, where the restaurant was situated alongside the other shopping outlets and the charity shop. In the passageway there were several easy chairs where some of the hospital patients were sitting talking to their friends and relatives. They were holding supplies of newspapers, chocolate bars and soft drinks that they had just purchased from the shops.

4

David looked in at the Cash Office and saw two ladies working, it was quite small, and even the quickest of glances made David understand why Linda Barrett would have wanted to be on her own when she was dealing with the travel claims presented by Zoe Ferguson and Rik Jeffreys.

He knocked on the door of the room marked 'Interview Room' which was opened by Peter Daley who was working alone.

"Good morning Peter, having a nice time?"

"Oh wonderful David, apart from the fact that I've been swamped with black bin bags full of fraudulent travel claim forms. Actually, the type of fraud is fairly straightforward; I don't think there will be a problem with Zoe Ferguson and Rik Jeffreys. They've been completing the travel claims for over two years, knowing their daughter was only in hospital for a couple of weeks. They're going to struggle to dispute the evidence, the problem we have is the vast numbers of claims. The staff have been very helpful especially Simon Gardner and I am certain that Linda Barrett is involved"

"I've been speaking to Stuart Bradley; he's going to suspend Linda when she returns to work tomorrow. I know you've numbered itemised lists of all the travel claims and all the forms have been bundled to agree with the numbers on the lists, so we'll pick a sample and use this for our interviews with Zoe and Rik. We'll disclose this sample to the legal representatives prior to the interview under caution, which will, of course, be taped. I'd like you to assist me with the interview, if that's okay"

25

"No problem David, I have a sample here ready for you to examine"

David and Peter spent about an hour going through the sample of travel expense claim forms, David thinking that he agreed with the thoughts of Peter, that the evidence was overwhelming, before referring back to Peter.

"I think that we'll have enough by the end of today in order to contact them, explain who we are, and arrange interviews under caution, here at the hospital. Do you have their telephone numbers?"

"Yes, I've got two mobile numbers. If we don't make contact, they don't live far away, the address given on the travel claims is always Basingstoke but an elderly lady, Cyridwen Roberts, has provided their correct address"

"Good, I think it's time for a lunch break, let's go taste the delicacies of the hospital restaurant"

As they both stood up, the telephone rang and Peter picked it up.

"Hello"

"This is Tracy Dickinson from the Cash Office next door, I thought you should know that I have Zoe Ferguson at the Cash Office window, she has handed in a travel expenses claim form for visiting her daughter"

"Is she on her own?"

"No, there is a man with her"

"Could you hang on for a few seconds while I talk to my colleague?"

"David, Tracy Dickinson from the Cash Office is on the phone, Zoe Ferguson is at the window, with a travel expenses claim form. There's a man with her"

"We might as well speak to them now, purely to stop this claim, let them know that we are making checks and wish to arrange a taped interview under caution. Tell Tracy that we'll be out straight away"

"Tracy, we're coming out now to speak to them"

David walked out of the office and saw Zoe talking to a man, presumably Rik Jeffreys. His initial impression was, perhaps, one of surprise. This couple were immaculately dressed and you could tell that some of their new source of funding was being spent in the more expensive boutiques in London. He then approached the couple.

"Hello, my name is David Parish, I would like to speak to you about your travel claims, I know that you are Zoe Ferguson, am I correct in thinking that you are Rik Jeffreys?"

"Yes, but we're a bit busy at the moment, we'll call back later"

"I think we all know what's been happening for the past couple of years with all the travel claims. It would be in your best interests if you co-operate with us"

David pointed to the office door, Zoe looked at Rik, who shrugged his shoulders and they both followed David into the office.

As they entered the room, David pointed at the two chairs this side of the desk and said.

"Take a seat please; this is my colleague Peter Daley"

David walked around the desk and sat next to Peter, facing Zoe and Rik.

"Both Peter and I are Fraud Investigators with the National Health Service, we have been completing a check on all the travel claims that you've made for visiting your daughter in this hospital. They go back some two and a half years, but as you'll be well aware, your daughter was only in hospital for a couple of weeks. We also know that you live locally and not in Basingstoke as you have recorded in all the claims. Clearly, you need to take some legal advice and we will not discuss the claims today. We'll arrange to see you both separately, but we would recommend that you are accompanied by your solicitor as the next interview will be a formal interview, taped and under caution. Who is your solicitor?"

Rik seemed more agitated than Zoe and he turned to look at Zoe before speaking.

"You're not the police; do you mean you are going to ask them to come to this meeting?"

"No, there will be two interviews. I will attend with Peter and you will be with your solicitors. I'm sure you will find this easier than dealing with the police"

Rik again looked at Zoe who said.

"Tell them"

"My solicitor is John Harrison"

Peter replied

"I know John, if you'd like, I'll give him a ring now and arrange a meeting"

"Okay"

Peter opened his diary to look up the telephone number; he then picked up the telephone and dialled the solicitor's office.

"Good morning, John Harrison, Solicitors"

"Good morning, may I speak to John Harrison, its Peter Daley"

There was a slight pause while the call was directed.

"Hello Peter, what can I do for you?"

"Morning John, I have two of your clients with me, Rik Jeffreys and Zoe Ferguson. My colleague David Parish and I have been looking at some travel claims made at Euston General Hospital by Rik and Zoe"

"Did you say David Parish, Mr Fraud?"

"Yes, do you know David?"

"No, but I've heard about him, it must be a big fraud?"

"Yes, early indications suggest three hundred thousand pounds but we will provide all the information when we see you. This is the intention of this telephone call, to arrange two taped interviews under caution. We'll hold the interviews here in the hospital, what's your diary like for next week?"

28

"Wednesday looks best"

"I'll just check that David is available"

"David, can you make next Wednesday?"

"Yes, I'm in Manchester on Monday, but will be able to make Wednesday"

"That's fine John, we'll inform your clients now and we will send letters confirming the times"

"Okay, next Wednesday, will you ask Rik and Zoe to contact me later today?"

"Yes, see you next week, bye for now"

Peter then put the telephone down and said to Rik and Zoe.

"Next Wednesday, we'll send you letters confirming the times and the office where the meetings will be held. John Harrison said will you give him a ring later"

Rik looked at David and asked

"What other people will you be interviewing besides us two?"

"I am sure you know the answer to that"

David knew from that question that Linda and probably Keith were definitely involved in the fraud. He stood up and opened the door, letting Zoe and Rik out of the office.

"Bye"

No reply was received.

Peter and David eventually went for their lunch and then worked the rest of the day preparing the documentation for next Wednesday; they would need to provide a sample of documents, by way of disclosure, to John Harrison before the interviews commenced next Wednesday. They also completed the letters inviting Zoe and Rik to attend the interviews. Once this had been completed, David then discussed the arrangements for tomorrow morning when Linda Barrett was due to return to work.

"Linda will be suspended tomorrow morning, we'll need to

be around to speak to her afterwards and arrange an interview under tape with her solicitor. We should be here before she arrives; will you be here at eight thirty a.m.?"

"Yes, that will be okay, where shall we meet, Stuart Bradley's office?"

"Yes, I'll let Stuart know, see you in the morning"

David had not booked any accommodation and using the internet he booked a hotel near South Kensington Tube station, he had used it several times before and there was a nice Italian Restaurant across the road where he would be able to have a meal later that evening. He would take a walk to Russell Square Tube station and then get the Piccadilly line direct to South Kensington.

David went to Stuart's office to update him on the events of the day.

"We are interviewing Zoe Ferguson and Rik Jeffreys next Wednesday; we've already made the arrangements with their solicitor. What is the best room to use?"

"I'll arrange for you to use the Interview Room in Human Resources, I can let you have it for the full day"

"I've arranged to meet Peter here tomorrow morning at eight thirty a.m. and then we'd like to see Linda Barrett after she has been suspended"

"That's fine, see you tomorrow"

Rik Jeffreys arrived back at their flat and rang Keith Simpson on his mobile in Marbella. After a couple of rings it was answered.

"Hello"

"Hi Keith, its Rik. Our travel fiddle's been rumbled, two Fraud Investigators caught us today, they know all about it and we're being interviewed on tape next Wednesday. We had to tell them who our solicitor is and he'll also be there. They said that the fiddle was worth around three hundred grand, I didn't realize it was that big. I think they also know that other people are involved probably Linda and maybe you, I thought that you should know before you get home tomorrow"

"Linda will go berserk; she has wanted to stop this for months. I'm not sure what the hell we're going to do, I'm going to have to go and tell her. I could do with a fix tonight, I brought a small supply of drugs but they have all gone. Cheers Rik"

The following morning David met Peter as promised in Stuart Bradley's office. Stuart had arranged for one of the Human Resources Managers to be present when Linda was to be suspended, but it did not work out that way.

Linda did not turn up for work. Louise Elliot, Stuart's Personal Assistant, rang Linda's home address but there was no answer. When she tried Linda's mobile, it was switched off.

Stuart was clearly concerned and his frustration showed.

"You hear of criminals going to Spain and never returning, I don't suppose we'll ever see Linda Barrett again, do we have any influence or contacts in Spain?"

David smiled before telling Stuart and Peter. He was, of course, thinking of Alisa Garcia, they are still very good friends.

"Yes, I do have contacts but how much information can you give me to help trace Linda Barrett and Keith Simpson?"

They all spent the next few hours talking to staff with David calling at Linda's home address and talking to a couple of the neighbours, using the excuse that the Hospital were concerned that Linda had not returned to work. They were also able to find out where Keith worked and Peter called at the garage.

They reconvened later that afternoon when David and Peter examined all the information that had obtained from a variety of sources. They now knew the name of the hotel where Linda was staying in Marbella, they had travelled by easyJet from London, Stansted and were due home early evening. A check of the flights on the easyJet website showed that the Flight 3116 would leave Malaga at 16.10 and arrive at Stansted at 18.05. It was known that they had hired a car when they arrived which was due to be dropped off at Malaga Airport.

Keith Simpson had not turned up for work and no telephone call had been received at the garage giving an explanation. They had provided Peter with the mobile telephone number of Keith. The Garage Manager had also informed Peter of Keith's drug habits which had affected his performance and timekeeping at work, he had been given a final warning. A recent photograph of Linda and Keith was received which had been taken at a work colleagues party.

David and Peter then made some telephone calls. David had a contact with security at the airport who had found out that Linda and Keith were due to get the easyJet Flight 3116 but had not boarded the plane. He was also informed that easyJet had not had any requests for further flights. Peter had discovered that Linda and Keith should have left the hotel yesterday but had stayed another night and had finally left that morning. Apparently, one of the receptionists had said it looked as though he had a bad hangover and she looked really angry. He did see their car take the road towards Malaga, but this would pass Fuengirola, Benalmadena and Torremolinos. Peter tried ringing Keith, but his mobile was also switched off.

David felt that they would get no more information and turned to Peter.

"There's no reason to stay in London now, I'll return home tonight and make enquiries in Spain. I'll see you next Wednesday for the interviews but I'll let you know what I find out. Will you bring your tape machine and tapes, saves me bringing mine up on the train?"

"That's no problem; I'll see you next Wednesday morning. Good luck"

David then made his way quickly to catch the 17.17 train from Euston which would arrive in Liverpool at a quarter to eight. The train journey was uneventful, he did get a bite to eat and did some work on his laptop. He caught a taxi at the station and arrived home at 8.15pm. It was an hour later in Spain, but David knew Alisa never went to bed until after midnight. He decided to make the phone call straight away and dialled a number that he would never forget and made the connection.

"Hola"

"Good evening Alisa, this is the love of your life"

"Senor Fraudo, it is nice to hear from you David, a friendly voice, it has been one of those days"

"I was going to ring you and say nice things about your favourite football team, Sevilla, I see they and Barcelona are top of the Spanish La Liga. I presume you are still their biggest fan?"

"Yes, I still never miss a home match and still travel to some of the away games, but I know you David Parish, what other reason have you got to ring me?"

"I do not need a reason to ring you Alisa, I should do it more often and should come out to Seville to see you, but work never stops. I do have a favour to ask you though concerning work. A lady, who works at a London hospital and her partner have been involved in a big fraud and are currently in Marbella on holiday. You do not have to make any notes; I will send you an email message with a photograph attachment in a minute. They are Linda Barrett and Keith Simpson, who should have arrived back in London yesterday, but they never arrived and we think must have been informed we were on to them by their two accomplices, who we spoke to yesterday. I'll send you details of their hotel and car-hire. I think they will have been headed towards Fuengirola, Benalmadena or Torremolinos. Before you say it, I know they are big places with thousands of tourists and this isn't in your area but there's some hope of finding them. Keith Simpson is a drug user and he will be looking to buy drugs, presumably, on the Costa del Sol. Is Sergio Lopez still in charge of the La Policia Drugs Team in that area, he will know some of the dealers and may be able to find out something?"

"How big is this fraud David?"

"Three hundred thousand pounds or nearly five hundred thousand euros"

"I'll give Sergio a ring and check my computer to see what information you are sending me on the email, but only as a favour for you"

"You are wonderful, Alisa. I promise that I'll come and see you in Seville soon"

"I will keep you to the promise Senor Fraudo, give me a few days, I will speak to you next Monday or Tuesday"

"Thanks Alisa, my love, I'm interviewing the other two accomplices who are involved in this fraud next Wednesday, I'll speak to you soon. Bye for now"

David put the telephone down and thought about what Alisa had said. He had been meaning to contact Alisa and arrange a visit. He would arrange this within the next few weeks.

5

David drove his car the short journey to Liverpool South Parkway Station in order to catch the 8.04 train to Manchester, Oxford Road. This would arrive just after 9 o'clock and it was only a short walk to the Human Resources Department of the Local Authority. He had arranged to meet Brian Lewis at 9.30 a.m. and the interview with Carl Sutherland was due for 10.30 a.m.

On entering the Local Authority building, he made his way to the second floor and followed the signs for Human Resources. The reception was on the left and David enquired of the lady behind the desk.

"My name is David Parish, I've come to meet a colleague, Brian Lewis, we are competing interviews in one of your rooms"

"Yes, I have all the details, there are two rooms available, Brian has already arrived and he's in the second room on the right. Brian has asked that I show Carl Sutherland and his Solicitor, Mark Weston to the first room on the right and let you know when they have arrived"

"Thank you"

David knocked on the door before entering and seeing Brian setting up the tape machine.

"Good morning Brian, nice to see you working hard, everything okay?"

"Yes, give me a couple of minutes and I'll update you on a couple of things and go through the paperwork, I presume

35

you'll then want to discuss tactics?"

"Yes, hopefully it should be fairly straightforward, at least I hope so"

David and Brian then made the necessary preparations, obtained a jug of water and some glasses, and were having a general chat when there was a knock on the door and the receptionist popped her head round.

"They are both in the room next door"

"Thanks, we'll bring them in shortly" said David.

David then turned to Brian.

"I'll bring in Mark Weston first, give him some background information and present him with the pack of disclosures, he will then be able to go back to his client and discuss the documents that we've given him"

David went to the office next door.

"Hello Carl, I am David Parish and I presume you are Mark Weston?"

"Yes, are you going to provide me with some disclosure documentation?"

"Yes, if you'd come with me, we are only next door; I'll go through the disclosure pack"

Mark and David left Carl Sutherland alone in the room and walked to the next room to join Brian who knew Mark fairly well, having met him on several previous occasions.

"Good morning Brian"

"Good morning, a present for you Mark" and Brian handed him the Disclosure Pack before both David and Brian opened their copies.

David then explained some of the contents to Mark.

"We have enclosed the death certificates of Francis and Mary Sutherland, the informant was Carl Sutherland on both of them dated nineteen ninety five and nineteen ninety seven respectively. There're several bank statements showing receipt of the pensions and the withdrawals together with copies of some of the cheques used to withdraw monies. You'll see that they have been signed by Carl who was authorised to withdraw from his parent's bank accounts when they were still alive. There are also copies of some of forms sent by the Pension Agencies to his parents verifying that they are still alive which have been signed by Rita Sutherland. There are some other documents for you to examine but we have no other causes of concern, both state pensions were stopped at the date of deaths. You will also see that we're looking at a fraud in the region of one hundred and sixty thousand pounds and do feel that admissions of guilt will be better for your clients, but you'll understand that"

"Have you verified that these are the signatures of my clients?"

Both David and Brian expected this question and David replied.

"Not yet, this is our first formal meeting, you will know that we did not ask any questions prior to today"

Mark left the room with the Disclosure Pack to join Carl Sutherland and discuss the contents. Brian turned to David.

"Do you think that Carl will admit to everything and say that he signed his sister's signature on the letters verifying his parents were still alive?"

"I'm certain he will, if he does and his sister sticks to the story during her interview, we may struggle to prove her guilt. We could refer the signatures to hand writing experts but we may have to settle for Carl and let Rita go free and Carl may well have forged his sister's signature. Let's see how it goes"

There was only a delay of about ten minutes before Mark Weston returned to the room with Carl Sutherland who looked quite pale and probably needed a good nights sleep. They all sat down and David turned to Carl.

"I just want to check that you understand what we are going to do. Brian will operate the tape machine and you will hear a loud noise before the start of the interview, this is normal. Has Mark explained what we are going to discuss and the procedures that will take place?"

"Yes, I understand, let's get it over with"

"Okay, Brian will you start the tape please?"

Brian started the tape and the noise appeared before David started the interview with the opening procedures.

"This Interview is being tape recorded, it is the twenty third of April, two thousand and seven and the time by my watch is ten fifty a.m. I am David Parish a Fraud Consultant for the Public Sector Authorities representing North West Transport. The other officer present is"

"Brian Lewis also a Fraud Specialist representing the North West Transport Authority"

"I am interviewing, please state your full name, address and date of birth"

"Carl Sutherland, Thirty seven Templeton Avenue, Levenshulme, Manchester. Date of birth, tenth of August nineteen fifty"

"Also present is"

"Mark Weston, AGK Solicitors, Manchester"

"We are in the Human Resources Department of the Local Authority, Oxford Street, Manchester. At the end of the interview, I will give you a notice explaining the procedures for the dealing with the tapes and how you can have access to them. Before the interview begins I must caution you."

"You do not have to say anything, but it may harm your defence if you do not mention when questioned something which you later rely on in court, anything you do say may be given in evidence. Do you understand the caution?"

Carl looked a little bit shaken but replied.

"Yes"

"You are not under arrest and you are free to leave at any time. The reason for this interview is that we are investigating allegations that you failed to disclose the death of your father, Francis Sutherland, to the North West Transport Authority in nineteen ninety five and continued to receive and withdraw pension payments made on behalf of Francis Sutherland. You also failed to disclose the death of your mother, Mary Sutherland to the Local Authority in nineteen ninety seven and continued to receive and withdraw pension payments made on behalf of Mary Sutherland. Do you understand the reason for this interview?"

"Yes"

"If at any time you wish to speak to your solicitor in private or if you wish me to stop the interview for any reason, then tell me and I will stop the interview"

At this stage, Carl Sutherland looked at Mark Weston, who moved his hand by way of acknowledgement, and then spoke.

"I know that you're going to ask me lots of questions but I want to say something now before you start, is this okay with you?"

David had an idea what Carl was going to say but replied.

"I will listen to what you have to say but this will not stop me asking questions if this is necessary, we may need clarification on some of comments that you are going to make"

Carl had made some notes on a piece of paper and took a deep breath before he started.

"I have looked at the documents in the pack with my solicitor and admit that I failed to inform North West Transport when my father died in nineteen ninety five. I was authorised to sign to withdraw money from the joint account because my parents were unable to go to the bank and got very confused with money. It was a mistake to begin with; I did not realize for a couple of months until the next bank statement arrived which were always sent to my address. I know it was wrong but I thought the extra money would help my mother and it just continued. When my mother died in nineteen ninety seven, I was very upset and felt unable to inform the Local Authority, North West Transport or even my sister. She did not know anything about this, when the letter came to confirm that my dad was still alive, I used my sister's signature, it is easy to copy. I then carried on drawing the pensions out every month, I was unemployed then and the money helped. I know it was wrong, I shouldn't have taken the money but I couldn't stop once I had started. My sister didn't know anything, she is really upset with all this and I have hurt her badly, it's my fault, I admit everything"

Carl then broke down in tears and David waited a couple of minutes.

"I will need to clarify a few points which should not take too long, do you want a break for ten minutes or should I continue when you are ready?"

David glanced at Carl and Mark and was about to inform Brian to stop the tape but Carl suddenly mumbled.

"I want you to carry on and finish this once and for all"

David looked at Mark who then nodded his head.

"I've listened to your statement but need to confirm a few answers that you have given, most of which you will be able to answer yes or no, is this okay?"

"Yes, I suppose so"

"Did you fail to notify the North West Transport Pensions Agency in nineteen ninety five that you father had died and did you continue to receive the pension and draw the proceeds from the bank?"

"Yes"

"Did you fail to notify the Local Authority Pensions Agency in nineteen ninety seven that your mother had died and did you continue to receive the pension and draw the proceeds from the bank?"

"Yes"

"Do you agree that fraudulent payments from North West Transport Pensions Agency total Ninety seven thousand, seven hundred and fifty pounds?"

"If that's what you've worked it out as, then Yes"

"Do you agree that fraudulent payments from the Local Authority Pensions Agency total fifty eight thousand nine hundred pounds?"

"Yes, I suppose so"

"Who has signed the annual forms received from both Pension Agencies confirming your parents are still alive?"

"I have"

"They are signed Rita Sutherland"

"I know that but I signed them as Rita Sutherland. She didn't know that I had signed her name"

"Can you repay the money?"

"I don't have that amount of money, it's been spent"

"How much money would you be prepared to pay back?"

"I don't know"

"Do you own your own house?"

"Well, yes"

"When did you buy the house?"

"It will have been in nineteen ninety eight, just after my mother died. I'd just got a job and I was left enough money to put down a deposit"

"Have a think about what I've said and let your solicitor know"

David turned to Brian.

"Is there anything else that we need to mention Brian?"

"No, I think we have enough for today"

David then asked a further question to Carl.

"Do you wish to add anything further or clarify any point or anything you have told me?"

"No"

"Here is the notice which explains your entitlement to a copy of the tape used in this interview. This interview is concluded at eleven twenty five a.m. on the twenty third of April, two thousand and seven. Switch off the tape recorder"

Carl turned to Mark Weston and asked

"What happens now?"

Mark looked at David who informed Carl.

"We will refer our findings to the Pensions Agencies but we'll advise them that this should be referred to the Solicitors who represent the Department of Works and Pensions and also act for some other Public bodies. They will then instigate court proceedings"

Carl signed a copy of the tape that had been sealed by Brian and would be made available to Carl's solicitors when the matter was referred for court action. Both Carl and Mark Weston then left the room.

The interview with Rita Sutherland was due to take place at 1pm; Rita was due to be accompanied by another solicitor, Cathy Pointon, from the same practice as Mark Weston. David turned to Brian and asked

"What do you think of our chances with Rita Sutherland, now that Carl had admitted everything with no help from anybody else?"

"I'd say we have virtually no chance"

"I'm afraid that I agree with you completely"

"But we'll still have to hold the interview, let's go get some lunch"

David and Brian completed the formal interview with Rita Sutherland, on tape, in the presence of Cathy Pointon. It went as expected, with Rita denying any knowledge, stating that Carl had told her the full story only after his initial contact with David. In fairness, it was possible that Rita may have been telling the truth; certainly no jury would ever convict her on the present evidence and the admittance of Carl.

Both David and Brian examined all the paper work and discussed both the interviews and the comments made by Carl

Sutherland. They agreed to take the case against Rita no further and David agreed to telephone Cathy Pointon, Rita's solicitor, the next day informing her of their decision.

They tidied the room, securing all the evidence correctly and David turned to Brian.

"Thanks for your help Brian. We'll need to keep in touch and monitor the progress of the legal team. We'll both be receiving letters from the witness support staff letting us know what progress is happening in the Magistrates Court and then the Crown Court"

"It'll probably be a few months David"

"I'm sure you're right"

They then left the office and made their separate ways home with David making his way to the train station for the return to Liverpool. The journey again took just less than one hour, when he got off the train and walked to where his car was parked. He made a slight detour on the way home in order to pick up some ink cartridges for his printer and a few packs of A4 paper.

6

The next day, Tuesday, David had set aside to complete all the paperwork and court documentation to be given to the solicitors in order to proceed with the case against Carl Sutherland. He also had to prepare for the meetings with Zoe Ferguson and Rik Jeffreys, being held the next day in London. He was also hoping to hear from Alisa Garcia with any developments in the search for Keith Simpson and Linda Barrett.

David had to work from home on many occasions and he had set up an office at home for this purpose, it contained all the necessary computer equipment, research documents, paperwork and a good filing system. He spent a couple of hours copying documents, numbering exhibits which would be required by the Court and checking all the statements that had been taken. It would be necessary to arrange a transcription of the taped interviews which he would read through prior to placing this with the other documentation. Once this had been completed he would then be able to contact the legal team for a meeting.

A check on the food cabinets showed that some shopping was required and as David also felt the need for a short brisk walk, off he went. He left his house and walked towards the park which was at the end of his road. It was a lovely park with a wide variety of trees and plants, the ducks were swimming around the lake as he made his way to the far end of the park. He then crossed the dual carriageway before turning right and making his way to the next main junction which had traffic lights. About 50 yards up on the right of Beaconsfield Road was Strawberry Fields, made famous by the Beatles song. It was originally a home operated by the Salvation Army but the dwindling numbers had now forced its closure. David wondered what would become of this in the fullness of time, probably more houses but one never knows.

A little further down the dual carriageway was the house were John Lennon lived with his Aunt Mimi from 1945 to 1963. The property know as The Mendips, 251 Menlove Avenue, is now owned by the National Trust and is a stop on one of the guided tours which tourists use to see parts of Liverpool. John Lennon was murdered in Manhattan, opposite to Central Park where he had an apartment in the Dakota Building. It happened on the 8th December 1980 which was, ironically, David's eighteenth birthday. The walk continued but David crossed Menlove Avenue and entered the golf course, he walked briskly, but making sure he was fully alert, watching for any wayward shots when the golfers were hitting the golf balls down the fairway. He had only played golf a few times and was never able to find the time and the interest to take the game more seriously. On leaving the golf course, he made his way past the local comprehensive school and walked down the gently sloping road before he turned right onto Mather Avenue.

He again crossed this dual carriageway and passed Forthlin Road, another Beatles landmark. Number 20 Forthlin Road was Paul McCartney's home and has also been purchased by the National Trust. This is also included on the guided tour and as he crossed Forthlin Road, one of the tourist coaches stopped, all the visitors getting off the coach and walking the short distance to the house numbered 20. There were, as usual, many Japanese tourists on the coach with their cameras all prepared and ready for action.

David continued straight on to the Tesco Supermarket where he did all the necessary shopping before finishing the walk and returning home. The total walk was about 4 miles, and it would be a good walk for the Beatles fans, but they tended to be more interested in the taking the guided coach rather than getting lost on what is a pleasant walk. It was now a good time for a coffee and some lunch.

After lunch, he then drove the short journey to the offices of the Local Authority and gave the tapes to one of the ladies in the Secretariat, who would complete the transcription of the taped interviews that had taken place with Carl and Rita Sutherland. He had just returned to his house when the telephone rang and he picked up the handset quickly.

"Hello"

"Hola Senor Fraudo"

"Hola Alicia, it's nice to hear from you, how are you?"

"I am fine. I have some news for you. Sergio Lopez has seen Keith Simpson"

"Oh, that's brilliant, has he detained him and what did Keith Simpson have to say?"

"He has said nothing but he is definitely not going anywhere. Wait for it, he's dead"

"Dead! How?"

"Yes, he is muerto. He was drunk and got involved in a dispute with a drugs dealer about the money for the drugs. It happened in Torremolinos on Saturday evening and he ended up getting stabbed. He was taken to the Carlos Haya Hospital in Malaga City but died in the early hours of Sunday morning from his wounds. The noise of the argument was heard by an officer from La Policia, who rushed to the scene and the drug dealer was arrested, but it didn't help your Senor Simpson"

"Was Linda Barrett with him?"

"No, they had an argument earlier that evening apparently and Keith went out alone, Linda stayed at their hotel room in Benalmadena"

"How did the police find her?"

"Keith had a new Spanish mobile phone and so did Linda. Her Spanish phone number was the only number on his phone. His British driving licence was in his wallet which is how they found out he was from the England. They were not sure of the relationship between him and Linda but an English speaking officer then telephoned her to find out what their relationship was and then gave her the bad news. She is in a terrible state, he is dead and she thinks the English police will be waiting to arrest her as soon as she arrives in England or that she might also end up spending years in a Spanish prison. They have also informed the British Embassy and your police, I understand that his father died a few years ago and his mother has remarried and now lives in Birmingham. She will be informed today but apparently Keith has not seen her for a couple of years and there is little contact, he did not like her new husband. There are no brothers or sisters. I have spoken to Linda on the telephone and explained that the English police are not involved at this stage but that you are in charge of the fraud. I also told her that the Spanish Police will not arrest her at this stage unless she fails to co-operate with you. I have her mobile phone number and said that you will contact her and that you'll be coming out to Spain"

"Why am I coming to Spain?"

"I have a slight problem and I hope that you will be able to help, I need to see you"

"What type of problem?"

"The Mitchell gang are buying property in Murcia"

David knew what that meant to Alisa and offered his immediate help.

"I will arrange a flight as soon as possible but it may be a few days, is that okay?"

"Yes, David, let me know when you are arriving, as I would like Felipe to come down from Murcia for a couple of days. He will probably stay the one night at my flat. I will send you an

47

email with the La Policia contacts, the Hospital details and the phone number and hotel address of Linda Barrett"

"Thanks, Alisa, you are a treasure, I will speak to you shortly, bye for now"

"Bye-bye David"

Any mention of the Mitchell's, brings great anger to Alisa Garcia and her family, David is fully aware of the reasons.

The Mitchell family live in a five bedroom, luxury, detached house, in Cheshire, which has a market value in excess of £1,500,000. The property has obviously been purchased with the proceeds of criminal activity but the police have never been able find the evidence from the crimes which allowed the purchase to take place. They also tried to involve Inland Revenue suggesting that if the income was legitimate which allowed the purchase, had this income been declared. Whilst an investigation did take place, the Mitchell family did manage to overcome all the questions, but it alerted them so that they knew that they would have to be more careful as this type of investigation might happen again.

Steve Mitchell, aged thirty four, is the elder brother who has always been involved in criminal activities, his younger brother Alan Mitchell, aged thirty one, tends to follow his brothers activities, usually guided by his elder brother. They have a younger sister Sarah, aged twenty five, who has never been involved in any misdemeanours and has tried to steer clear of any involvement in her brother's activities, although she has reluctantly accepted the rewards of some of their activities, usually in the monetary field. It is quite clear that Sarah has a dislike of her elder brother and has recently acquired a rented flat in Manchester City Centre, which she shares with a friend, Karen Lucas. Sarah obtained a degree at Liverpool University and is currently a consultant for a Commercial Property leasing and letting company in Manchester. The only reason that she returns to the family home is to visit her mother.

The brothers live with their mother, Paula Mitchell, age fifty six who does not work, but always made a point of knowing, without their knowledge, what her sons were up to. Their father Frank Mitchell was serving a ten year prison sentence in a Spanish prison for his involvement in a robbery on the Banco Costa del Sol. This took place over five years ago but he died from cancer six months into his sentence.

The total amount involved in the robbery which occurred in December 2001 was nearly two million euros; the euro was becoming the official currency of Spain on the 1st January 2002 and Frank Mitchell was taking advantage of the delivery of the new currency notes to the Bank. The robbery took place after the bank had been closed for two hours but they gained access when they threatened a bank employee who was leaving the premises. The robbery became violent leaving the bank employee confined to a wheelchair. It was known that Frank Mitchell had not fired the shot but his accomplice was never captured, it was widely believed to be Steve Mitchell, who had fired the gun which crippled the bank employee. A third robber was waiting in a stolen van.

The bank employee was Luis Alvarez, a cousin of Alisa Garcia.

Whilst Alicia is a senior officer in the Guardia Civil, her brother Felipe Garcia is an Inspector in La Policia based in Murcia on the Costa Blanca.

There are three police organisations in the Andalucia region and they are all armed:

The Guardia Civil (Civil Guard) are recognised by their green uniforms and are responsible for national security, customs and crowd control. You will usually see them on the motorway in either cars or on motorbikes as they do speed checks.

The National Police (La Policia) wear either a black uniform and a white shirt or a blue military style uniform. Their duties include guarding public buildings, the Royal Family and Government figures. If you are a victim of street crime these are the police that will deal with your case. If you are a victim of such crime, you need to make a statement (denuncia) at a police station.

The Municipal Police wear blue and white uniforms. They are responsible to the mayor and town hall in each municipality, and their duties include controlling local traffic and parking violations.

The Garcia family involvement in the different police organisations and the shooting of a family member made the Spanish police even more determined to arrest the culprits. They had escaped from the scene using a stolen white van which was found, burnt out, a few miles away. There was no sign of the money but several car tracks were found in the immediate vicinity.

The robbers had a problem, the stolen money was all new euros and the numbers of the notes had all been recorded, they would have been better stealing the old pesetas, which would have still been legal tender for a couple of months and longer if paid into a Spanish bank. The police did know the robbers were English speaking but they did not have any more leads at this stage. All banks had been informed of the numbers on the stolen euros and some were beginning to be received by banks in Murcia, but they were being paid in by shops, bars and restaurants and only as part of their normal takings.

Finally, La Policia had a lucky break. They had good news when they visited a restaurant in San Javier that had paid some of the euros into the bank. The restaurant owner had no idea who had given the euros but he then spoke to other members of staff and one of the girls suddenly had a thought. Four guests had paid a bill of a hundred and fifty euros with three new fifty euro bills but as they left, the man who paid the bill had slipped a tip into her pocket. She had thanked him but then forgot about it until she got home when she pulled out a new fifty euro note, which was a very big tip. It was the policy of the staff to put all the tips together and then share them out, so she told the manager the next day about this fifty euro tip and this was sorted out when the tips were shared that night. She still had that note on her dressing table at home and when she gave the police the number of the note the next day, it was found to be on the stolen list. The group were not regulars at the restaurant but the booking had been made in the name of Mitchell. The waitress also remembered a lady calling this gentleman by the name of Frank and there were also two younger men at the table, possibly the sons of the older couple.

La Policia in Malaga made enquiries with Interpol and they responded by contacting the English Police. The Mitchell family were known to both Greater Manchester Police and Merseyside Police, who were also able to provide them with an address in San Pedro del Pinatar, Murcia. This is one of the main tourist destinations on the Murcia coast and faces the tranquil waters of the Mar Menor. Felipe Garcia headed the La Policia raid on the apartment in San Pedro del Pinatar where they found Frank Mitchell alone, his family having returned to England the day before. A thorough search of the property uncovered only twenty thousand euros which had been stolen on the raid on the Costa del Sol. No other money was ever located.

He pleaded guilty at the subsequent trial, saying that he fired the gun, but refused to give the names of the other accomplices and was sentenced to ten years imprisonment. It was soon discovered that he knew that he had a terminal illness and his sentence would be over in a short time. It was clear that he had decided to complete this bank robbery as a closing highlight to his criminal career and had no intention of implicating anybody else, especially his family.

Felipe Garcia and La Policia also knew that he did not fire the shot that crippled Luiz Alvarez. They had also discovered that his two sons, Steve and Alan, were in Spain at the time of the robbery. Naturally Frank and the other accomplice inside the bank were masked, but the subsequent investigation suggested that the bodily shape of the second accomplice who had fired the gun may well have been Steve Mitchell. They did not have the evidence and Steve had never been brought to trial, but Felipe Garcia and his sister Alisa did not forget and would always seek justice for their cousin, Luiz.

Alisa could not really understand why Steve Mitchell and his family would want to buy another place in Spain; surely he would know that he was still a wanted man in Spain even though they had no evidence to put him behind bars. She also wondered how he was going raise the money to pay for the purchase of the property and was the money in Spain or in England. Maybe the opportunity to gain some type of retribution for the injuries sustained by a member of their family was about to happen and Alisa decided that she wanted the help of the man she still loved, David Parish.

7

Alisa had first met David in March 2000 when he was investigating holiday travel insurance claims on behalf of several U.K. Insurance Companies. His investigation was centred on the Costa del Sol but arrangements had been made to visit the Guardia Civil in Malaga for their assistance. Alisa was English speaking and would usually be asked to assist fellow Police Officers or Investigators from the United Kingdom in their enquiries.

When this English Investigator walked into Alisa's office, it was a pleasant surprise; he was tall, probably about 6 feet 3 inches, with dark wavy hair, obviously very fit, in his mid-thirties and once he spoke, introducing himself as David Parish, he captured the full attention of Alisa. Their initial meeting lasted a couple of hours and David explained the details of his investigation and amused Alisa with some of the holiday travel claims that people had been making.

David mentioned one case, a man claimed for "recuperation costs" when recovering from a heart attack while holidaying in West of Africa, but it turned out the bill was for the cost of visiting a local brothel.

According to research by the Association of British Insurers, nearly half of holiday makers would not rule out making a fraudulent insurance claim in the summer. They had also discovered that there were fraudsters based on the Costa del Sol who were offering their services to assist people in making false holiday insurance claims. The fraudsters also referred the claimants to La Policia, if necessary, in order that details of non-existent thefts were recorded. In order for a claim to be successful, Insurance Companies always insisted crimes were reported to La Policia. Claims were also being made for illnesses and injuries that had not taken place and an assistant in a clinic was giving false receipts and documentary evidence at a cost of one hundred euros to each claimant.

It was to eliminate these services that David was seeking the help of Alisa. The promise of assistance was immediate and it did not take the Spanish Police long, headed by Alisa, to arrest and charge these 'Holiday Insurance Claim Assistants'.

David then arranged to take Alisa for a meal by way of thanks before he returned to England. They discovered that they both loved walking and hiking and took holidays in pursuance of this passion. Alisa then mentioned that she had booked a week's walking holiday with Walk Andalucia in three weeks time, and jokingly asked David if he would like to join the walk. David quickly checked his diary; he was due some holidays and agreed, hoping that there was a spare place available on the walk. Alisa immediately contacted the organisers of Walk Andalucia who confirmed that a place would be made available. The walkers would be based in the delightful mountain village of Torrox Pueblo which is situated south east of Malaga. They would be staying in old Spanish houses but with modern conveniences, apparently there would be fifteen walkers sharing four houses and David would be in separate accommodation to Alisa.

It was three weeks later that Alisa met David again, at a welcome meeting held by the organisers of Walk Andalucia. The fifteen walkers were in different sized groups, some were single like David and Alisa, others were in twos or threes, but like many walkers, they all soon become a friendly group. They had met up in one of the Spanish houses but then all went for a meal in a typical Spanish Restaurant. David and Alisa soon found they had many other common interests, travel, sport, walking not to mention a love of wine and food. They had not married before, Alisa was now thirty-four and David was thirty-seven.

The holiday was based in the two ranges of mountains, the Sierra Tejeda and the Sierra Almijara. All the walkers would meet in the morning at a car park in Torrox Pueblo and be transported for about a half an hour to the start of the different walks. The walks would involve steep climbs but most of the walkers were able to manage and were well equipped. Certainly David and Alisa were able to complete all the walks but they were often strenuous and a well earned bottle of San Miguel was required at the end of each walk.

The walking holiday was not the most romantic of holidays, but David and Alisa did manage to talk a lot and did become closer as the holiday progressed. There was a free day for the walkers so David and Alisa went to Nerja on the Spanish coast and spent a pleasant day, having lunch at a Tapas bar and sharing a bottle of Rioja before returning in the evening to join the rest of the walkers.

On the final evening, the meal was in a restaurant noted for its fish dishes and the surroundings were typically Spanish with a picturesque view overlooking the mountains. Telephone numbers and email addresses were exchanged by many of the walkers, who were saying that they should meet again on some future walks. David had Alisa's contact details but on the walk back to their different Spanish houses, David asked Alisa if they could see each other again, not on a walking holiday, but to spend some more time together. Clearly, Alisa was delighted; she wanted to see David again, and a week's holiday was fixed, but not for a couple of months time, due to Alisa's work. They reached the house were Alisa was staying and David gave Alisa a kiss, which was interrupted by cheers from the other three walkers staying with Alisa who were looking over the balcony. They both had to smile and David waved to the other walkers as he left to go the house where he was staying. Alisa went upstairs where she joined her houseguests, who were all English, for a final drink. They all commented that they could see romance in the air and it was often the talk of the walkers as they were climbing the mountains.

It was during this drink, no more than fifteen minutes after David had left, that Alisa's mobile telephone rang. It was David, saying that he had contacted easyJet and would be able to delay his return home to Liverpool for 24 hours and he would like to spend his final day with Alisa. She was more than happy with this delay and would discuss the arrangements in the morning when they were leaving Torrox Pueblo at the end of the week's holiday.

The following morning, Walk Andalucia transported the walkers to Malaga Airport. All, apart from Alisa, had flights arranged from Malaga Airport to other airports. David and Alisa did not enter the airport but caught a taxi to Mijas Costa, where they had booked a room in a super hotel which overlooked the sea. It was a hotel that David had heard about on his visits to the Costa del Sol, he had never stayed there but it was the perfect romantic setting. Alisa had heard of the hotel and its facilities and fully agreed with David's choice. On arrival they thought that they would take a stroll along the beach but would first book into their room and get rid of the luggage. They found their room easily but it was more than two hours later before they started their stroll along the beach, hand in hand.

Over a couple of San Miguel beers in a beach bar, David and Alisa spoke about how they could manage their relationship and be able to see each other, with David being based in Liverpool and Alisa in Malaga. David agreed to return to Malaga in three weeks for a long weekend with Alisa flying to Liverpool a couple of weeks later. They would still go on the week's holiday in two months time.

They had a lovely romantic meal that evening in the hotel at a table overlooking the sea. A bottle of Faustino V Rioja made the meal even more pleasant and they retired to their room, placing the 'Do not disturb' notice on the door. They were late down the following morning for breakfast before visiting a local street market. David then had to catch a taxi in time for the easyJet Flight 7182 to Liverpool which was due to depart at 5.40 p.m. and he had to be at the airport about 4 p.m.

David and Alisa caught the taxi from the hotel in Mijas Costa and headed for Alisa's flat in Malaga, where David said his goodbyes, before returning to the taxi for the short journey to Malaga Airport in order to catch the flight to Liverpool. It was to be three weeks before David made the first of many weekend flights to Malaga with Alisa completing the reverse journey when work allowed.

They took their planned week's holiday in June in Paris. David was able to fly direct with easyJet from Liverpool to Paris, Charles de Gaulle, with the return flight a week later. Alisa had no direct flight from Malaga to Paris but was able to change at Madrid although there was a direct flight from Paris to Malaga for the return journey. She flew to Madrid with Air Europa the day before to see a friend, and left the following morning on an Iberia flight to Paris Charles de Gaulle in order to meet up with David.

They stayed at a four star hotel in the Latin Quarter close to the River Seine and were able to take in most of the sights in Paris. The Louvre was wonderful and the trip up the Eiffel Tower was spectacular, they walked and walked which is always the best way to see Paris. One night they had a romantic meal on board a boat cruise on the River Seine and then were spoilt for a choice with the restaurants available in the Latin Quarter and around the River Seine on the other nights. Paris lived up to its reputation as a city of romance and they were saddened in having to depart, separately, to their different parts of Europe.

Their long distance romance continued for another year before David made the decision to try and use Spain as a base for his fraud consultancy, specialising in cases which involved the United Kingdom and Spain. They rented a villa near Benalmadena Pueblo on the Costa del Sol for three years, but it was becoming more difficult for David to act as a Fraud Consultant without having to return to his Liverpool home on many occasions due to work pressures. Alisa was then offered promotion in work, which would involve a move to Seville. After much heartache, they decided that they would go their separate ways, which meant that David would be better returning to Liverpool and Alisa should take the promotion being offered by the Guardia Civil and move to Seville. Although they are now over two thousand miles apart, they still have strong feelings for each other and happily they have remained good friends, very good friends. There is a direct flight between Liverpool and Seville and whilst they have continued with their long distance romance, their meetings are now sadly becoming less frequent.

It was during the time that David and Alisa were in Benalmadena, that the Bank robbery took place and the shooting of Luis Alvarez. His support to Alisa and her family was wonderful at this time and his knowledge and assistance had helped the British Police to name the Mitchell family and lead La Policia to Frank Mitchell. Alisa now wanted the help of David Parish again, but she was also missing him and wanted to see David again for herself. This would be happening within a matter of a few days.

8

David was in his office at home completing his research and documentation for the interviews with Rik and Zoe, which were taking place the following morning. He had used the internet to book the seat on the train from Liverpool to London Euston, but, due to the late booking, he would need to collect the tickets at the Train Station in the morning. He was printing off the details, when the email message arrived from Alisa, providing, as promised, the La Policia contacts, the Hospital details and the mobile number and hotel address of Linda Barrett.

He decided that he would give Linda a ring and looked at the phone number on the email, as there was a chance that he might get some information, which would help in the interviews tomorrow morning. Anything said in this phone call could not be used as evidence; he would have to give details of any information he obtained from Linda at the beginning of the taped interview. He picked up the handset and dialled the phone number provided by Alisa.

There was a slight delay before the call was answered.
"Hello"
"Hello, is that Linda Barrett?"
"Yes"
"My name is David Parish, I understand that Alisa Garcia from the Spanish Police, told you that I would be ringing you"
"Oh yes, she said that you were investigating the travel claims

at Euston General Hospital and that you're not the police"

"That's correct Linda. My role is to investigate cases of fraud and, in this case, I'm working for the National Health Service at the hospital. I have seen Rik Jeffreys and Zoe Ferguson and will be formally interviewing them again concerning these travel claim frauds which have gone on for more than two years. First of all, I would like to assure you that you are free to return to London and there'll be no police waiting for you when you arrive back at the airport"

"Thank you very much; I have been worried out of my mind"

David could sense the relief in the way Linda was speaking.

"I know you're in a terrible situation, with the murder of Keith and knowing that we have discovered the fraud. Book your flight back from Malaga to Stansted Airport, go home, and I will contact you there. I'll be coming out to Seville later this week and will not be back until the beginning of next week. I really think that you should book your flight as soon as possible"

"The Spanish Police lady said that I could trust you, she also said that you might be able to meet me at the airport, I'd rather wait until you are back in England. I have been asking the police here about Keith's body, but they said that it may be some time before his body is released, it won't be in the next few days"

It was the first time that David had heard that he was supposed to meet Linda at the airport, Alisa hadn't told him.

"The Spanish Authorities do move rather slowly at times and it may be some time before the body is released. The meeting you mention can be arranged, I suppose, I will have to let you know when I'm returning back to England, in order that I would be there when you arrive"

"The Police lady also said that it might even be possible for you to meet me in Spain and get the same flight back to London when you are going home"

More news for David, he did not know what else Alisa has

said that he would do, but it was possible to catch the same flight and it would ensure that Linda returned to London.

"Okay, I will contact you when I'm in Seville, and arrange to accompany you on the same flight home"

"Should I come to Seville or will you be coming down to Malaga?"

"When I have finished in Seville, I will drive down to the Costa del Sol and arrange to meet you at Malaga Airport or Benalmadena if you prefer"

"That's great. Thanks for your help"

David was thinking to himself what information he might get by prolonging the conversation and decided to keep chatting to Linda.

"How did you get involved in this?"

"It was a terrible mistake. Zoe and Rik were claiming travel expenses from Basingstoke to see their daughter in hospital. I didn't know that they lived local and certainly didn't know that their daughter had left the hospital. One evening, Keith came home and mentioned that Rik had called at the garage and spoke to him about the fraud that Zoe had planned, which they were doing at the hospital. He said that it was at the cash office where I worked and I might start to get suspicious if they carried on, but if I ignored the deceit, Keith would get a share of the money that they were claiming. I went mad to begin with, but Keith persuaded me to let them carry on, the extra money would be useful and he said I wasn't doing anything criminal. I thought it would only carry on for a few weeks but it went on for a couple of years and I was terrified to say anything. I know that Keith and Rik used to meet every couple of weeks and Keith would receive some money, but I've no idea how much money Keith received; he did give me a couple of thousand pounds every now and then. I know he had used some of his money to buy drugs and now look what has happened, he's been murdered all because of drugs. I just wish this had never started and I'll never forgive Rik and Zoe. Rik actually rang Keith in Spain and told him that they'd been caught by you. If he hadn't made that call, we would've got the plane home the next day and Keith would still be alive. I hope that Rik gets what he deserves, it's his fault Keith's dead"

"Do you still have any of the money?"

"I don't have much of the money, Keith took care of it, and I've no idea if he's still got some of the money. I suppose there may be some money at home as he wouldn't have put it in the bank. Rik probably only gave him a small share and he could of easily cheated Keith. Thinking about it, Keith asked me a couple of times how much they had claimed, but I refused to check in case somebody caught me going through the records"

"That's okay, but I'll need to formally interview you after you have arrived back in London. It will be on tape and you should be accompanied by a solicitor but I'll explain all that when I see you. In the meantime, I'm putting my trust in you, do not leave your hotel and do not run away. I will see you safely back to London and let you know what happens. I'll give you a ring over the weekend when I am in Seville"

"Thanks David, I promise that I'll not run away. All I want to do is get home and get all this business finished and get on with my life, give me a ring as soon as you can"

"Bye for now Linda"

"Goodbye David and thank you once again"

David put the phone down as another email arrived, this time from Peter Daley, who was confirming the arrangements for tomorrow. Rik would be interviewed first at 10.30 am and Zoe Ferguson at 1 pm, with both interviews taking place in the Human Resources Department of Euston General Hospital as agreed with Stuart Bradley. Interview Rooms 1 & 2 have been arranged and the Receptionist in Human Resources is aware that we are coming. John Harrison would be representing both

Rik and Zoe which may cause some minor problems as John would be able to update Zoe on what had happened earlier. It was always difficult to prevent information being passed to a second suspect when two were being interviewed on the same day, usually the first suspect would contact the second, and in this case Rik would be able to warn Zoe. This was, however, a fairly clear case of fraud, the evidence was substantial and David was not unduly concerned. He also felt he would be able to get as much information as he required from Linda Barrett.

He did a quick reply to the email message from David confirming he would be catching the 6.27 a.m. Virgin Express from Liverpool, Lime Street to London Euston which was due to arrive just before 9 o'clock. He would then make the short walk to the hospital and should be there around 9.30 a.m. and he also reminded David to bring his tape machine for the two interviews that were taking place with Rik and Zoe.

9

Zoe and Rik were sitting in their flat preparing for a meeting with their solicitor, John Harrison. Rik was clearly getting a bit agitated.

"What excuses are we going to make?"

Zoe had obviously given it plenty of thought.

"I don't know, I think they already know everything, there isn't much that we can say tomorrow. I've seen it on television; I think it was on 'The Bill', when the bloke being questioned by the police kept saying no comment. I don't know if we could say that, we'll ask John Harrison when we see him later, but if we admit everything, they may take it easier on us. I've got Alice to worry about and take care of; don't you think that you should take most of the blame?"

"What, this was all your idea. I am not as stupid as you think; I've been keeping a record of the money that you gave to me and also the money that you told me to give to Keith Simpson. I've given Keith around fifty thousand pounds, which he would have to share with Linda and I've received just over fifty thousand pounds. We agreed to do three equal shares which would be a total of a hundred and fifty thousand pounds, but the fraud bloke told John Harrison that the total amount fiddled was three hundred thousand pounds. That means you must have got away with two hundred thousand pounds, not fifty thousand pounds and you've cheated on Keith and Linda, not to mention me. Where's the rest of the money?"

"I don't know what you're talking about, they must have made a mistake, it couldn't have been as high as that, I gave you fair shares. I may have kept a little bit extra myself but I deserved it and it was my idea and I was taking the biggest risk"

"You are lying through your teeth. If they say three hundred thousand pound has been taken, then they've probably got the correct information, don't start trying to tell them that their calculations are wrong, they'll have the evidence already. I've heard about these types of investigators, they wouldn't say a figure unless they knew they were correct. What have you done with the money?"

"Maybe Linda took some of the money before she handed it to me"

"Don't talk a load of crap, if you were given less than your claim, you would've gone berserk and created a scene, or waited for her outside the hospital. You would've told me and I used to see you checking the cash when you came home, just to make sure it was correct"

"I haven't got much money"

"Who has got it then, your bloke on the side?"

"What the hell are you talking about, I haven't got another bloke, there's only you, but I'm beginning to wonder why"

"I've already told you once, don't think I'm stupid. You had a night out last Saturday when you said you were going to see Sally Bridges for a drink and meal"

"That's right, I did"

"No you didn't, I was in the pub on Monday night and I saw Sally Bridges with her bloke. We had a little chat and she mentioned that she hadn't seen you for a couple of months and wondered how you were getting on. I also remember you saying that you were going out with Sally last month as well, just tell the truth Zoe"

"We've got to get ready to go and see your solicitor, we'll talk later"

"If you think that I'm going to be the fall guy, while you split the two hundred thousand quid with your new bloke, you've got to be joking. This was all your idea and you're the leader of the fiddle, take what's coming and don't pass the blame on to me"

"What about Alice?"

"Your mum will take care of Alice; you know that, you've probably already made the arrangements. Don't try and deny there is another bloke on the scene, you have been cool on me for the past six months and sex is now virtually non-existent, I presume that you've been getting plenty off him?"

"Why can't we blame Linda Barrett and Keith Simpson? You warned Keith and they haven't returned from Spain. They'll easily hide themselves in Spain and no one will ever see them again"

"Keith has become a good mate of mine and I don't do the dirty on my mates, not like you. Linda never wanted to get involved and as you know, she has wanted to stop for some time. They'll be back and will admit their parts and face the music. Linda is probably persuading Keith to come back soon"

Linda got up off the chair and made her way upstairs shouting.

"We have got to agree on something before we see our solicitor"

Rik picked up his phone and went to the kitchen where Zoe could not hear him. He dialled the telephone number of his solicitor, John Harrison.

"John Harrison, Solicitors"

"Hello, this is Rik Jeffreys, can I speak to John Harrison?"

"He's with another client at the moment, can I take a message?"

"Yes, I'm seeing John at four o'clock with my partner Zoe Ferguson"

"That is correct"

"Will you tell him that I want him to represent me but will he get somebody else in your firm to represent Zoe. He was going to represent both of us, but I don't want him to represent Zoe. I will explain when we arrive, and will you ask him if I can have five minutes alone before Zoe joins the meeting?"

"Yes, I'll let him know what you have said, see you at four o'clock"

"Thanks see you then"

Rik put the mobile in his pocket and went through to the lounge to wait for Zoe.

They left the flat for the fifteen minute walk to the solicitors office. They turned into Tottenham Court Road before turning left into New Oxford Street. They then joined High Holborn before making their way to Holborn where the office of John Harrison Solicitors was located.

They did not speak until they reached the beginning of Holborn when Zoe had had enough of the silence.

"What story are we going to tell your solicitor?"

"Yes, for your information, he's my solicitor and he's not yours, you are going to see somebody else"

"I don't know what you mean, we both spoke to him last week and he agreed to represent both of us"

"I phoned him before and left a message telling him that I didn't want him representing both of us. I wanted him to represent me and I asked could he arrange somebody else to represent you"

"When were you going to tell me?"

"Now, I've just told you. I reckon that this is the best thing to do, just tell the truth, admit everything and when it gets to court, you or your brief can start whingeing about who will look after Alice. They will probably then reduce your sentence. If you pay back some of the two hundred thousand pounds, your sentence may be made even more lenient. In fact if you do pay some of the money back, it should help us all to get a smaller sentence. How much can you give back?"

"I'm not giving them a penny, I'll take my chances. I don't have a police record like you do"

"They were only minor offences and I've been clean for three years. They will not hold those against me when they look at sentencing me for my small part in this fiddle"

"Small part, you must be joking, who was it that got Keith and Linda involved? You arranged it all with Keith. Anyhow, you said at one time that Keith had been to jail"

"A few years ago, before he met Linda. I'll tell John Harrison how we involved Linda and Keith and I'm sure they will say the same when they return home"

"They may never return home and they may never be found"

"When we met John Harrison last time, he mentioned that the Investigator, David Parish is a bit special and is known as Mr Fraud in this country. He has contacts everywhere and he'll soon find out where Keith and Linda are staying. We might find out some more news when we see him tomorrow and John Harrison might be able to give me some up to date information when we meet"

"Where is the office?"

"It's just a bit further up on the right"

Rik walked up the few steps to the front door of the old building with a sign on the door stating 'John Harrison, Solicitors'. They pushed the door and walked towards the reception desk.

"Hello, I'm Rik Jeffreys, I have a meeting with John Harrison at four o'clock"

"I'll let him know you are here, please take a seat"

Rik and Zoe sat on the two chairs and heard the receptionist say.

"Hello John, I have your four o'clock appointments, Rik Jeffreys and Zoe Ferguson in reception"

They waited about five minutes when John Harrison came out of his office and walked towards them.

"I believe you want to see me first Rik?"

"Yes, do you have somebody else to represent Zoe?"

"Yes, Anna Young will be speaking to Zoe, once I've had a quick conversation with you"

John then turned to Zoe.

"Will you stay here until I have had a quick word with Rik?"

Zoe was clearly in a foul temper and about to explode.

"I've got nothing else better to do at the moment"

Rik then followed John Harrison into his office, closing the door behind him. They both sat down before John spoke to Rik.

"You'd better tell me what's going on and why you want somebody else to represent Zoe"

"We've had a row about what we should be doing now, and some things have happened since we last spoke to you and I think it's best if I tell you everything"

"I am your solicitor, I'd expect the truth if you want me to help you"

"I agree, I think my best chances are if I admit everything but Zoe may tell a different story"

"Forget Zoe for the moment, she will be seeing Anna in ten minutes"

Rik shrugged his shoulders and ran his hands through his hair before he started speaking to John Harrison.

"We heard the fraud bloke saying that the amount that had been fiddled was about three hundred thousand pounds, would this be right or would he exaggerate it to make it look worse?"

"If Peter Daley and David Parish say that three hundred thousand pounds has gone missing, then this is going to be an accurate figure. They know their stuff and they'll be providing some documentary evidence tomorrow. Why?"

"We met a married couple with their daughter when we took Alice to the hospital. They told us that they lived in Basingstoke and were allowed to claim all the travel costs because they were on benefits. Zoe decided that we would tell the hospital that we lived near Basingstoke. Her mother lives there and she decided to use her mother's address. We then started to claim the same travel costs as the other people. It was never queried and when Alice came out of hospital after a couple of weeks, Zoe carried on claiming, but we knew that we couldn't carry on claiming for ever as somebody would soon realize that there was a fiddle going on. I'd seen Linda Barrett in the cash office and found out that she was in charge. I know her bloke, Keith Simpson, and Zoe suggested that I went to see him in the garage where he works. I called in one day and arranged a meeting in the pub around the corner. I told him what we'd been doing and we could carry on if Linda would turn a blind eye and pretend not to notice us. Zoe would normally make the claim but I used to go occasionally. He told us that Linda was straight and would not get involved, but when I said that they might get five hundred quid per week, he eventually decided that he would speak to Linda. Keith persuaded Linda not to notice anything and Zoe carried on making the travel claims. I'd told Keith that we would share the money between three, Zoe would get a third, I 'd get a third and Keith would get a third which he was going to share with Linda. I used to go and see him every couple of weeks and give him the cash"

John Harrison was listening intensely as Rik was talking.

"I kept a record of the cash that I was given by Zoe as well as the money that Zoe gave me to give to Rik. It worked out that I received around fifty thousand pounds and Rik was given another fifty thousand pounds. I'm not an expert at sums but even I can work out that Zoe gave us one hundred thousand quid. If the fiddle was three hundred thousand pounds, then Zoe must have kept two hundred thousand pounds for herself. She won't tell me where the money is, but I know that she's got money hidden somewhere. I've also just found out that she's seeing another bloke and if she thinks that he's going to get some of the money, there's going to be trouble"

John suddenly interrupted.

"Rik, you are in enough trouble, don't start anything else, and don't be so stupid"

"Our relationship is over; she's fiddled me out of the money as well as having another bloke. That's why I wanted to talk to you alone and I want you to represent me, not Zoe"

"I understand that, Anna Young will take care of Zoe"

"Listen John, I'm prepared to admit what I have told you and face the consequences. I told Zoe that if she paid some of the money back, it might lighten our sentences but she wasn't interested"

John looked at the notes that he was making.

"Where are the other two, Keith Simpson and Linda Barrett?"

"They're in Spain, they were there on holiday but I gave Keith a ring and warned him that we'd been caught. They haven't returned and are probably hiding somewhere in Spain. I don't think they will stay long though. Linda has wanted to stop the fiddle for a while and I reckon that she'll make Keith return and face the music"

"I don't think that you should admit that you gave Keith a warning, it will not look too good"

"Okay then, my lips are sealed. Zoe also wants to pass the blame onto Keith and Linda, but Keith is a mate of mine. I'll tell the investigators what I've told you and I think Keith will do the same when he comes home"

"This conversation is confidential; do you want Anna and Zoe to know what you've told me and what your intentions are?"

"Yes, I don't mind. I've already told Zoe but she mightn't believe me. She probably still thinks that I will take the wrap. That's not going to happen; I could live with the fact that she didn't share the money but not with her having another bloke. I know that Alice will be okay with Zoe's mother as they get on really well"

"Should I bring Zoe and Anna into this office and let them know what you are going to say and do?"

"That's fine by me"

There was a wait of ten minutes before John, Anna and Zoe came into the office and sat around John's desk. John then spoke to Rik.

"I have informed Anna and Zoe briefly about your intentions. I would like to give them a summary while you are here before they go into Anna's office"

"That's okay with me"

John then turned to Anna and Zoe.

"Rik has admitted his part in the travel claim fraud. He has stated that he has received fifty thousand pounds and has given Keith Simpson a further fifty thousand pounds from the money given to him by Zoe. He has no knowledge of the remaining two hundred thousand pounds which is the balance of the total fraud of three hundred thousand pounds. I have been informed that the total is three hundred thousand pounds by Peter Daley but haven't seen the documents yet. They will be provided tomorrow and I have no doubts that Peter Daley and David Parish, known as Mr Fraud, will have all the incriminating evidence that they require"

John then spoke to Zoe.

"I know that Rik has asked you to repay some of the two hundred thousand pounds. This would be a good gesture and may allow the judge to be more lenient when passing a sentence. I would think that you'll both be looking at a prison sentence of about two years but that is only my thought"

Zoe was clearly furious but managed to stay calm and say.

"I'm not going to give anybody any money, I will take my chances and you can't prove that I have the money" John replied.

"That is your choice Zoe. I think that you and Anna should now go and discuss what you are planning to do and prepare for the meeting with David Parish tomorrow"

Both Anna and Zoe then left the room, leaving Rik with John. John then said to Rik.

"I think I have enough background information. I will be presented with a disclosure pack tomorrow morning and we'll then be able to discuss this in a separate room. Do you know where we are meeting?"

"Yes, the Human Resources Department of the General Hospital, I know where that is. We have to be there at half past ten"

"Do you still have contact with Keith Simpson?"

"No, I spoke to him to warn him and I've tried a couple of times since but I can't get through; he must have thrown the phone away in case anybody else tries to get hold of him or Linda. I've also tried Linda's mobile but I can't get through on that either. I think that they must've got some new phones. Keith has my number but he hasn't tried to contact me"

"Well, thanks for that Rik. I'm sorry about you and Zoe and hope that Anna can persuade her to co-operate but I have my doubts"

"So do I, I'll try again later if she comes back to the flat. I'll wait outside until she's finished with Anna. See you tomorrow"

Rik then left John's office and sat down in reception. He picked up a magazine and started glancing through while he was waiting for Zoe, but his mind was on his relationship with Zoe, which was as far as he was concerned, well beyond the point of no return. It was all over and what would happen to their daughter, Alice.

Anna had taken Zoe to her office in order to discuss what John Harrison had said.

"It would appear that the fraud is three hundred thousand

pounds and Rik is saying that he and Keith only received one hundred thousand pounds, is this true?"

"Don't believe what he is saying and don't listen to Keith or Linda if they come back from Spain. I don't think that they will come back and they've had a lot more than a hundred thousand pounds. I've shared most of the money with them and I'm not going to give any money back"

"As John said, it may make the Judge more lenient if you show some retribution and pay money back"

"I'm not giving any money back. I have a daughter, Alice; surely the Judge will take that into account when he makes a sentence. The job of the barrister must be to try and keep a mother with her child"

"That is not always the case Zoe. You are looking at a custodial sentence for a fraud of three hundred thousand pounds"

"I'll take my chance"

"The interview is planned for one o'clock tomorrow at the Human Resources Department. The investigators will give me a disclosure pack and we'll then be able to discuss it further. Will you be there just before one o'clock?"

"Yes, I'll be there"

"Have a think about what has been said today, I'll see you tomorrow"

Zoe then left Anna's office and walked past Rik in reception without making a comment. Rik got up, placed the magazine back on the table and followed Zoe out of the building onto the road, and made the return fifteen minute journey back to their flat. Not a word was spoken by either of them until they entered their flat.

Rik then spoke.

"What are your plans, this is my flat and I have no intention of throwing my daughter out of her home?"

"I will be moving out in a few days"

"Where will you go?"

"That's none of your business"

"Alice is my daughter and I want to know where she is going"

"I'll go to my mother's house for now; you'll be able to contact me there until I find somewhere else. I've got to go and collect Alice from her friends, I'll be back later"

The door then slammed as Zoe left the flat.

10

Steve Mitchell was in a buoyant mood as he finished packing his case for a few days trip to Spain. He had been negotiating the purchase of a villa to be built in La Grande Club, near to the Mar de Menor in Murcia. It was to be built to the specifications agreed by Steve and the owners of La Grande Club but he had made a couple of previous visits, viewed other properties and examined the different plans which the owners were able to provide.

The Mitchell family had owned an apartment in San Pedro del Pinatar, which they had sold for 150,000 euros, about £105,000. He had used this to place as a holding deposit on the land and had since transferred out a £150,000 making the required deposit of 25% which allowed the building to commence. The total cost of the four bedroom luxury villa, which has its own swimming pool was agreed at a price of 1,500,000 euros, just over a million pounds. It was expected that it would take a further six to nine months to complete the villa and Steve was going out for an inspection visit. He was going with his girlfriend, Linzi Owens, his brother Alan and his girlfriend Tanni Flowers. They had booked a couple of rooms at the super five star hotel, which is on the site of La Grande Club.

Steve had been concerned and took great care in ensuring that the money being used to buy the property was not subject to an investigation. He had, over the years, since his involvement in the bank robbery, managed to spend and change the stolen euros allowing large amounts to be held in different banks in Spain and the U.K. The bulk of the stolen money had reached U.K. destinations and had been used to help in buying their current house in Cheshire.

He had updated himself on the Money Laundering Regulations which came into effect in 2004 and the checks that were being made to uncover money laundering, especially when transferring money from British banks to Spanish banks. He had decided that it would be safer to use the facilities being offered by one of the Money Transfer Organisations, based in Manchester, who specialised in the movement of funds for the purchase of foreign properties. At his first meeting it became obvious that the transfer of funds was an important part of their business and they encouraged the use of this facility.

They were advertising the most competitive exchange rates available, saving money. You could get fixed exchange rates for future settlements, which would protect you from adverse currency movements, fast international money transfers and no commission charges. They also quoted friendly, expert staff to guide you through what are sometimes complex issues. Steve had noticed, on this initial visit, that the Manager was Phillip Harris who used to go to the same university as his sister Sarah. He thought that Phillip might have asked Sarah to go out on a date a few times, but presumed that Sarah had never taken him up, although they had remained friends. He recalled Sarah telling their mother that she had seen him around Manchester a couple of times and had chatted to him when they met. Steve thought that this acquaintance of Sarah may be a possible future benefit, if any difficulties were to arise when he was required to send the money to Spain to purchase the villa.

The doorbell rang and Steve's brother Alan answered the door. It was Linzi and Tanni fully laden with luggage for their trip to Spain.

"Good morning ladies" said Alan who then looked at their luggage.

"We are only going for a few days, you know"

Tanni walked over to Alan and gave him a kiss and then said gleefully.

"I'm so excited, I'm really looking forward to the trip and staying at a five star hotel"

Steve walked down the stairs carrying his suitcase and a smaller bag for use as hand luggage. Linzi walked over and gave him a hug and kiss before speaking.

"Good morning darling, I see you're ready to go"

"Yes, everybody ready?"

A chorus of "yes, yes, yes" was received from Alan, Tanni and Linzi.

Steve shouted "Mum, we're going"

Paula, his mother, came through from the kitchen, smiling.

"Enjoy your holiday boys and girls; I'll have some peace for a few days once you've gone"

Alan and Steve walked over to Paula giving her a cuddle before Alan said.

"Bye Mum, see you next week, take care. You've got our mobile numbers and the number of the hotel. Any problems, give us a ring"

"I can take care of myself, get going"

They all made their way to Steve's car, loading the cases into the boot, before getting into his big 4 x 4 car. Steve started the car and they all waved to Paula, before making their way on the fairly short journey from the Mitchell family home in Cheshire to Manchester Airport. The car journey was uneventful apart from the non-stop chat of the girls who were obviously looking forward to this break. Steve parked the car in the Multi-Storey car park at the airport before they all made their way to Terminal 1 departures and the check-in for the Jet2 flight, LS863, leaving at 11.10 am for Murcia. This was due to arrive at 3 o'clock in the afternoon. They waited in the queue which was moving quite briskly before getting to the check-in counter, where they got rid of their suitcases and made their way to the departure lounge.

The girls must have looked in every clothing, perfume and jewellery shop both before the security check in and then after the security check in. Surprisingly, they did not buy anything, probably because Steve and Alan did not put their hands in their pockets. It was a bit early for a drink even for Steve, so they settled for a coffee in Starbucks, knowing they would have to be fairly quick as boarding would be due to start shortly.

Alan kept checking the screens for information on departures and when it came up he announced.

"Boarding Gate number seven, let's get going"

They walked to the Boarding Gate and waited ten minutes before they were called to show their boarding cards and passports to the flight attendants. They then joined the queue to board the bus to the aircraft. The bus completed the small journey and they entered by the front of the aircraft, again showed their passports and boarding cards to the flight attendants at the entrance to the aircraft and found their seats. Steve was sitting with Linzi and Alan sitting next to Tanni. Shortly after take off, Steve was feeling a bit hungry when the stewardess arrived and he turned to the others.

"Think I'll have the five pounds package, a sandwich, coke and small tub of crisps. What would you like Linzi?"

"That's fine by me, but a diet coke for me"

"Alan"

"Yes, same for me Steve"

"Tanni"

"Yes please, but diet coke"

The stewardess handed out the orders and said.

"Anything else?"

Steve felt like celebrating, having looked at the drinks list.

"Oh yes, could we have two of the half bottles of the Pannier Champagne"

"Certainly"

She handed one bottle to Steve and the other bottle to Alan.

"That will be forty-six pounds please"

Steve handed over £50 and received the £4 change.

"Enjoy your trip" said the stewardess.

On the stewardess's next trip down the aisle, the trolley was loaded with various fragrances and aftershave. Steve saw the trolley getting nearer and said to Linzi.

"Would you like any perfume?"

Linzi had already been looking at the flight magazine in the back cover of the seat in front and soon selected a fragrance that she would like. She showed the picture of the fragrance to the stewardess who handed over the little pack.

"That will be twenty-five pounds please"

Steve handed over the cash and Linzi turned to Steve gave him a little kiss and said.

"Thank you"

Alan and Tanni were seated behind Steve and Linzi and the stewardess then approached them.

"Which one would you like Tanni?"

Tanni had already decided which fragrance she would like and pointed it out to Alan and the stewardess. Once again the little pack was handed over.

"That will be twenty-two pounds fifty please"

Alan handed over £25 and received the change and the stewardess said.

"Thank you, I've tried that fragrance, it's very nice"

Tanni turned to Alan and gave him a kiss.

The rest of the flight was uneventful and they arrived at San Javier Airport, Murcia on time at 3 pm. They all got off the aeroplane and walked to the terminal in order to reclaim their baggage.

As they arrived Steve turned to Allan.

"Will you take care of the cases with the girls, and I'll go and sort out the hire car?"

"Sure, see you by the hire car office"

Steve made his way to the hire car office and joined a small queue. He pulled out the documents that he would require, having booked the car on the internet. When it was his turn, Steve walked over and handed in the email paperwork, his passport and credit card. He had already written his contact address in Murcia and his mobile telephone number, knowing that this would be required by the lady at the desk. The paperwork was completed and the lady pushed over one of the forms saying.

"Sign here please"

Steve duly signed the slip of paper and was given back all his other documents as well as the car key.

The lady then pointed the direction that Steve should take and said.

"Go to the top, turn right and cross into the compound. You will find the car at Bay twenty-eight"

"Thank you" said Steve before turning round to see Alan, Linzi and Tanni waiting with all the suitcases.

Steve walked over and picked up his suitcase. They then followed Steve to the car compound and soon found the 4 x 4 car in bay twenty-eight. They loaded the luggage and got into the car with Steve driving. They left the airport and made the half-hour journey to the complex, La Grande Club, and soon found their way to their hotel. After registering they made their way to their rooms before Steve turned to Alan and Tanni.

"We'll have a look to see how the villa is getting on and have a drive around the complex. See you downstairs in about an hour, say five o'clock"

"Sure, see you later" said Alan.

Their room was next door to Steve and Linzi's.

La Grande Club is one of the world's finest all-round sports and leisure resorts, located in Murcia on sunny south-eastern Spain's Costa Calida near Mar Menor, Europe's largest saltwater lagoon, a delight for water sports enthusiasts. It has everything to offer.

No matter what time of year you choose to visit, there are plenty of things to keep you entertained and busy, always with assurance of five star facilities and service. You will find a seemingly endless variety of activities: golf, tennis, spa, swimming, fitness, squash, paddle tennis, cricket, professional football, lawn balls, pitch & putt, crazy golf, mountain biking, jogging and walking routes, beach, water sports, horse riding, go-karting, cultural tours, shopping, over 20 restaurants and bars, lively nightlife.

The resort is made up of a number of in excess of 20 different communities or 'villages', each with its own style and characteristics. There are also individual villas made to suit the requirements of the owners.

La Grande Club also offers two distinct types of deluxe accommodation: the five-star hotel and super self-catering accommodation available in one of the villages.

It is a perfect destination for sports-lovers, couples, children, friends, in facts it is ideal for everybody, including the Mitchell family.

Steve Mitchell was purchasing an individual villa to suit his needs.

They all met downstairs in the hotel lounge and decided to have a drive around the resort before having a drink. Steve knew the resort fairly well and was soon able to make his way through some of the communities before heading to the area where the new villas were being built, including the plot belonging to the

Mitchell family. He had not been out for a couple of months and was hoping to see some building on what had been an empty plot.

Once he arrived at the site, he was pleased to see that some work had clearly started and foundations were now evident although no higher than ground level. He knew that once the Spanish builders had got going, there was every chance that the building work would progress remarkably quickly, at least that is what he had been told by the Agent.

They all got out of the car and Steve pointed to the site.

"This is ours and the villa should be completed in about six months, at least I hope so, I'll be having a word with the Agent tomorrow morning. Are you coming Alan?"

"Yes, I'll come with you"

The surrounding area was picturesque and Steve felt really pleased with what he was about to achieve.

Alan had been out once, but before Steve had signed the contracts. He then complemented his brother.

"You've made a good choice; it's going to be brilliant"

The girls were really impressed, not that there were lots to see at this stage, but they could see other villas in the near vicinity. Tanni remarked.

"Is it like one of these other villas?"

Steve looked around and pointed to one saying.

"It'll be a bit like that one over there, I saw it when I first came out and thought it was one of the best ones"

They all got back into the car and stopped at an Italian Restaurant on site to see if they could book a table that evening. Alan went inside and spoke to one of the staff.

"Can I book a table for nine o'clock for four people?"

"No problem, what name is it?"

"Mitchell"

"That is booked and we'll see you at nine o'clock sir"

Alan retuned to the car.

"Nine o'clock is fine; shall we go back to the hotel for a drink?"

"There is a nice little bar just around the corner from the hotel, we'll go there" said Steve.

They then drove back to their five-star hotel, parked the car and soon made their way to the bar.

The next morning Steve met Alan in the hotel restaurant for some breakfast.

"We had a good time last night, good meal, few drinks. Where is Tanni, in bed like Linzi?"

Yeah, I told her we were going to have some breakfast and then go and see the bloke from property sales, what's his name?"

"Greg Collins, he's English comes from somewhere in the Midlands. Most of the business they do is with English people or Germans who speak English"

"Have you arranged a time or are we just going over?"

"No, it's not very far. We'll just walk over, if he's not there, somebody else will be"

The waiter came over.

"What would you like for breakfast sir?"

"Full English" said Alan

"Same for me" said Steve.

The breakfasts did not take long to arrive. It consisted of bacon, sausage, fried egg, mushrooms, hash brown, baked beans, toast with coffee. Both the brothers soon cleared their plates and waved to the waiter as they left the restaurant.

They then took a leisurely stroll to the Property Sales office. Greg Collins was at his desk when Steve and Alan opened the door and walked into the office which was lovely and cool with the air-conditioning blowing a pleasant gust of air. Greg immediately got off his chair and walked towards the two brothers.

"Good morning Steve, how are you?"

"I'm fine; I think you've met my brother Alan"

"Yes, I met you the first time Steve came to make some initial enquiries about property here in La Grande Club"

Greg shook hands with both Steve and Alan.

"When did you arrive?"

"Yesterday afternoon" replied Steve.

"Have you been over to the plot yet?"

"Yes, I see the foundations are being put down"

"That's right. I was up there with some other clients a couple of days ago, looking at a plot nearby and watched a group of builders working on your villa. It should be ready on time, but you know the Spaniards, they have spells where property seems to really get going and other times when nothing seems to happen. It'll be just the same with English builders"

"You're probably right. We're here for a short break with our girlfriends and staying at the hotel. Alan has not had the chance to be involved and I thought we'd get an update and check out a few things"

"No problem, take a seat"

Steve had made some notes on a previous visit but wanted to confirm the details and he had wanted to get Alan involved at this stage.

"The purchase price is one and a half million euros, which works out as just over a million pounds. I was asked for a deposit of twenty-five percent which has been forwarded to one of the lawyers that you recommended. That was around two hundred and fifty thousand pounds, is twenty-five per cent the normal deposit?"

"Yes, you find in Spain that twenty-five percent is required for new property and ten per cent for re-sales. I know that you selected Pepe Fernandez as your lawyer and he acted for you on the sale of your apartment in San Pedro del Pinatar. He also said that the balance of the deposit came in three different instalments. He then decided to combine the money and sent it in the one payment to our bank which is what we preferred"

"Pepe said that his fee would be three quarters of a percent, which is Seven thousand, five hundred pounds. That seems high but you did say they would charge between a half and one percent"

"That's right and you'll find that the five lawyers that we recommend will all charge the same. I'm sure they probably get together over a few drinks and agree a fee. It stops purchasers phoning round them all asking what the fee will be and they'll then find out that they charge the same and they're not prepared to take anything less"

"The VAT is seven percent and you reckon that we should allow for ten percent of the property cost, which allows for the lawyers costs and any other fees which may occur?"

"It isn't VAT in Spain, it is IVA but it's the same type of tax. We advise all our clients to allow ten percent, but they will generally end up paying a little less than that"

"What is it like selling property here, not that we are going to sell the villa?"

"Villas tend to sell quicker than apartments or town-houses. You tend to pay a premium for property on La Grande Club as it is established and tends to follow the London property market and not necessarily what is happening in the rest of Spain. You are buying into an instant social life and it's, therefore, more than a simple property purchase, it is often a lifestyle decision. Perhaps not so much for you now as you're not retiring here now, but it will be later. This place has won prizes for its golf courses and other facilities and is recognised as one of the safest places to live in Spain"

"When do you think the completion date will be, six months?"

"Possibly, they have started, but you'll find that we will not give a definite date at this stage, you have to allow for the Spanish manana process. We will let you know when we require more money"

"We'll send the money in several lump sums to our lawyer and he'll pass it to you when the villa is completed"

"That's okay, it's a bit unusual, but if Pepe Fernandez is happy, that's fine by me, and hopefully it shouldn't be too long"

They all shook hands and Steve and Alan left the office.

Greg then opened his telephone directory and looked up the phone number of Inspector Felipe Garcia of La Policia in Murcia. He dialled the phone number and heard the dialling tone.

"Hola, La Policia"

"My name is Greg Collins from La Grande Club; may I speak to Inspector Felipe Garcia?"

"One moment, I'll put you through to him"

"Hola, Felipe Garcia"

"Hola Inspector, it is Greg Collins. I spoke to you a few months ago about Steve Mitchell looking at property here in La Grande Club"

"Yes, I remember speaking to you Greg, how are you?"

"I'm fine. I just thought that I'd let you know that he has paid a deposit of three hundred and seventy-five thousand euros on a new villa which is being built. He is also here in La Grande, staying at the hotel. He's with his brother and their girlfriends"

"When will he be paying the rest of the money?"

"In about six months when the building should be nearly finished. He's going to send the money in several lump sums to his lawyer, Pepe Fernandez. Do you know Pepe?"

"Yes, I know Pepe very well. I'll start making some enquiries here and also in England. Thanks for your help Greg, it is appreciated"

Greg remembered being visited at the Estate Agents where he used to work by officers from La Policia. It was a few years ago, after a bank robbery on the Costa del Sol, and they were asking him to let them know if anybody called Mitchell was looking to purchase property. Although nothing happened then, he remembered the name when Steve Mitchell started coming in to look for property. He had contacted La Policia who immediately put his call through to Inspector Garcia. He had asked Greg to keep him in touch with any updates. He was also told that it was a relation of the Inspector that had been shot in the bank robbery.

People from many different backgrounds and different countries were buying property in La Grande Club but Greg had never really taken to Steve Mitchell. He did not know but from his brief discussions with Inspector Felipe Garcia, he thought that Steve Mitchell must have been involved with this bank robbery. There was something about this English bloke that he didn't like and he didn't really trust him. At the same time, he didn't want the purchase of the villa in La Grande Club to fall through because there would be a good commission on its sale.

11

Steve and Alan returned to the hotel and found Linzi and Tanni sitting in the bar having a couple of cups of coffee.

Alan was the first to speak.

"Good morning girls"

Tanni was first to reply and Linzi waved in acknowledgement.

"Morning Alan, where've you two been?"

"We've had a meeting with the property guy about the villa"

Steve walked over to Linzi and gave her a peck on the cheek before asking.

"What shall we do today, any ideas?"

There was no immediate reply to Steve's question but he then came up with an idea of his own.

"How would you like to play a game of bowls. Not ten-pin bowling, there are some lovely greens just around the corner? I played the last time I came with some people that I met in the bar. It was good fun and I wasn't too bad"

Tanni was again quick to reply.

"My Dad plays crown green bowls a lot at home, he's in a bowls club. I've played a few times with him, but not for about four or five years. It's great fun, especially in this lovely weather. I'd love to have a game. I think they aren't crown greens here in Spain, they play on flat greens, I remember Dad saying that when he played on his holidays in Spain. Can we hire the bowls; actually, I think there called woods not bowls?"

"Yes, we can hire them at the Sports Club Reception. Are you a good player?"

"I know the rules and wasn't too bad, but like I say, I haven't played for a few years now and you need to play regularly to be any good. We'll need to wear flat shoes but you'll be able to get way with trainers"

Linzi remarked.

"I've never played and don't know how to play"

Alan smiled and said.

"I've only ever played once and that must've been about ten years ago and I can't remember the rules, but Tanni and Steve will show us"

Steve responded.

"Okay, game on; let's get into casual clothes or shorts and something on our feet. We'll meet back down here in half an hour"

All four made their way to their rooms in order to get ready for the Mitchell Open Bowls Tournament and were all dressed, ready and downstairs in the hotel twenty-five minutes later.

They all walked slowly to the Sports Centre and Steve approached the Centre Receptionist asking.

"We'd like to hire four sets of bowls please"

The girl said.

"Are you playing the one game together or two different games?"

"We're playing the one game together"

"You'll only need the one jack bowl then and I'll give you two sets of men's bowls, they're called woods and two sets of ladies woods. The men's woods are a bit heavier than the ladies woods. The cost for the hire of the woods and green number three for two hours will be thirty euros. Do you want to pay cash or shall I put it on the room bill"

Steve handed over three ten euro notes and they all collected their own woods.

There was some good hearted laughter whilst they practiced bowls, especially with Linzi's attempts at bowling, not that Alan was that much better, but there was some semblance of the understanding of the game, helped by the fact that both Steve and Tanni had played before.

Steve then announced that it was time to start the game proper.

"I'll bowl the jack first and then we'll take turns with the first bowl and then again with the second bowl. The nearest to the jack gets one point but if one person ends up with both his bowls nearer the jack, they'll then get two points. The winner is the first person to get to twenty-one. The winner can buy the first round of drinks in the bar tonight, so that will probably be me"

Steve bowled the jack and they all took their turn to have a bowl, with the nearest to the jack in the first end being Alan. Alan then earned the opportunity to bowl the jack in the second end and they went in the order of who was nearest to the jack in the last end. Linzi, not surprisingly was last to bowl but with the last shot, she finished the nearest and gained her first point, which was followed by great laughter and jumps in the air. The score was now Alan 1, Linzi 1, Steve 0, Tanni 0.

The game then settled down eventually with Steve leading the scoring. It was, at the halfway stage, Steve 11, Tanni 6, Alan 3, Linzi 1 but everybody was having great fun. The game continued but Tanni started to improve and the score was now Steve 19, Tanni 19, Alan 5, Linzi 1. Alan had the jack and started the next end, with Steve second, Linzi third and Tanni, who made a mess of the last round, was fourth. After the first seven woods had been bowled, Steve was nearest with Tanni second, which meant Steve would get a point unless Tanni got nearer with her last wood.

Tanni bowled her last wood and knocked Steve's nearest wood out of the way which left Tanni with both her woods nearest to the jack, giving her two points and victory by 21 points to Steve's 19.

Linzi was the first to comment.

"You've won Tanni, brilliant, that was a great game"

Alan was also delighted.

"You've got hidden skills Tanni, anything else that I need to know?"

Steve then said.

"That was a fluke to finish with, you didn't deserve to win"

He then left the bowling green leaving the other three to collect the woods and return them to the Sports Centre.

As they left, Linzi spoke to Alan and Tanni.

"He isn't the best of losers and he'll probably be in a bad mood for a few hours, ignore him, he'll get over it"

They then made their way to bar near the hotel and found Steve having a San Miguel beer. Tanni then said.

"It's my turn to pay for the first round of drinks as I was the winner. That's what we agreed. What would you like to drink, Linzi?"

"White wine please"

Alan.

"A San Miguel please, Tanni"

Steve.

"No thanks, I've already got a drink"

"Have another one"

"No thanks, I'm going to our room after this drink"

Tanni ordered the drinks at the bar.

"Two glasses of white wine and one San Miguel please, I'll pay cash"

The barman prepared the drinks and placed them on the bar.

"That will be nine euros, please"

Tanni handed him a ten euro note and said.

"Keep the change"

"Thank you, enjoy your drinks"

Tanni then took two of the drinks to the table, where they were sitting, for Alan and Linzi, and returned to collect her glass of white wine. As she sat down, Steve got up and said to Alan.

"I'm going to my room now Alan. I think that I'll go out for a meal with Linzi tonight. You and Tanni can go out on your own"

He then left the table leaving Alan, Linzi and Tanni a bit confused but then Alan picked up his drink.

"Cheers. Where are you off to tonight Linzi?"

"I haven't got a clue, first time that I've heard that we're going out, just the two of us. He's sulking, can't stand losing to a woman"

They then all laughed together and enjoyed their drinks before Linzi left to go to their room and see what type of mood Steve was in.

Alan and Tanni had a short walk around the complex before they returned to their room to have a quick siesta before getting ready for their evening meal together. They were both quite happy with the idea of going out on their own and decided that they would go to the little Spanish village which was about four miles away. There was a good choice of restaurants and Alan knew they would be able to get a table fairly easily. They decided that they would get a taxi so that they would be able to have a few drinks.

Shortly after Steve had returned to his bedroom the dialling tone on his mobile rang out.

"Hello"

"Hello Steve, its Ron Thomas here"

"What's up?"

"I just thought that you should know that Bill Kennedy has been arrested. The Police were doing an investigation into the car crash scams and were speaking to some of the drivers. They found out that Bill was involved in two of the crashes and that he gave different names but I wouldn't worry about Bill. He won't involve us and he'll tell the police that the crashes were his own idea and he'll follow our instructions that the cars belonged to friends of his who've gone abroad. We might have to think about winding down the car scam for a bit, if the cops are questioning lots of the other drivers. I know they've set up an investigation team and the Insurance Companies are doing the same thing. What do you think?"

"Yeah, stop it until I get back. We might have to think about some other scams, I've got some ideas. We've been doing this for about two years now and the London gang have been doing it for four years. Anyway, thanks for letting me know, Ron"

"That's okay boss"

12

Steve Mitchell ran his criminal activities like a military organisation. He had, in his late teens, joined the Territorial Army but had been thrown out after a couple of years because he was considered to have the wrong attitude for military life. He was not sorry to go but had learnt a few lessons during his stay.

Ron Thomas had been made a Service Manager by Steve and was very loyal employee. Steve had a high regard for Ron, but Steve was not the type to tell him that. He has become quite dependent on Ron and even more than his own brother, Alan. If Steve wanted a good job doing, he would always rely on Ron, so his payments to Ron did reflect this loyalty. Steve, himself, however, did inflict and enjoyed handing out violent punishment. Many of their business ideas had come about from discussions between Steve and Ron; it was only afterwards that Alan Mitchell became involved. In many ways, Steve thought that Alan was a hindrance and often wondered what role to give to Alan, but he knew he thought the world of Steve, his older brother, and would do anything he said.

The idea of a car crash scam had been instigated, initially, in London but Ron knew the leader of the gang that were involved from his time in prison. He arranged a meeting and went down to London where he was given some of the background into how this scam was operated and some of the methods that they used. It was made perfectly clear to Ron that whilst they were prepared to give him advice to start a car crash scam, they should steer well clear of London and the South West. He was told to inform the Mitchell family that they should stay north of Birmingham.

He then returned and completed a report for Steve which highlighted the way the scheme was operated. A meeting was arranged with Steve, and Alan was present when Ron Thomas made his report on the fake car crash scam which had now been going on for a couple of years.

A criminal gang is orchestrating crashes in London as part of a £3million a week insurance fraud. In a recent sting, gang members used two cars to force a lorry to slam into the back of one of the vehicles so they could make bogus claims for the 'accident' and personal injury.

In the course of the con, the first car is being driven close in front of a lorry to give the innocent driver no chance of braking in time. To make the accident seem realistic the second car veers in front of the first car on the A40 forcing it to slam on the brakes. After the lorry crashed into the back of the second car the other car sped away leaving the shocked truck driver to exchange insurance details with the gang.

One woman driver who willingly joined the gang and took part in crashes at up to 70mph told me that it is like waiting for your own funeral, waiting to be hit by a massive lorry. I was crying the first few times - but the gang members liked that because it was a bit realistic after the crash. We must go at high speeds and then slam on the brakes in front of the targeted lorry. It is like a bad dream, but it is really exciting.

Another crash on the same night resulted in a car being shunted 40 yards down the A406 after the same getaway car in the first

*incident had been used again to stage the accident. Afterwards
the Asian driver in the team got out of the car and leaned over
the back of it claiming his back had been injured.*

*A variant trick used by the gang is to brake heavily in front of
a lorry just before a set of traffic lights. The gang target Lorries
because they have long braking distances and cause far more
damage than cars.*
*The gang is trying to trap lorry drivers all around the capital,
with stunt crashes attempted on the A4, the M4, the A406 North
Circular and the A316 between Chiswick and Mortlake.*

*The fraud works because drivers who crash into the rear
of other vehicles are almost always ruled to be the party at
fault. The use of the second car to force the crash is enough
to convince the lorry drivers that they have been involved in a
genuine accident.*

*Claim firms are then exploited by the gangs, who use the
details of different people each time, to rake in payments for
crash repairs as well as money for personal injury. Because
the claims are kept at no more than £600 per person involved,
insurance companies are not prompted to investigate in greater
detail. Meanwhile, large haulage firms see accidents as
inevitable and also fail to check details closely.*
*This gang has been operating the con for at least two years
and had a stockpile of up to 60 cars stored around London
waiting to be crashed.*

*Ron has also been told that Insurance companies, which
estimate fraudulent claims cost them £208m a year, are so
concerned that they have set up the Insurance Fraud Bureau to
share information of suspicious claims.*

The conclusion in his report stated that Ron felt his scheme was practical and could easily be put into operation in the North of England

The report was studied by Steve and shown to Alan and they both agreed with Ron's findings that they could instigate this scam and it would now be put into operation.

Steve and Ron decided that they would not operate this staged car crash scam in the local area which included Manchester, Liverpool and Cheshire. They thought that the drivers they would use may be known in this area and if they staged a car crash they might know the other parties involved in the crash. In the end, they ruled out the North West of England altogether and decided to operate the scam in Yorkshire, with the main centre based in the area surrounding Bradford and Leeds.

They built up a stockpile of forty cars and set up a vehicle repair garage which specialised in getting their crashed cars in and fitting replacement parts, which were mainly required for the rear of the cars. They would keep a stock of parts which were usually obtained from scrap yards involved in the demolition of cars which they would then paint to match the colour of the car. That meant that when one of their cars was hit in the rear it could be returned to the garage and new parts immediately fitted, which allowed the cars to be back on the road quickly. They then had a team of ten drivers who would be trained on how to operate the staged car crash scams. The team contained three ladies and three Asian lads as they were operating in an area in which there was a mixed community.

The staged accidents were similar in nature to those in London, in that their team would operate alone or in pairs, but the car immediately in front of a lorry would break hard in front of the vehicle at junctions or lights. The stopping speed of a lorry would be longer than a car making the crash more inevitable and the team knew how far in front they should break to lessen the chance of any injury to themselves. When two cars were used, the first car would speed away, leaving the second car driver to say the first car had braked hard, and he had no choice but to slam on the breaks. If the damage was severe and the garage thought that the Insurance Assessor would consider it not repairable, they would let the Insurance Company treat it as a write off. Their garage would then ask the Insurance Company if they could retain the car for spare parts which would avoid then the costs of removing the car and having it scrapped. The Assessor would normally agree and their garage would make a temporary repair before putting it back on the road with a different driver and different insurance details.

On some occasions, the value of the repairs may have been considered too high by their garage staff, and they would arrange for the car to be vandalised beyond repair and then make the insurance claim.

The original intention was to try and limit the claims to around £600 which was the figure used by the London gang, but Steve and Ron decided, after a couple of months, to make bigger claims which meant there was often an investigator sent out by the Insurance Companies. Their team were trained well, and they did not fine it difficult to pacify the investigators and get their claims cleared through the Insurance Companies.

They then hit on the idea of purchasing some old mini-buses. One of their team would drive the mini-bus with about half a dozen other team members sitting inside as passengers. A second team member would drive a car and then swerve in front of the mini-bus who would be prepared to brake hard on the signal of the car driver. The mini-bus would then brake leaving the car or lorry behind little chance to break in time causing the inevitable crash into the back of the mini-bus. The mini-bus team driver and all the team passengers would then claim whiplash and other injuries as well as claiming for the cost of the repairs to the mini-bus.

In the two years since they started the car crash scam, none of their team had received any serious injuries. Steve considered that they had been well rewarded for their efforts and he paid them 10% of the insurance claim. There had been over a thousand crashes and his team members had been paid a hundred and ten thousand pounds between them. He kept meticulous records on his laptop computer and the scam had earned almost one million, one hundred thousand pounds over the past two years. Deducting the 10% payment to the team members, the cost of the repairs and the purchase of the vehicles, his profit was still in the region of six hundred thousand pounds.

This car crash scam was highly profitable and the profits were to be used for the purchase of the villa in Spain, but Steve was a cautious person and would not continue with any business if the risks were becoming too great. He would continually monitor the progress and would have no hesitation in stopping the whole scam if he thought it was a risk, even if it was still profitable.

Ron Thomas was a good source of information and had contacts in all sorts of places. He had found out that the police had set up two investigation teams at the request of the Insurance Companies and they were being supported by the Insurance Companies Fraud Investigators. The two areas were London looking around the M4 and Yorkshire around the M62. They were calling a meeting shortly, which would be attended by the man well known in the fraud world, David Parish, Mr Fraud. Ron's contact in the police had indicated that they were looking at about twenty-five cases very closely. It was this contact who had told Ron about the arrest of Bill Kennedy.

Ron had also discovered from one of his sources that the Association of British Insurers were actively involved and that it was very likely that the costs of car insurance was to be increased in this area of Yorkshire. It was, with this in mind, the reason why and he had phoned and warned his boss, Steve Mitchell, in Spain.

13

David had arranged for a taxi to take him to the Train Station in order to catch the same 6.27 am Virgin Express that he had used the previous week. He collected his tickets from the ticket booth at the station and made his way to the platform in order to board the train. He found his coach and seat in the second class compartment that he had booked. As he placed his luggage on top, another female passenger sat down on the opposite seat to him. It was, however, not a young attractive female who would accompany him on the trip to London. This was a little old dear, probably in her seventies.

Before David had the chance to speak, the lady asked David.

"Would you be so kind as to put my bag on top, I can't reach?"

"No problem. How are you this fine morning?"

David placed the small suitcase on the top and as he sat down, the lady replied.

"I'm fine, thank you. Are you going to London?"

"Yes, I have some business down there, and you?"

"Oh yes, I'm going to visit a friend for a couple of days. She lives by the Oval cricket ground where Surrey plays. She'll meet me at the station with her son and then he'll take us downstairs to get the tube. It's only the one journey on the tube and his car will be parked near the tube station that we get off"

The train had not even left the station and David began thinking that this journey may not be quite so peaceful and quiet as last time.

"How often do you make this journey to visit your friend?"

"I'd say about twice a year and she comes to see me in Liverpool twice a year. We're going to the London Palladium tomorrow to see a show"

"Oh, which show is that?"

"The Sound of Music. Did you watch the television programme when they picked the female lead for the show?"

"No, I didn't see that"

"The programme goes on for weeks and weeks and they vote somebody out each week until there is only the one left. She's supposed to appear in the show at the Palladium every night but I know two people who have been to see the show and she hasn't been on. She must have been sick or something"

David smiled and pulled out his laptop as the train was leaving the station. He plugged it in and switched on thinking this may lead to many more questions from his elderly friend but was surprised when she commented.

"I have a laptop at home and it's the same make as yours. I don't know how you can manage without one these days. All my records are kept on the computer such as people's addresses and birthdays. I often use it to purchase things and booked this train ticket on the internet. Not bad for an eighty-five year old, hey"

"You're eighty-five. You don't look it and you're able to use a computer, brilliant, I'm impressed"

She smiled and pulled out her novel. David glanced at the book, the author was Lee Child and he recognised it as one of the Jack Reacher novels. Not what he imagined an old dear would be reading.

"Do you like the Reacher novels?" asked David.

"Yes, I think that I've read most of them. Do you like them?"

"Yes, they're a very good read. I've just started on one of his most recent books"

"Which one is that?"

"It's called Bad, Luck and Trouble"

"I don't remember that title, what's it about?"

"I'm only about a quarter through, but it's when his old army unit are called together to investigate why one of his team had been murdered. He was thrown from a helicopter"

"I haven't read that one"

David then started to read up his notes on the interviews that he would be completing today and thinking back to the telephone conversation that he had with Linda Barrett. He had not informed Peter Daley that he had spoken to Linda, or that Keith Simpson had been killed. He doubted that Zoe or Rik would know about his murder, Linda had not told them so he would probably bring this up during the interviews. The news of the death of Keith may have a greater effect on Rik, who had obviously been quite friendly with Keith, whereas there did not appear to be a great involvement between Zoe and Keith. They were about an hour into the journey when Keith switched the laptop off and placed it into the side of his luggage bag. He was now feeling it was time for a drink and a bite to eat.

"I'm going for a coffee and a roll, would you like me to get you anything?" he said to his fellow traveller who was engrossed in the novel.

"No thank you, I've got a flask and a buttered scone in my bag. Would you pass it down please?"

"Certainly"

David stretched up and placed the bag on the spare seat next to his elderly friend"

"Thank you"

David then walked to the next carriage where the cafeteria was situated and being a creature of habit he collected his usual, Premium Bacon Roll and Large Americano, before paying at the counter.

He then made his way back to his seat, where his elderly female travelling companion was enjoying a cup of coffee and a scone.

"This will do me until lunch time" she said

"Enjoy yourself" said David as she smiled back to him.

"What have you got to eat?"

"A bacon roll, I always get one of these when I'm on the early morning train"

"Bon appetit"

The train slowly pulled into Euston station just before 9 o'clock and all the passengers started to gather their belongings and make their way to the exit doors on the train.

"Do you need a hand with you bag"

"No it's not very heavy and I don't need a trolley"

They got off the coach together and walked along the platform where she was greeted by her friend and a younger man, presumably the son.

"Enjoy your trip and the show"

"I will, it's been nice meeting with you, cheerio"

This time David took the short walk and headed straight for Euston General Hospital before again entering at the front. This time, however, he made his way to the Human Resources Department where he would meet up, initially, with Peter Daley. He soon found the Human Resources Department and entered where he found the receptionist behind her desk.

"Good morning, my name is David Parish; I understand that Stuart Bradley has booked us Interview Rooms one and two. My colleague, Peter Daley may have already arrived"

"Yes, he's in Interview Room one" pointing out the entrance to the room.

"Thank you, we'll be here for most of the day"

David knocked on the door and entered to see everything had

been set up by Peter. The tape machine and documents were already prepared on the table.

"Morning Peter"

"Morning David"

"I see you've prepared everything, thanks a lot. I've got some news and need to update you on a few things. We've got an hour, which is plenty of time, if that's okay with you?"

They sat at the desk and checked through all the documents that they were going to give John Harrison, the solicitor for Rik Jeffreys. It was, in fact, quite a small pack as they only intended including twenty samples of the fraud, as well as the evidence and financial details of the total fraud. There were well over a thousand other claims which had been itemised and placed in about thirty folders. Once David and Peter were up to date with all this documentation, David turned to Peter saying.

"A lot of things have happened over the past few days. You know that I mentioned that I had some contacts in Spain and that I'd make some phone calls"

"Yes, any luck?"

"I suppose you could say yes. I spoke to Alisa Garcia asking her to see if she could find Linda and Keith. Although it was a long shot, I did mention that Keith was a drugs user and may be looking to purchase drugs when he is in Spain, and it may be worth contacting the Head of the Drugs Squad in that area, Sergio Lopez. She rang me back a couple of days ago saying they had been able to contact both of them. The only problem being that Keith is dead; he had been stabbed to death in Torremolinos, following some dispute with a drugs dealer. Linda wasn't with him at the time but La Policia was able to contact her when they found a mobile number on Keith's new mobile phone. Alisa then spoke to her on the phone and told her that a fraud investigation was going on into the false travel claims at a hospital in London and that I was the person in charge of the investigation. She was apparently in a terrible state, thinking that the police would arrest her as soon as she arrived back in this country as well as having to sort out the problems surrounding the death of Keith. Alisa then suggested that it might do her some good if I was to telephone her"

"And did you?"

"Yes, I spoke to her last night. I did make some notes but they can't be used in evidence at this stage until we formally speak to her on tape"

"Is she coming back?"

"Yes, early next week. She did give me quite a bit of background information and we may be able to bring some of this up with Rik and Zoe, depending on how the interviews go. A lot of the information we already know, but she did clarify a few other things. She said that Rik and Zoe had started the travel fraud when their daughter went into hospital and had carried on after she left, but they then thought that the people working in the cash office, including Linda, would get suspicious. Rik then approached Keith, who he already knew, and suggested that Linda should turn a blind eye to the claims and they would then share the money. At first, Keith knew that Linda wouldn't agree but in the end he persuaded her and she admitted to receiving some of the money, but not a great deal. I think that the other three must have shared the bulk of the three hundred thousand pounds between them. She is really angry with Rik and Zoe, blaming them. Rik rang Keith in Spain warning him that the fraud was over and that they'd been spoken to by us. That's why they never returned to this country. As far as Linda is concerned, if that phone call had not been made to Keith, he would still be alive today"

"She might have a point"

"Interestingly, Linda did not know the fraud was taking place until she was informed by Keith. She thought that Zoe and Rik did live in Basingstoke and the claims were legitimate"

Peter was listening intently and suddenly thought.

"Do Zoe and Rik know that Keith Simpson is dead?"

"No, I'm sure they don't. I'm also pretty sure that they don't know that I have spoken to Linda and that I've gained some more information"

"Are you going to disclose this to John Harrison before the interview?"

"No, I've got nothing in writing to show them. We'll use the information as and if it becomes a help to us"

"It's good to know that you and Alisa are still on speaking terms"

"Yes, we've always remained very good friends and have met a few times since we split up and we chat regularly on the phone"

"You may end up seeing her again then?"

"Funny you should say that. She has asked for my help in trying to help catch some gangsters from Cheshire who may be laundering money, probably stolen or some other criminal act, to be used to purchase property in Murcia. It's a long story but a nephew of Alisa was shot and crippled during a bank robbery on the Costa del Sol about six years ago. The father of this family, Frank Mitchell, was convicted but later died in jail. The Garcia family and La Policia believe that Steve Mitchell, the elder son, fired the shot but he's never been convicted and the Garcia's want their revenge. I'm going to see her in Seville in a couple of days to discuss what she knows and how I may be able to help. I've also agreed with Linda Barrett that I will then go down to meet her on the Costa del Sol and accompany her back to this country. I've also told her that we will give her a few days to sort herself out and make any arrangements to do with Keith Simpson, but we will then want to make formal arrangements for an interview with us"

"Don't get too close to this David, leave a distance between you and Linda, especially when you meet her in Spain. You don't know what state of mind she may be in, you should have some safeguards"

"I've thought about that Peter, I will be travelling with Alisa to meet Linda in Benalmadena. Alisa will then accompany us to Malaga Airport and we'll then join the crowds and get the flight home. I was then looking for a friend to pick us up at Stansted Airport and drop Linda off at her flat in Hackney. So, how about a lift please, Peter?"

Peter started laughing.

"Let me know the flight and times, and I'll pick you up"

14

There was a knock on the door of the interview room and the receptionist walked in.

"John Harrison and Rik Jeffreys have arrived and I've sat them in Interview Room two. Do you require a drink?"

"Thank you" replied David. "A jug of water and four glasses or tumblers would be fine, thanks a lot"

"I think we'll get John Harrison in now, Peter, I'm still not keen on him representing both Rik Jeffreys and Zoe Ferguson, but we'll have to live with it"

Peter who knew John Harrison knocked on the door of Interview Room 2 and entered.

"Good morning John, Good morning Mr Jeffreys"

"Good morning Peter, do you want to see me alone and give me a disclosure pack prior to the interview?"

"Yes John, if you pop next door, we'll have a quick chat and give you a copy of our disclosure pack"

John turned to Rik.

"I'll only be about five minutes, wait here till I return"

John then followed Peter into the Interview Room next door and Peter introduced him to David,

"David, this is John Harrison"

"Hello John, nice to meet you. We'll show you what we are disclosing at this stage"

Both Peter and John then sat down and David handed John a file of documents.

"There is not a huge amount of paperwork to show you at this stage. We have enclosed twenty copies of fraudulent travel claim forms, ten of which have been completed by your client, Rik Jeffreys and the other ten by his partner Zoe Ferguson. We also enclose a detailed list of all the travel claims made by your clients over the period in question which stretches over two and a half years. The total fraud is in excess of two hundred and ninety six thousand pounds and there are just short of fifteen hundred claims, some of which are for two or three journeys. The vast majority of the travel claim forms have been completed by Zoe; there are less than a hundred which have been completed by Rik"

John was glancing at some of the documents and said.

"This looks fairly straightforward to me. You did say that both Rik and Zoe Ferguson were my clients. For your information, I am not representing Zoe now, she will be represented by a different solicitor from our firm, Anna Young"

Both David and Peter were a little surprised, but David thought he would still ask the question, even knowing he might not get an answer.

"Why the change, is there anything that we should know?"
John smiled.

"I am sure it will all be revealed in the next hour"

John then took the disclosure pack to go and discuss with Rik.

David turned to Peter.

"It sounds as though they have fallen out big time. We might get more than we expected from Rik Jeffreys"

Peter nodded his head.

"I think you may be right, but it probably suits us now that John is not acting for both Rik and Zoe.

"I tend to agree"

They had to wait about a half of an hour before hearing the

knock on the door and seeing John Harrison and Rik Jeffreys enter the Interview Room. All four then sat around the desk before the interview under caution began.

"I just want to check that you understand what we are going to do. Peter will operate the tape machine and you will hear a loud noise before the start of the interview, this is normal. Rik, has John explained what we are going to discuss and the procedures that will take place?"

"Yes, I understand, he has told me"

"Okay, Peter will you start the tape please?"

Peter started the tape and the noise appeared before David started the interview with the opening procedures.

"This Interview is being tape recorded, it is the twenty fifth of April two thousand and seven and the time by my watch is eleven ten a.m. I am David Parish a Fraud Consultant for the National Health Service representing Euston General Hospital. The other officer present is"

"Peter Daley also a Fraud Specialist representing Euston General Hospital"

"I am interviewing, please state your full name, address and date of birth"

"Rik Jeffreys, Flat four, seventeen Chineham Street, Bloomsbury, London. Date of birth fifteenth of October, nineteen seventy seven"

"Also present is"

"John Harrison, John Harrison Solicitors, Holborn, London"

"We are in the Human Resources Department of the Euston General Hospital, London. At the end of the interview, I will give you a notice explaining the procedures for the dealing with the tapes and how you can have access to them. Before the interview begins I must caution you."

"You do not have to say anything, but it may harm your defence if you do not mention when questioned something which you later rely on in court, anything you do say may be given in evidence. Do you understand the caution?"

Rik understood this and was quite calm.

"Yes"

"You are not under arrest and you are free to leave at any time. The reason for this interview is that we are investigating allegations that you were involved in making fraudulent travel claims at the Euston General Hospital between October, two thousand and four and April, two thousand and seven knowing the information on the claim forms was false. The total number of travel claims is One thousand, five hundred and twenty-one and the cost of these claims totals two hundred and ninety six thousand and thirty pounds. Do you understand the reason for this interview?"

"Yes"

"If at any time you wish to speak to your solicitor in private or if you wish me to stop the interview for any reason, then tell me and I will stop the interview"

"Okay"

"I would like you to open the Disclosure Pack and have a look at the first ten travel claim forms which are numbered DP one to DP ten"

Rik duly opened the folder and looked at the first ten items in the pack.

"They are all travel claim forms which have been completed by you and signed by you. Do you agree?"

"Yes"

"The address on the claim forms is in Basingstoke but you have just informed us that your address is Flat four, seventeen Chineham Street, Bloomsbury, London. Have you always lived at Chineham Street since two thousand and four?"

"Yes"

"You are saying that the address in Basingstoke is incorrect and the information on the travel claim forms is fraudulent?"

"The address in Basingstoke is Zoe's mother. We've never lived there and the address and the details concerning the travel journeys are not correct. I admit that they're fraudulent"

"Will you have a look at the next ten travel claims in the pack, which are numbered DP eleven to DP twenty"

Rik again quickly glanced through the copies of the travel claims which were in the pack.

"The address on those travel claim forms is also Basingstoke, but they have all been completed and signed by Zoe Ferguson. Would you agree that they are also fraudulent?"

"Yeah, they have been filled in by Zoe, it looks like her writing and it's her signature on the forms"

"Did you know that Zoe was also completing the travel claim forms incorrectly and that the claim forms were fraudulent?"

"Yes, we were both completing the forms but most of them were completed by Zoe. I've no idea how many forms there are, but I know that they are all fiddled and we weren't entitled to make the claims"

"Turn to the next page and you will find a summary of all the claims. There are one thousand five hundred and twenty-one listed and there is a sum of money relating to these fraudulent claim forms which totals two hundred and ninety six thousand and thirty pounds. Do you agree that these figures are correct?"

"I haven't got a clue how much money has been taken over the past couple of years. If you say there are fifteen hundred forms and they total over two hundred and ninety thousand quid, you're probably correct but I haven't got any idea. All I know is that Zoe was in charge of all the money and she gave me about fifty thousand pounds. She also gave me around fifty thousand pounds which I then gave to Keith Simpson which he shared with Linda. I know those figures are right because I kept some records. Zoe will have taken her share but I don't know what's happened to the rest of the money, you'd better ask Zoe"

"Are you saying that you are only aware of approximately one hundred thousand pounds?"

"I've seen a hundred thousand pounds and I know Zoe had her share which I thought might have been another fifty thousand pounds, which makes three equal shares. Your figures are a lot higher than that, but like I said, I haven't got any idea what other claims were made. I'm not sure that you can pin all this on me. I'll have a chat with my solicitor later. I'm not going to say that I haven't been involved, let's face it, the evidence is pretty strong"

"If you are saying that Zoe is responsible and that she must have nearly two hundred thousand pounds. Then, where is the money?"

"I don't know and I haven't seen any money round the house. I've had a good look over the past couple of days but I can't find it and I can't find any bank statements or bank books showing lots of money deposited"

"Where is your fifty thousand pounds?"

"It's all gone, I've spent it"

"Has Zoe spent all her money?"

"She hasn't spent two hundred thousand quid, at least not around the house and it's not been spent on Alice or me. I'm certain that she's got another bloke. I don't know who but he might be able to help. You'd better ask Zoe about him"

"You've no idea who he is?"

"No, but it's probably been going on for at least six months"

David put his copy of the Disclosure Pack to one side and then said to Rik.

"I've got a few other questions. You have mentioned the involvement of Keith Simpson and Linda Barrett. They went to Spain and haven't returned. Do you know why?"

"No, they must have found out that we'd been caught"

"Did you tell them?"

"No"

"That's not what I've been told"

"What do you mean?"

"I spoke to Linda Barrett on the phone last night. She said that you had telephoned Keith the day before they were due to leave and warned him. Keith then told Linda and they decided to stay in Spain for a bit longer until things cooled down and hear what was happening to you and Zoe"

"Why would Linda speak to you, did she ring you?"

"No, I phoned her on her new mobile"

"How did you get the number, I don't know of any new phone numbers for Keith and Linda?"

"The Spanish police gave me the number"

"Have they been arrested in Spain?"

"No, Keith Simpson has been murdered in Torremolinos, he was stabbed to death"

"You mean Linda has killed him?"

"No, he was stabbed during an argument with a drugs dealer"

"Keith is a mate of mine; I don't know what to say. It's terrible. When was he killed?"

"On Saturday, they should have returned home on Friday, but once they were warned, they decided to stay on. They left their hotel on Saturday morning and went to Benalmadena and he was killed that evening"

"That means if I hadn't of warned him, they would've returned on Friday and he would still be alive. I just tried to help him but he was stabbed because he stayed on. Linda must hate me"

"I think it's fair to say that you are not the most popular of people with Linda and neither is Zoe. She didn't really want to be involved in the first place. She did tell me that you approached Keith suggesting that he asked her to turn a blind eye to the claims being made by you and Zoe"

"That's true. Zoe thought Linda might find out about the fiddle and we agreed that we'd try and include Keith in the scam. We thought that he might be able to persuade Linda. I thought that

I had problems with Zoe, but they don't compare to Linda's problems"

David turned to Peter.

"Is there anything else that we need to mention at this stage, Peter?"

"No, I think we have enough for today"

David then asked a further question to Rik.

"Do you wish to add anything further or clarify any point or anything you have told me?"

"I have admitted to my part in this fraud. I can't help you with all the money that has been taken. You will have to ask Zoe. I'm a bit taken back by what has happened to Keith. He was a mate of mine. I feel sorry for Linda but there's nothing that I can do to help. I've probably said too much today but maybe you'll put a word in with the Judge when it gets to court"

"I can't make any promises but your co-operation will be noted"

"Thanks"

"Here is the notice which explains your entitlement to a copy of the tape used in this interview. This interview is concluded at eleven forty five a.m. on the twenty fifth of April, two thousand and seven. Switch off the tape recorder"

David then turned to Rik and John Harrison.

"You have co-operated and provided us with some information. I would like you to co-operate further but this is up to you. I can't stop you contacting Zoe after you leave this office before we see her later today. If you wish to help further, don't speak to her and don't let her know the outcome of this interview this morning"

"That's fine by me and I've no intention of helping Zoe. I won't go back to the flat and I'll switch my mobile off"

"John, how would this affect your relationship with your colleague, Anna Young, who is representing Zoe?"

"My job is to help my colleague. It wouldn't look good if I

didn't disclose some information that I had, which may be of help. If my client asked me not to discuss this interview, then I would have to accept that instruction"

Rik then reacted to the last comment.

"By client John, do you mean me?"

"Well, yes"

"In that case, I would like you not to disclose what's been said today. Don't tell Zoe or her solicitor anything"

"That's okay with me Rik, I won't say a word to Anna Young, just explain that it is a direct request from you"

"Okay"

Rik signed a copy of the tape that had been sealed by Peter and would be made available to Rik's solicitors when the matter was referred for court action.

John and Rik then left the Interview Room, leaving David and Peter to discuss the information that had been provided by Rik Jeffreys and the progress made to date.

David turned to Peter.

"What do you think? Is he telling us everything and is he telling the truth?"

"He's owned up to his part in the fraud and told us of the involvement of the others. I think there has been some big argument with him and Zoe and it looks as though Zoe is seeing some other bloke. Rik is obviously upset about this and has no intention of helping Zoe. He was taken back when we told him about Keith Simpson. I'll tell you something else. Zoe will not be as co-operative as Rik and I think that we may be in for a hard time with her"

"I tend to agree with you. We've got enough to sort out Rik and we've got plenty of ammunition to use against Zoe. She's got plenty to hide and I don't think that she'll be in any mood to help us, especially when she knows that Rik has spilled the beans"

"I think she may be in for a shock"

"Yes, I don't think that Rik or John Harrison will say anything"

"Neither do I. Shall we go and get something to eat before we meet the wonderful Zoe Ferguson?"

Good idea. Let's settle for a sandwich from the shop"

15

David and Peter had returned to the Interview Room in Human Resources and prepared for interview with Zoe, when the receptionist knocked on the door.

"Anna Young and Zoe Ferguson are next door"

"Thanks" replied Peter.

David got to his feet and told Peter.

"I'll go and get Anna Young"

He knocked and entered the room next door saying.

"I'm David Parish"

The dark haired lady on the left quickly replied.

"Anna Young from John Harrison Solicitors, representing Zoe Ferguson"

He returned a minute later with Anna Young and said to Peter.

"Anna, this is my colleague, Peter Daley"

Peter smiled in acknowledgement.

David then sat next to Anna and showed her the Disclosure Pack which was a copy of the one given to Rik Jeffreys. He then made the same initials comments that he had said to John Harrison earlier in the day.

"There is not a huge amount of paperwork to show you at this stage. We have enclosed twenty copies of fraudulent travel claim forms, ten of which have been completed by your client, Zoe Ferguson and the other ten by her partner Rik Jeffreys. We also enclose a detailed list of all the travel claims made by your client over the period in question which stretches over two and a half years. The total fraud is in excess of two hundred and ninety six thousand pounds and there are just short of fifteen hundred claims, some of which are for two or three journeys. The vast majority of the travel claim forms have been completed by Zoe Ferguson and there are less than a hundred which have been completed by Rik Jeffreys"

"I'll have a look at these with Zoe, but is there anything else that you are going to disclose following the meeting you had this morning with John Harrison?"

"No, why do you ask?"

"Zoe has not been able to contact Rik Jeffreys and John has told me that his client has forbidden him from disclosing any information which came up this morning"

"I will be asking some questions around what arose this morning but I think you'll find that Zoe already knows what Rik has said. He did tell her last night what he was going to say this morning"

"I may be a little while next door as I think I may need to have a good talk with my client"

David smiled "Take as long as you want, we understand"

Anna then left the Interview Room with a slight look of anger on her face.

It was almost an hour later when Anna returned to the room with Zoe Ferguson and they both took their seats facing David and Peter.

"I just want to check that you understand what we are going to do. Peter will operate the tape machine and you will hear a loud noise before the start of the interview, this is normal. Has Anna explained what we are going to discuss and the procedures that will take place?"

"Yes, I understand, carry on"

"Okay, Peter will you start the tape please?"

Peter started the tape and the noise appeared before David

started the interview with the opening procedures.

"This Interview is being tape recorded, it is the twenty fifth of April, two thousand and seven and the time by my watch is two fifteen p.m. I am David Parish a Fraud Consultant for the National Health Service representing Euston General Hospital. The other officer present is"

"Peter Daley also a Fraud Specialist representing Euston General Hospital"

"I am interviewing, please state your full name, address and date of birth"

"Zoe Ferguson, Flat four, seventeen Chineham Street, Bloomsbury, London. Date of birth twelfth of January nineteen seventy eight"

"Also present is"

"Anna Young, John Harrison Solicitors, Holborn, London"

"We are in the Human Resources Department of the Euston General Hospital, London. At the end of the interview, I will give you a notice explaining the procedures for the dealing with the tapes and how you can have access to them. Before the interview begins I must caution you."

"You do not have to say anything, but it may harm your defence if you do not mention when questioned something which you later rely on in court, anything you do say may be given in evidence. Do you understand the caution?"

Zoe understood this and snarled at David.

"Yes"

"You are not under arrest and you are free to leave at any time. The reason for this interview is that we are investigating allegations that you were involved in making fraudulent travel claims at the Euston General Hospital between October, two thousand and four and April, two thousand and seven knowing the information on the claim forms was false. The total number of travel claims is One thousand, five hundred and twenty-one and the cost of these claims totals two hundred and ninety six thousand and thirty pounds. Do you understand the reason for this interview?"

"Yes"

"If at any time you wish to speak to your solicitor in private or if you wish me to stop the interview for any reason, then tell me and I will stop the interview"

"Okay"

"I would like you to open the Disclosure Pack and have a look at the travel claim forms which are numbered DP eleven/DP twenty"

Zoe opened the folder and looked at the first ten items in the pack.

"They are all travel claim forms which have been completed by you and signed by you. Do you agree?"

"Yes"

"The address on the claim forms is in Basingstoke but you have just informed us that your address is Flat four, seventeen Chineham Street, Bloomsbury, London. Have you always lived at Chineham Street since two thousand and four?"

"Yes"

"You are saying that the address in Basingstoke is incorrect and the information on the travel claim forms is fraudulent?"

"I suppose so"

"Will you have a look at the next ten travel claims in the pack, which are numbered DP one to DP ten"

Zoe slowly looked through the copies of the travel claims which were in the pack.

"The address on those travel claim forms is also Basingstoke, but they have all been completed and signed by Rik Jeffreys. Would you agree that they are also fraudulent?"

"Yeah, it looks like Rik's writing"

"Did you know that Rik Jeffreys was also completing the travel claim forms incorrectly and that the claim forms were fraudulent?"

"Yeah"

"Turn to the next page and you will find a summary of all the claims. There are one thousand five hundred and twenty-one listed and there is a sum of money relating to these fraudulent claim forms which totals two hundred and ninety six thousand and thirty pounds. Do you agree that these figures are correct?"

"I don't know unless I look at every form. If you've got all the forms and added them up then you're probably right, but I don't know how much money I've had and I don't know how much money Rik's had. What did he say?"

"Rik said that you gave him around fifty thousand pounds and you gave him another fifty thousand pounds which he gave to Keith Simpson. That leaves nearly two hundred thousand pounds which has not been accounted for"

"He's lying through his teeth. I don't know what I've given to him or what he's given to Keith Simpson but I haven't had two hundred thousand pounds, you must be joking"

"I think it's fair to say that you will be jointly charged with a fraud of two hundred and ninety thousand and thirty. We are interested to know if you have any money that you are prepared to return to us. It may help you when the case gets to court"

"I've got no money to give back"

"What is the involvement of Linda Barrett and Keith Simpson?"

"Linda Barrett works in the cash office. She's given me most of the money when I've made the travel claims. I don't know how much Keith Simpson is involved, for all I know, he mightn't be involved. Rik said he met him and it was arranged that the travel fiddle would carry on and Linda would ignore it. I don't know Keith's role but Rik's had money which he says he gave to Keith. For all I know, Rik mightn't have given him the money. They've gone to Spain and you'll probably never see them again"

"I have spoken to Linda Barrett in Spain and she'll be returning early next week. She has admitted to turning a blind eye after Rik had approached Keith Simpson. She's never had a great deal of the money"

"That's what she says. She's probably lying as well. Have you spoken to Keith Simpson?"

"No"

"Is he coming back next week as well?"

"No, he's dead"

"What"

"He was murdered last Saturday night"

"Did Linda Barrett do it?"

"No, it was the result of an argument with a dealer when he was buying some drugs"

Suddenly Zoe broke into tears and began sobbing uncontrollably. David looked at Peter and Anna all of who were completely confused by this outburst as Zoe had been in full control of herself during the interview.

David then turned to Anna and said.

"Should we stop the interview for a break?"

Before Anna was able to reply, Zoe started speaking.

"He can't be dead, I love him. We've just got our own place and we're going to move in next week. I've been trying to phone him but I couldn't contact him. I was going to tell Rik that we were finished and Keith was going to tell Linda when they got back from Spain"

Anna then said.

"Please stop the tape Peter, I will take Zoe next door to let her calm down and I'll let you know what is happening"

As Anna and Zoe were leaving the office, David said.

"It is two thirty pm on the twenty fifth of April, two thousand and seven and this interview has been suspended at the request of Anna Young, solicitor representing Zoe Ferguson"

Peter then switched the tape machine off.

Peter then asked David.

"Did you have any idea about Zoe and Keith Simpson?"

"No idea, whatsoever, I don't think that Anna was aware of that either. If I had known, I might have been a bit more delicate with the information"

"I've never known of you to be so concerned David"

"Well, I suppose that there's always a first time. I'll go and see if they want a drink or anything"

David left the room returned within seconds.

"The receptionist had given them some water. She's still sobbing but Anna said that she will return as soon as she can. In actual fact, the interview was nearly finished. If we are able to continue, the only thing that I would be asking is the whereabouts of the money again"

It was about fifteen minutes later when Anna returned to the Interview Room and informed David and Peter.

"She'll be okay in a moment, I think she wants to carry on with the interview and get it finished but I said that I would talk to you first. I presume that you didn't know about Zoe and Keith Simpson either?"

David replied.

"No, I had no idea. It was a bit of a surprise"

"How much more have you got to ask? If it's not a lot, she may be able to continue but I don't think that you should be asking a lot of personal questions concerning her relationship with Keith Simpson at this stage"

"The interview was nearly over and I haven't got much more to question her about. What do you know about the relationship, which may avoid me asking Zoe?"

"I didn't know about it before. Apparently, they started going out together about six months ago after Zoe had taken her car to the garage where Keith Simpson worked. They got chatting when she collected the car and it went on from there. This fraud was going on a long time before they got together"

"At this stage, I don't need to ask many more questions, but I would like to formally finish this interview as it may save us repeating it all again"

"I understand that. I will go and get Zoe"

Anna then left the room and returned a minute later with Zoe.

David spoke to Zoe before the interview was formally restarted.

"First of all Zoe, I did not know about your relationship with Keith. If I had known, I wouldn't have told you about him the way that I did"

"I know, it was a secret, nobody knew"

"Okay, let's restart the tape"

"This Interview is being tape recorded; it was suspended and is now being recommenced. It is the twenty fifth of April, two thousand and seven and the time by my watch is two fifty five p.m. I am David Parish, others present are"

"Peter Daley"

"Anna Young"

"Zoe Ferguson"

"I would like to ask you again, do you have any knowledge concerning the whereabouts of any money that you've received in respect to fraudulent travel claims?"

Zoe thought for a little while before answering the question.

"I gave Keith some money but I don't know how much. I do have some money which I am prepared to return"

"How much are we talking about?"

"I'm not sure but I think it will be about fifty thousand pounds. I'll let my solicitor know the exact amount"

"Where is the money?"

"It is hidden and I'm not saying where"

"Is it in a bank or are you talking about cash?"

"It's cash"

"I would like that money returned very quickly"

"It will be, I'll give it to my solicitor"

"There are no more questions at this stage. It's possible that we may have to interview you again. Here is the notice which explains your entitlement to a copy of the tape used in this interview. This interview is concluded at three five p.m. on the twenty fifth of April two thousand and seven. Switch off the tape recorder"

Zoe signed a copy of the tape that had been sealed by Peter and would be made available to Zoe's solicitors when the matter was referred for court action.

Anna and Zoe left the room leaving David and Peter to clear away the machinery and documentation.

Peter asked.

"How much money will she have left after repaying us fifty thousand pounds?"

"I think she will be left with a nice little nest egg and she'll be hoping for a shorter sentence by making that gesture. It was probably Anna who suggested that she returns some of the money"

"Sounds like good advice"

"Yeah, I'll keep hold of the tapes for now Peter. I won't refer it to our legal boys until we have spoken to Linda. It's probably going to be in about a week's time but I'll let you know when I get back from Spain with Linda"

"You'll let me know the flight times and when the plane is due to arrive at Stansted?"

"Yes, I'll just give Stuart a ring to let him know where we're up to with this case and about Linda and Keith. Thanks for your help Peter"

"Are you going to tell Linda about Zoe and Keith's relationship?"

"No way, unless she knows about it and tells me, but I'll just listen if that's the case"

"I don't blame you. I'll see you some time next week"
Peter then left the room as David said "Cheers"

David phoned Stuart Bradley on his direct line.
"Hello, Stuart Bradley"
"Hi Stuart, its David Parish. We've just interviewed Rik Jeffreys and Zoe Ferguson and they have admitted their parts in the fraud, so if we're lucky you might get about fifty thousand pounds returned by Zoe"
"I suppose that's no great surprise but will you take civil action after the prosecution and sue them for the rest of the money that they've taken?"
"I will need to find out what assets they have, but it's always a possibility"
"Do you have any further news on Linda Barrett?"
"Yes. She's been found by the police in Spain and I've spoken to her on the phone. I'm going to Spain on some other business within the next few days and have arranged to bring her back to this country. There's some bad news though. Her partner, Keith Simpson, was murdered in Spain last Saturday so you can guess what sort of state she's in"
"What happened?"
"He was stabbed following some dispute about buying drugs. I know that neither you nor Human Resources have been in touch with Linda Barrett. It's normal policy for the Hospital to speak to her, formally suspend her, and then confirm this in writing. She would then be paid whilst an investigation is undertaken and she'd normally face a disciplinary hearing once I've reported to you after my formal taped interview"
"That sounds right"
"In this case it mightn't be possible. I'm hoping to arrange our interview towards the end of next week but I doubt if you'd get her in before then. You should be able to write to her, formally suspending her because of her failure to return to work and the

fact that you haven't been notified. But no mention of the fraud investigation at this stage, what do you think?"

"I can't see a problem. It may not be correct policy but I'll chat to the Director of Human Resources, Mike Williams"

"Thanks Stuart, I'll let you know more information when I get back from Spain"

"That's fine, enjoy your trip"

"Bye Stuart"

David then packed his belongings and left Euston General Hospital for the short walk back to the Train Station

16

David was again catching the 17.17 train from Euston, but there was no need to rush as he had three quarters of an hour to get to the station. He knew that the train would arrive in Liverpool at a quarter to eight. The train journey was again uneventful, he was sitting alone and did some work on his laptop. He had bought a baguette at the station which held off the pangs of hunger.

This time the train was delayed for half an hour due to some work on the tracks and he caught a taxi at the station and arrived home just before nine o'clock.

He did a check on his diary for the next week and decided that he would have a few days break when he returned from Spain. He would then be able to go to the Lake District and take in a few walks. A check was made on the various websites to get suitable flights and he booked a seat from Liverpool to Seville leaving on Friday at 16.55 with Ryanair. He also checked that there were seats available from Malaga to London Stansted with easyJet leaving next Monday at 16.10 and, hopefully, Linda Barrett would be in the second seat.

David then phoned Alisa.
"Hola"
"Hi Alisa, its David"
"Hi David and what have you got to tell me?"
"I have booked a flight from Liverpool to Seville for Friday evening and will, hopefully return from Malaga to London on

Monday with Linda Barrett"

"That's super, I did speak to Felipe and he said that he would be able to come to Seville on Friday morning, but would prefer to leave late on Saturday because he has to go to Madrid. He can get a flight from Alicante to Seville on Friday morning and then a flight from Seville to Madrid on Saturday evening. He'll be staying with me on Friday"

"That's fine. I'll be arriving late on Friday and will book into the Hotel Emperador on Calle Jose Laguillo"

"David. You only need to book the one night as you can stay at my flat on the other two nights. Felipe will not be there then. It'll be best if we arrange a meeting on Saturday morning at my office, the Guardia Civil in Seville. You know where that is don't you?"

"Yes, what time?"

"How about ten o'clock and we'll then go out and have some tapas for our lunch"

"That's okay but I will need to go to the Costa del Sol on Monday and meet up with Linda before we catch the flight from Malaga to London. Will you come with me?"

"Yes. I'll arrange a car. It will take about three hours"

"Thanks Alisa. I will see you on Saturday morning. I'm looking forward to seeing you again"

"Me too, David, bye for now"

David then looked up the hotel on the internet and booked a room for the one night on Friday.

The following morning, David rang a contact he had with the Cheshire Police.

"Good morning, Cheshire Police"

"Good morning, may I speak to Chief Inspector Anne Graham"

"Yes, who is it calling?"

"David Parish"

"Good morning David, what can we do for you Mr Fraud?"

"Actually, I'm not sure Anne. Hopefully you can help me or I can help you. You know the Mitchell family?"

"Yes, I'm afraid so"

"I'm going to Spain tomorrow investigating a couple of frauds that have taken place. I have a meeting with the Spanish Police and I know they are going to bring up the Mitchell family. Steve Mitchell is buying a property worth over a million pounds and they are curious where the money is coming from. It seems possible that he is placing cash deposits into several different bank and building societies in this country and this will then be transferred to Spain. The accounts in this country have probably been opened okay, but where's he getting the money from, any ideas?"

"We're off the record now David and I don't really know, and you will have to give me a few days to make more enquiries, but something has cropped up recently. You know these fake car crash scams where gang members use either one or two cars to force another vehicle to slam into the back of one their vehicles. They then make bogus claims for the accident and personal injury?"

"Yes, I've had some reports sent to me recently from both Insurance Companies and some of my fraud contacts who have been raising concerns. I'm going to attend a meeting within a couple of weeks"

"There has been a big increase over the past few months in the North around Leeds and we liaised with Yorkshire Police and carried out some preliminary investigations, talking to the people who have been caught up in the scams. We asked for a brief description of the car drivers who were driving the cars that they crashed into. A couple of the drivers gave a similar description and mentioned seeing a tattoo of a snake on his arm. This rang a bell with one of the officers and he obtained a mug shot from our records and showed it to the two drivers, who confirmed that he was the other driver. Different names were given but we've now arrested this man, Bill Kennedy. He's known to us but we don't think that he has the brains to organize this sort of scam. He's probably the foot soldier who's doing what he's told to do and getting paid on results. He has been questioned but denies the involvement of anybody else, saying it's all his own idea and all he's done is drive a friend's car, and used his friends name to get their car fixed. The car crashes weren't his fault and the other drivers ran into the back of him. When asked about the different names, he admits it was wrong but he's saying that they're friends of his, who've gone abroad for a few months and let him use their cars. We do know that he has worked for Steve Mitchell in the past and we wouldn't be surprised if there was a connection, now that it seems he is raising lots of cash. It's possible but we've got no evidence at this stage. I think that we should consider having a word with our friend Steve Mitchell but he covers his tracks very well. A similar scam may have also happened around London"

"I should be able to get more information from the Fraud Divisions in the Insurance Companies who are dealing with this type of Fraud. It may be worth considering an official get together to try and get to the bottom of these car crash scams before it gets much worse. I'll let you know Anne if I find out any more"

"Thanks David, I'll give you a ring in a few days once I've made some more enquiries. They still have the bloke in custody who was involved in these car crashes and he is still being interviewed. We can't be sure, at this stage, if there is a connection with Steve Mitchell but I'll get back to you. If you find out anything in Spain, let me know"

"I'll do that Anne, thanks a lot"

Liverpool John Lennon Airport was fairly busy when David made his way to the check in desk for the Ryanair flight to

Seville. The flight was due to leave on time at 16.55 which meant that he would be arriving at Seville Airport just before nine o'clock. It was only a fifteen minute ride by taxi from the Airport to the Hotel.

He then made his way to the departure lounge, managed a cup of coffee before making his way to the boarding gate before walking to the plane which took off on time. David then looked at the price list for the drinks, five euros for a small miniature bottle of French merlot. He would need two of the miniatures which equalled about a half bottle of wine. Drink prices are never cheap on aeroplanes, ten euros which was about seven pounds in sterling.

The stewardess soon arrived at David's seat.

"Would you like a drink?"

"Yes please, two red wines, the merlot please"

David then held out the ten euro note which was exchanged for the wine.

The flight arrived on time and David collected his luggage fairly quickly before walking out of the airport and getting into the taxi.

"Hotel Emperador, Calle Jose Laguillo, por favour"

"Si Senor"

The journey took less than fifteen minutes and cost David eighteen euros.

David went to the hotel reception and handed in the booking details that he had downloaded from the internet and printed out. He was then given the entry swipe card for room 215 on the second floor. A quick visit to the room where he left his luggage unpacked and he then made his way to a little family run Spanish bar that he knew, which was only about fifty metres from the hotel.

It was warm enough to sit outside even though it was nearing ten o'clock. He was known to the staff and smiled when the young girl arrived.

"Tapas por favour, Calamares y Tortilla Espana. Una copa de vino tinto rioja"

The girl did not speak any English but David did speak Spanish, having lived there for three years and having a good teacher in Alisa. He enjoyed squid, Spanish omelette and a glass of rioja. The meal arrived including the basket of bread, which was soon demolished and he went to the bar to collect a second glass of rioja and pay the bill which came to less than ten euros, excellent value he thought and what a nice way to spend your first hour in Seville. It is a beautiful city and David thoroughly enjoyed walking through this city but he doubted if he would have much chance for walking on this visit.

"Adios" he shouted as he left the bar.

"Adios Senor Fraudo" came the reply from the man who owned the bar. Oh to be so popular.

David then made his way back to his hotel but not taking the direct route. He thought a half hour walk would help him sleep better and always enjoyed walking the side streets of Spain, even at eleven o'clock in the evening. There was still activity in the bars and restaurants although many people were now making their way back home or returning to their hotels.

He approached the hotel reception to collect his entry card and was given a message by the girl on reception. It was a handwritten note of a telephone call from Alisa stating.

'Alisa Garcia rang to confirm that you had arrived safely and booked into the hotel. She will see you in the morning'

David smiled and made his way to his hotel room.

17

The young couple, both in their mid-twenties were sitting at a table in the corner of an Indian Restaurant in Manchester. She had striking features with long blond hair, was elegantly dressed in a colourful top and long flowing skirt. He was smart and casually dressed with short dark curly hair. You could tell by their actions and their eye contact that love was in the air.

The waiter walked over to the table and asked.
"Are you ready to order yet?"
The young man finished reading the menu and spoke to the waiter.
"Yes, we'd like two pappadums, the mixed starters for two, and one chicken tikka tandoori and one chicken balti please"
"Would you like a drink?"
"Yes please, two bottles of the Indian beer"
"Do you prefer the Kingfisher beer or the Cobra beer?"
"The Kingfisher beer will do fine, thanks"
"Thank you, I'll bring the drinks over now"

The young lady, Sarah Mitchell started chatting to her boyfriend, Phillip Harris.
"How was your day today in the world of money?"
"It was okay, actually, your brother Steve came in today and was making some enquiries with Jenny Percival at the counter. He had just returned from Spain and was talking about buying the property in Murcia and sending the money over to

his solicitor, but then mentioned that he'd be sending us about fifteen lots of fifty thousand pounds. Our job would then be to send these amounts individually to the solicitor and presumably his solicitor would then make the one payment to the sellers of the property. Jenny called me over and I then went to have a word with Steve. I told him that we have to verify that the sender is legitimate before we transmit any monies to foreign countries, mainly to comply with money laundering regulations.

In his case, we knew he was Steve Mitchell so there would be no problems in sending the money to Spain. Checks are made, usually by our Internal Auditors, and they'd probably find it unusual that a person wanted to send three quarters of a million pounds in fifteen instalments. If it was a one off payment of seven hundred and fifty thousand pounds, that would not be unusual as we get many people buying foreign properties, not just in Spain, but all over the world. I got the impression that he thought it may seem less obvious if small payments were made, but that would not be the case for this type of transaction. We do get people paying us with cheques or transfers from different sources, but that's not altogether unusual, because they have their money and savings with different banks. You'll find that some will sell their property in this country and the solicitor will send us the proceeds or their may be a sale of shares. It will, though, only be one transfer from us to the foreign solicitor. He said there was no immediate need for the transfer and he would think about what I had said. He may ask you about it. He doesn't know about us does he?"

"No, mum knows but she won't tell Steve or Alan"

"I don't know how he gets his money and I think that I'd rather not know"

"You're best keeping your distance, Phil, I don't get involved. He thinks that he is an entrepreneur and he does have lots of different types of businesses. I know that he has a bar and he's got a few of those tanning and sun bed shops. He's got a beauty shop where they do false nails and things and, using his words, he buys and sells all sorts of stuff often on market stalls and the internet, I think. He does get involved in some property deals and tends to pick my brain when property is involved. There was some type of investigation when he bought the house in Cheshire but nothing really came of it and he's never been in trouble with the police, but I'm sure they know him. I'm his sister and I don't trust him, the money comes from somewhere but not those little shops and market stalls"

Their beer arrived with the pappadums and they kept quiet for a few minutes while they ate the pappadums and the relishes which came with them. Phillip took a sip of the beer and spoke to Sarah quietly.

"It's not our job to check the source of how the money came to Steve, for all we know a lot of it may be honest money, but then maybe not. Think I'll keep my distance"

"Couldn't agree more and I'm sure Mum doesn't know either or maybe she does. She probably knows a lot more than she lets on. After all, Dad was a criminal and spent time in jail; he even died in a Spanish prison"

"I know all about that Sarah, but you've made an honest life for yourself and I love you Sarah Mitchell"

"I love you too, Phillip Harris"

They didn't even notice the waiter arriving with their mixed starters, a good selection of onion bhaji, sheesh kebab, samosa and pakooras.

Sarah has, for the past couple of years, shared a flat in Manchester with her friend Karen Lucas but she knew that Karen was moving to London to be with her boyfriend. Karen was spending the weekend in London and had phoned Sarah and given a date when she was moving out, just before she came out to meet Phillip.

"Karen is definitely going to London in two weeks" which brought a smile to the face of Phillip.

"I'll be moving in the day after" said Phillip.

"That's if I let you" grinned Sarah

"I'd better go home soon and start packing"

"Funny guy"

"I suppose Steve will then find out about us" said Phillip.

"Yeah, I've told Mum but I'm sure he'll find out when you move in. He's probably having me watched to make sure I'm safe. It's a family thing even though I can't stand him"

The main courses of chicken balti and chicken tikka tandoori arrived, which Sarah and Phillip shared. The food was excellent and Indian food was certainly one of the favourites of both Sarah and Phillip.

After they finished their meals, Phillip asked Sarah.

"What type of property is Steve buying in Spain?"

"He hasn't mentioned it to me yet, but Mum has told me all about it. He's buying a big villa in Murcia. It's on one of those big complexes called La Grande Club and has its own swimming pool. I do know some people who have property there and it's supposed to be excellent. He will probably ask me about it soon. I haven't been to La Grande Club but we'll be able to go there sometime in the future"

"Will he charge us rent?"

"No, I'm his lovely sister" and they both laughed.

"I know some blokes who went there and played golf, apparently the facilities are super"

Phillip paid the bill and they left the restaurant, hand in hand, and walked down the road to catch a taxi to Sarah's flat.

They had now been together for some five months but it had taken Phillip a few years to find the right moment and persuade Sarah to go out together. He had only seen her a few times since they left Liverpool University but she was always with some other men. The only time that he had seen her out with Karen and no bloke in tow, he was with a previous girlfriend, so it wasn't the right time, even though he'd had strong feelings for Sarah for several years ever since they'd met at University. He didn't know that the feelings were mutual.

The taxi arrived at Sarah's flat and Sarah opened the main door as Phillip paid the Taxi driver. They made their way to Sarah's first floor flat and opened the door. The light on the phone was flashing indicating that there was a message and Sarah pressed the button.

"Hi Sarah, its Steve. I want to pick your brain about a property deal that I'm doing in Spain. Are you coming over tomorrow to see Mum, give me a ring and let me know? Bye for now"

"I'll give him a ring tomorrow morning. I was going to go over to Cheshire to see Mum tomorrow afternoon anyway. He'll be asking me about making the payment for the villa in Spain and he'll probably mention that he's spoken to you. I'll have to act a bit stupid as though it's all new to me"

Phillip couldn't resist the reply.

"That shouldn't be too hard"

He then braced himself as Sarah gave him a playful dig in the ribs before heading for the drinks cabinet.

"What would you like to drink, the usual?"

"Yes please, my favourite, Ouzo and lemonade"

This was a drink that Phillip first drank when he had a holiday on the Greek island of Crete. Curiously, Sarah also had this drink when she was on holiday with Karen in Corfu and this was now her favourite aperitif or pre-bedtime drink.

They finished their drinks before heading to bed, and made a lovely end to what had been a perfect romantic evening. It took a matter of seconds to undress and scramble into bed.

18

David was awake by seven o'clock in the morning and leisurely took his time to have a shave and shower and was dressed by a quarter to eight. He then left his hotel room and made his way downstairs to the restaurant, where he had a continental breakfast. He quite enjoyed the breakfast, which consisted of yoghurt, fruit juice and then a couple of rolls with a selection of Spanish sliced meats together with a cup of coffee. He was the first down to breakfast which surprised him, but within the next ten minutes another dozen people had arrived, the vast majority being English tourists.

He made his way to the hotel reception to check out but there was no bill to pay as he had booked the hotel on line at a cost of just over fifty pounds. A receptionist was standing at the counter when David arrived.

"I would like to check out but you will see that I have already paid for the room, Room two one five"

"Yes, Mr Parish, the room was paid on reservation with the booking agency"

"I'll just go and get my luggage, is it okay if I leave the luggage in the hotel until this afternoon?"

"Yes, you may place it in the room next door"

"Thank you, I won't be too long"

"That's no problem"

David then made his way to the room on the second floor and collecting his luggage and other belongings. He then returned to the hotel reception and handed in the swipe card for the room, before he took his luggage to the room next door, which was allocated for luggage when guests arrived too early to get into their rooms, or like David, if they were leaving but did not want to carry their luggage around the city.

He turned left outside of the hotel and walked passed the Spanish bar where he had eaten the previous evening. This led to a circular road which goes round the city centre in Seville and he joined the Calle de Recaredo. He had almost an hour to spend before the meeting with Alicia and Felipe but thought a short walk and a coffee would be quite relaxing. Alisa lived in an apartment in a side street on the other side of the road, which he passed before finding a little coffee bar where he was able to sit outside and enjoy the pleasant warm day. The waiter walked towards David who spoke in his best Spanish language.

"Un Café con leche, grande, por favour"

"Si, Senor"

The coffee arrived within five minutes which David drank whilst contemplating what Alisa and Felipe were going to ask or discuss at the meeting. He then started to think about his relationship with Alisa, clearly they were still very fond of each other, David often thought if Alisa was in a similar job with the British Police living anywhere in England, they would still be together, which would probably be true. Alisa did not want to leave her job or lifestyle in Spain which was also understandable. If David had stayed in Spain, he was also sure they would still be together, but he did not want to stop working in England. He did not want to stop working in the specialist field of fraud and enjoyed being known as Mr Fraud or Senor Fraudo his nickname from Alisa.

Felipe and Alisa were also close, having a good brotherly sister relationship. Felipe tended to try and protect Alisa, not that Alisa needed any protection. They were living in different parts of Spain now, with David being based in Murcia and Alisa in Seville. It was probably about seven hundred kilometres from Murcia to Seville but there were now internal flights from Alicante to Seville, and Felipe only lived about an hour from Alicante using the main A7 motorway.

The relationship between Felipe and David was a bit cooler although professionally, they had respect for each other. The idea of a love affair between his sister and a bloke from England who failed to stay in Spain did not come naturally to Felipe. It would have been better for him if his sister had married a nice Spanish man and had a family. He failed to understand that his sister did not want a family; she loved her job, did not want to leave it and was in several ways happy to continue to with this relationship, although the meetings with David were becoming more infrequent. Felipe had asked David, on a couple of occasions when he was living in Spain, when they were getting married and settling down to have a family. David had told Felipe that he had better ask Alisa, but he never did.

David finished the coffee and stopped the waiter as he passed, in order to pay the bill.

"La cuenta, por favour"

The waiter gave David the bill for one euro eighty, and David gave him a two euro coin saying. "Gracias"

He then continued his walk to the office of the Guardia Civil where he had arranged to meet Alisa and Felipe. He arrived shortly before ten o'clock and found Felipe standing at the reception desk talking to the lady sitting behind the desk. He approached Felipe saying.

"Good morning Felipe. How are you?"

Felipe turned to David and smiled as they shook hands.

"I'm fine David and how are you?"

"Very good, is Alisa in her office?"

"Yes, she came in about eight o'clock. I stayed in her apartment to do some paperwork and make a couple of phone calls, so I've

144

only just arrived. I know where her office is, we'll make our way there now"

David then followed Felipe along a couple of corridors before arriving at the office with the name plate "Alisa Garcia". The door was open and Alisa got off her chair as soon as she saw David and walked towards him, giving him a hug and a kiss.

"It's lovely to see you David; did you have a good journey last night?"

"Yes, the flight was on time and I managed to down a couple of glasses of rioja with tapas"

"I suppose you went to the little bar by the hotel?"

"But of course, they know me there. The owner called me Senor Fraudo"

"I wonder where he got that name from."

"I think he's heard somebody called Alisa Garcia call me that when we've been there before"

Alisa gave David a playful punch before they all sat down in her office.

Felipe started the meeting by telling David what he had learnt about Steve Mitchell.

"I've been informed by a contact that Steve Mitchell is buying a villa at La Grande Club in Murcia for One and a half million euros. He's paid a deposit of three hundred and seventy five thousand euros and the balance is due on completion, which should be some time within the next six months. He was in Spain at La Grande Club last week with his brother and their two girlfriends. He and his brother had a meeting with the manager of property sales. They discussed the purchase details and apparently Steve Mitchell told the manager that they were going to pay for the property from several different sources in England, which is a bit unusual. Apparently, the deposit was made up with the sale of a property in San Pedro del Pinatar, which came to a hundred and fifty thousand euros, and the rest by three instalments of around seventy-five thousand euros which made up the deposit that was required. I don't know how, but from what I've heard about the Mitchell family, they wouldn't have raised that kind of money from legal sources. I don't think they have committed any offence in Spain in connection with this purchase but if they're up to something in England, I would love to help and have Steve Mitchell put in jail. We have never forgotten what he did to Luiz and we want our revenge. I did speak to Interpol and a police officer in England, but they didn't know of any robberies where Steve Mitchell may have raised some cash but would be looking into it further. We then thought, if it was some type of fraudulent activity, you may be the best person to contact as you tend to know plenty of frauds that take place. What do you think, David?"

"After I spoke to Alisa last time, I phoned a contact that I have with a Police Inspector in Cheshire and I've also had some information from some Insurance Companies. They've also invited me to attend a meeting shortly. She had no definite news and has promised to get back to me within the next week or so, but there has been a fraudulent scam taking place where cars are driven but then brake hard causing a lorry to crash into the back of the car. The driver of the car then claims for the damages to the car and personal injury. This type of incident has happened on a couple of hundred occasions, they think, and they believe that it may be an organised crime with somebody using a team of drivers and providing cars which they then repair. It appears that this type of scam has mostly occurred in London and Leeds and you would think that they're outside the areas where the Mitchell's may operate. Somebody has been arrested for taking part in a couple of the scams, but he used different names and he says that he arranged them, but the police don't believe him. The funny thing is that he has worked for Steve Mitchell in the past and this is the only connection they have at this stage. I don't think that it is a coincidence that this scam is going on, defrauding Insurance Companies at the same time that Mitchell is trying to raise money to buy this villa in Spain. There is nothing definite but the police will be investigating and I should be able to persuade the Insurance Company Investigators to look into it further and keep me updated. I'll also probably be able to get them to employee me on a consultancy basis to have a look at this type of fraud. Sorry, I don't know any more at this stage but things may happen soon, at least we hope so"

Alisa had been listening quietly but now remarked.

"When payments are sent from England to pay for property in Spain, would you be able to trace the source?"

"Possibly, but you would have to get some help from the solicitor acting for Steve Mitchell and the solicitor's bankers who received the money. I don't know who they are and whether they would help"

Felipe replied to that question.

"I know the solicitor, Pepe Fernandez, he will probably help us and I'll then contact his bank to see if they'll provide the information we want. It may take a few days but I'll let you know as soon as I hear"

There was a knock on Alisa's office door and a young lady arrived with three coffees which she placed on the desk before leaving.

"Gracias" said Alisa.

David was impressed.

"I didn't even have to ask for this, I trust you've arranged this before we arrived"

"I know what we all drink and I knew you'd both arrive on time. That's service for you"

Felipe then asked David.

"What are our chances of getting something on Steve Mitchell?"

"As I see it and it is the early stages. I don't see how you will be able to get him for any offence in Spain. It's a question of trying to find out where the money comes from and that may be difficult, but if the money reaches Spain for the purchase, he may have to provide some details of the source to please the Tax Authorities in England. If it hasn't been declared and he hasn't paid tax then he might have a problem. I'll speak to an investigator at the HM Revenue and Customs who covers Mitchell's area and give him some information on the amount of money being sent to Spain. They may become very interested"

Alisa looked at both David and Felipe.

"I don't know about the taxman in England but that sounds as though it may be our best chance of getting Steve Mitchell"

Felipe nodded his head.

"I tend to agree with you both. We would like him to end up in a Spanish jail but if we can't have that, we would settle for him spending time in one of your jails. We'll never get our justice for what he did to Luis but I suppose that would help a little. What type of sentence would he get, if found guilty?"

David held his hands in the air but said.

"I don't really know but there was a recent case of a London gangster getting seven years for money laundering and tax avoidance, but the sentence could be less than that. It often depends on who the judge is and how he feels on the day"

They all smiled before Felipe remarked.

"Alisa, my flight to Madrid is booked for five, forty five, but there is an earlier flight which leaves at one, forty and it would be better if I catch the earlier flight. I've got time now to make some enquiries concerning the transfer of money that Mitchell used to pay the deposit. I'll then be able get the one, forty flight, if that is okay with you?"

"Yes, that's fine Felipe. You can use this room, I'll take David to the meeting room and we'll discuss another fraud case that I've been investigating for David. We'll return in about an hour but we'll only just be down the corridor if you need us"

David and Alisa left the office leaving Felipe to make some enquiries and find out a few phone numbers. They collected a couple of coffees before making their way to the meeting room.

Alisa asked David.

"Have you spoken to Linda Barrett since you arrived in Seville?"

"No, I thought we'd have this meeting with Felipe first in case I was going to be delayed but I'll give her a ring later. I thought that I'd spend today and tomorrow here and then we could go to the Costa del Sol on Monday morning. I was going to fly back on Monday but I'll get a flight to London on Tuesday, if that's okay"

"Yes, I've booked a car and the journey should only take just over two hours. It might be best if you see her briefly on Monday to make sure there are no problems and then book the flight for Tuesday"

"That's what I thought. I don't think there will be any difficulties in getting a flight, there are quite a few available. What day do you have to return?"

"Tuesday morning"

"We'll have to book a hotel"

"That's already arranged David, I've booked a room at the hotel in Mijas Costa where we first got to know each other"

David walked across to Alisa and gave her a gentle kiss on the lips.

"Thank you. You think of everything. There's something else that I've found out concerning Keith Simpson. He was having an affair with Zoe Ferguson who is one of the others involved in this fraud. I don't think that Linda Barrett knows anything about it and according to Zoe, he was going to tell Linda when they returned home"

"Are you going to tell her?"

"No, not unless I have too"

"You're a coward"

"I agree"

A few minutes later, Felipe entered the room.

"I spoke to Pepe Fernandez and he then contacted his bank and he has just rang me back with the information that we require. There was the proceeds from the sale of the property in San Pedro del Pinatar which was transferred from the solicitors acting for a Spanish couple who bought the property. That is fairly straightforward and the remainder was three payments of seventy-five thousand euros which all came from the same place in England. It is called the Money Transfer Organisation, which is in Manchester, but it is quite normal for foreign transfers of money to be sent from these types of businesses or a Bureau de Change as well as the Banks. I've got the dates of the money transfers and the address of the Money Transfer Organisation"

Felipe then handed David a piece of paper showing the details of the transfers and the address of the Money Transfer Organisation.

"Thanks Felipe, I'll make some enquiries when I return to England, I'm dealing with a case which is based in Manchester so I do have a contact who covers that area. He will probably use the same place when he has to send the balance of the money to Spain"

"I've changed my flight to Madrid, I'm catching the flight that leaves at twenty to two and need to be at the airport an hour before. I've arranged for a police driver to pick me up in a quarter of an hour. Thanks for your help David, it is much appreciated by Alisa and I. Hopefully we might finally catch up with Steve Mitchell"

"That's okay Felipe, but it may be a few months before the money starts moving to Spain, which is when we might have some luck. I think that it might be much harder to catch him running this car crash scam. He will have covered his tracks, making it pretty impossible to catch him but you never know"

Felipe then shook hands with David.

"It's nice to see you two together again, take care of my sister, not to say that she's not capable of looking after herself. Bye Alisa"

They gave each other a hug and Felipe then left the room to make his way to the airport in Seville in order to catch the flight to Madrid, Barajas.

"That's that for now, David, do you fancy a short walk and some Tapas?"

"Fancy asking me that question, you know how I love Tapas. Where do you fancy going?"

"We'll take a stroll towards the centre and go to the Plaza Nueva, there's a good Tapas bar on Calle Albareda"

"I've got to collect my luggage from the hotel sometime; we'll get it on the way back to your flat after we've had our Tapas and a walk around the centre of your lovely city"

They made their way towards the centre of the city and started walking down Calle San Esteban passing the Church of San Estaban and then the Palace, Casa de Pilatos with its wonderful garden of flowers and exotic plants. The Convento de San Leandro is on the right where you can buy pastries made by the nuns which are sold through a revolving wooden stand. Their gentle stroll takes them along Calle Aguilas before they turn off and head towards El Divino Salvador a monumental baroque church which took nearly forty years to build and was completed in 1712. David and Alisa were walking hand in hand when they entered Plaza Nueva which is a popular meeting place with the inhabitants of Seville. They sat on a bench under the statue of the horse ridden by Ferdinand 111, which overlooks the Plaza, watching the people passing, both tourists and locals.

Alisa then smiled at David.

"Come on, let's go to the Tapas Bar and get something to eat"

They walked out of Plaza Nueva and made the short walk to Calle Albareda and entered the Tapas Bar where they managed to get a small table in the corner before David spoke to Alisa.

"Should I get a selection of tapas and a glass of red wine?"

"That would be lovely, you know what I like"

David walked over to the long counter where there was a large selection of tapas on show. The waiter came over to David.

"Si Senor"

"I'd like two glasses of rioja and a selection of tapas"

David pointed out six different tapas and the waiter placed portions on the small plates, some of which he placed in the microwave to be heated. He then served David with two glasses of rioja which he took to the table. The tapas were all ready when David returned and it took him two journeys to collect all the food and deliver it to their table. David raised his glass.

"Cheers"

Alisa tapped the two glasses.

"Cheers, enjoy your tapas"

After their meal, David handed fifteen euros to the waiter and did not take any change.

"Thank you"

"Gracias Senor"

They both left the bar and made their way through the Santa Cruz area of the city before heading towards the hotel where David had left his luggage. They entered the hotel and David made his way to the receptionist before he pointed to the room where he had left his luggage. The receptionist then waved as acknowledgement and David entered the room and collected his luggage before returning to Alisa at the front of the hotel. They then walked past the bar where David had eaten the previous evening and crossed the main road before turning left towards where Alisa's apartment was located. It was only another five minutes before they entered the apartment and Alisa made her way to the kitchen to make them a couple of coffees.

Alisa had always been interested in oil painting and had tried to copy from prints or some other photographs. As David glanced around the room he noticed two paintings which were of a very good standard and when taking a closer look he saw that they had been signed in the corner by Alisa. As Alisa entered the lounge with the two coffees, David remarked.

"When did you paint these Alisa, they are very good?"

"I've been on a couple of painting courses in Cordoba. I was chatting to a lady whose house had been robbed and I noticed a few oil paintings on the walls which were painted by her. She told me about this artist in Cordoba who holds four day courses so I made some enquiries and decided to go. I find it quite interesting and I was given several suggestions on how to improve my painting. They are my last two attempts and I'm quite pleased with the way they've turned out"

"They are absolutely superb, you know that I'm no artist but even I can see that they're really good"

"Thank you Senor Fraudo"

Later that evening they walked to another small Spanish bar just around the corner from Alisa's apartment who specialised in fish dishes. His special meal of the day was swordfish steaks which came with a salsa sauce and potatoes which tempted David.

"I think I'll have the swordfish"

"I'll have the same and for a starter I'll have the sliced chorizo with serrano ham and manchego cheese"

David looked at the three starters and besides the choice selected by Alisa, there were spicy chorizo, pan fried in red wine or meatballs in tomato sauce.

"I think I'll have the spicy chorizo in red wine and a bottle of the Faustino Red please"

They sat down with the bottle of wine while they waited for the starters to arrive and began a friendly chat without bringing up their own relationship. The meal was excellent and David settled the bill and they slowly walked back to Alisa's apartment.

Alisa made coffee while David found some music to play. After a while they turned to each other, got to their feet and made the way to the bedroom. Their absence apart had never destroyed their feelings for each other and they often wondered why they were both living and working separate lives in different parts of Europe. The distance between Liverpool and Seville may be covered in a two and a half hour plane journey but this now seemed too far away.

19

David was out of bed first in the morning and went to the kitchen and made himself a cup of tea and a coffee for Alisa which he took to the bedroom. He placed the coffee on the bedside table as Alisa opened her eyes.

"Good morning, a cup of coffee" he said.

"Thank you, what time is it?" was all Alisa could manage.

"Quarter past nine"

David smiled.

"I'll have my tea and then I'll shave and shower"

Alisa waved as David left the bedroom.

He finished his cup of tea, and made his way to the bathroom for his early morning shave and shower. Once completed, he returned to the bedroom to get dressed and found Alisa sitting up in bed. He walked over to Alisa and gave her a kiss before he managed to get dressed. Alisa put on her dressing gown before asking.

"What are your plans today Senor Fraudo?"

"I don't have any plans but I'll give our friend Linda Barrett a ring in about half an hour. It'll be ten o'clock; she should be out and about by then. I'll have a coffee and one of your muesli bars for breakfast, do you want anything yet?"

"No, I'll have a shower first and get ready. Have a think of where you would like to go"

David made a cup of coffee and ate one of Alisa's muesli bars. He then decided that he would ring Linda.

He picked up his mobile and found the number for Linda before pressing the button and listened for the dialling tone. The phone was quickly answered.

"Hello"

"Hello, is that Linda?"

"Yes"

"It's David Parish here, Linda"

"Hello David, I've waiting for you to ring, where are you?"

"I'm in Seville today, but I'll be driving down to Benalmadena with Alisa Garcia from the Spanish Police tomorrow morning. I imagine we should be there about mid-day"

"When are we going to fly back to England?"

"I'll arrange that after I've spoken to you but, hopefully, it will be some time on Tuesday afternoon. A colleague of mine will then pick us up at Stansted Airport and he'll drive you back to your flat in London. I take it that you're still happy to return to England?"

"Oh yes, I just want to get back as quick as possible and get it all sorted. I won't let you down"

"As soon as we've arrived in Benalmadena, I'll give you a ring and we'll meet you in the reception of your hotel"

"Do you know where it is?"

"Yes, I think so, but I'll be with Alisa Garcia and she knows where the hotel is"

"Thank you once again, David, I'll see you tomorrow"

David put the phone down as Alisa came out of the bathroom wearing a towelling robe.

"Did you have any problems with Linda Barrett?"

"No, she wants to go home as soon as possible. I said I'd ring her as soon as we arrived in Benalmadena, and arrange to see her in the reception area of her hotel"

"Have you decided where you want to go today?"

"No, not yet"

"Get a move on Englishman; I'll be ten minutes getting dressed"

"Do you want a hand to get dressed?"

"No, you stay here, David Parish"

"I did tell Linda that I'd book the flight after I had spoken to her tomorrow. I think I might as well book it now, is it okay if I use your computer?"

"Yes, go ahead"

The computer was in a small room that Alisa used as an office. He logged onto the computer and booked two flights with easyJet on flight 3116, which was leaving at 16.10 on Tuesday, arriving at London, Stansted at 18.05. He printed off the details with the reference number that he would need at the check in desk, it also showed the costs of the flight which he would be claiming back as part of his expenses. It wasn't a normal type of expense but he felt that Stuart Bradley at Euston General would not complain too much. He also went into a hotel booking website and booked a room for Tuesday night at the hotel in South Kensington that he frequently used.

Alisa walked into the lounge wearing a pinkish coloured top and three quarter length dark trousers with flat sandals ready for walking. She looked extremely attractive and asked David once more.

"Where are we going, Senor Fraudo?"

"I think we'll head for the Rio Guadalquivir and the Canal de Alfonso but stop at the Parque de Maria Luisa, which you Sevillians say is the most romantic park in Seville, with all those horse drawn carriages"

Alisa had to laugh as it was the walk they always tended to take whenever David was in Seville.

"We'll leave in about a half an hour, which will give us time for another coffee and I think I'll have a little snack"

It was probably about three quarters of an hour before David and Alisa left the apartment and walked out into the sun of Seville. It was the perfect weather for a slow stroll, not too hot, but warm enough to walk without any coats or jumpers.

They walked along the main road to begin with, looking at the shops and joining the hundreds of others making similar journeys. They made their way alongside the city centre passing the area of Santa Cruz which was on the right before they headed for the Plaza de Espana with its little canal, boats and the fountain. They spent half an hour walking around the plaza before going to the Parque de Maria Luisa, where they again found somewhere to sit and watch the world go by, but they resisted the temptation to ride on one of the horse drawn carriages. After sitting for a little while, David felt the need for food.

"Shall we have something to eat, where is the nearest Tapas bar?"

"Come on, I know another nice bar"

They then headed towards the bar.

The following morning Alisa and David went to Estacion de Santa Justa to collect an Opal Astra hire car which had been provided for their journey to the Costa del Sol. Restrictions had been placed on the driver and only Alisa was allowed to drive the car. They headed out of Seville at 9.30 am and took the A92 passing Osuna and Estepe before taking the A45 which headed south towards Malaga. The journey had been quite pleasant and there were very few traffic problems although it was getting busier as they reached Malaga. They then took the old coastal road towards Benalmadena. It was now just after mid-day and David picked up his mobile and rang Linda. She answered the very quickly.

"Hello"

"Hello Linda, its David. We will be arriving within fifteen minutes and we'll see you in the reception of your hotel"

"That's fine. I'm in the hotel reception now"

"Okay, see you shortly"

As they entered Benalmadena, Alisa said to David.

"It's just a little further down, we'll have to turn left towards the beach. The hotel is at the bottom of that road"

Alisa turned left and drove down the road, parking in the hotel car park and they both got out of the car. Alisa then turned to David.

"Have you ever met Linda Barrett?"

"No, I've seen a photograph of her and Keith Simpson, but I know that you've met her and you never forget a face. It must be your police background"

"Thanks for the compliment"

They walked into the hotel and saw just the one lady sitting in reception and David recognised her immediately from the photograph. Linda Barrett stood up but did not move from her spot. Alisa walked ahead and said to Linda.

"Hello Linda, this is David Parish"

David then shook hands with Linda and said.

"Let's sit down in the corner; I think it's a little bit more private here"

They walked to the corner and sat down but then Linda turned to Alisa and David.

"Would you like a drink, tea, coffee or a beer?"

David replied.

"Yes, I'll have a coffee, how about you Alisa?"

"Yes, I'll have a coffee as well"

Linda walked to the reception and asked the receptionist.

"I'd like to order three coffees please, put it on my bill"

"I'll arrange that for you, it'll probably be about ten minutes"

"That's okay"

Linda then returned and sat with Alisa and David.

"When are you going to book the flights home?"

"I've already booked two seats on the easyJet flight. It leaves at ten past four, tomorrow afternoon and is due to arrive at Stansted at five past six. We should aim to be at Malaga Airport before three o'clock, I think it best if we collect you from your hotel here at about quarter past two in case there's any heavy traffic"

"Quarter past two is okay, I'll be waiting here for you. I've spoken to the police here about having Keith's body sent back home, but they said that it might be a long time before they will be able to release the body. Is that right?"

Alisa replied.

"That is often the case in Spain as they don't always release a body until after the trial has taken place and that might be a long time. I will make some enquiries and I'll let David know after you have returned back to England"

"I don't know if Keith's mother has been informed. I've never met her and Keith hasn't spoken to her for a few years. The Spanish police told the British Embassy and they were going to try and make contact"

"I'll find that out as well and let David know"

"Thanks"

The waiter arrived with their three coffees. As they were drinking their coffees, David could see that Linda Barrett was in a dreadful state, thinking she had probably had not slept well for days.

Linda asked David.

"What do I owe you for the flight home, I want to pay you?"

David had to think for a second. The cost had been a hundred and eighty euros, including taxes for the two flights.

"It came to ninety euros including the taxes"

Linda immediately opened her purse and took out ninety euros in notes which she handed to David.

160

"I don't want the hospital to have to pay for my flight home"

"Thanks"

David thought that comment was quite ironic as the hospital was probably paying anyway, with the money from the proceeds of the travel fraud. He decided to make no comment though.

Linda then looked at David.

"Have you interviewed Zoe and Rik yet?"

"Yes"

"What did they say?"

"I can't tell you that, but you'll be able to tell me everything when I interview you. We'll discuss some possible dates for that on our way home"

"I spoke to my Mum and Dad about what had happened and told them about the fraud I've been involved in, they're heartbroken, but they contacted a solicitor and he's phoned me here in Spain. He's heard of you and thought it was a bit unusual that you were coming to Spain to bring me back"

David had to smile.

"He's quite correct, it is a bit unusual, but there were other reasons why I had to be in Spain at this time. It wasn't much of a problem to arrange to come back with you. It is what you wanted"

"I know, I told him it was my idea, but he did say that I shouldn't say anything about what we've done until I get home and we have the taped interview"

"He's right, and I've no intention of asking you any questions, but I will have to get his details from you so that I can contact him to arrange the interview. What's his name?"

"Darren O'Brien, I don't know who he works for but I'll give you the details later"

"I'm glad you've contacted a solicitor as it makes it easier for me. Anyhow, Linda, I think we'll leave you for now, but we'll call back tomorrow at about quarter past two. We'll meet you here in reception. Is that okay?"

"Yes, I'll see you tomorrow"

David and Alisa then left the hotel and made their way to their hire car. They got into the car and travelled down the coastal road to the hotel in Miraflores Playa on the Mijas Costa. It was now a few years since he had been to this hotel but it had many happy memories, both to him and to Alisa.

20

Alisa and David entered the hotel and were immediately recognised at reception, even though they had not been for a few years.

"Good afternoon, it is the lady police officer from Guardia Civil and Mr Fraud from England"

David was surprised to be recognised after all this time.

"You have a very good memory don't you?"

"I tend to recognise faces very well but sometimes forget the names but when Alisa booked the room, I was able to picture the faces from the names that I had been given. How are you both?"

"We're fine" replied David as they were given the registration cards to complete.

They both completed their own cards and David handed over his passport to the receptionist. This was not required for Alisa as she was a Spanish resident.

"You are in room one, zero, six on the first floor, it has a sea view as requested"

They walked up the stairs, the room being just down the corridor on the left hand side. As they entered the room you could see the wonderful view overlooking the ocean.

Alisa then said.

"Let's go for a walk along the beach and stop at the beach bar towards Calahonda. I think I'll change into shorts and sandals"

"I'll do the same but I'd better make a quick phone call to Peter Daley. He's agreed to pick us up tomorrow at Stansted Airport.

David took the mobile from his jacket pocket and looked up Peter Daley's number which he had recorded on the phone. He then rang Peter in London.

"Hello David"

The phone number for David had obviously shown on Peter's mobile.

"Hi Peter, have you got a pen handy?"

"Yes"

"We're booked on the easyJet flight three, one, one, six which leaves Malaga at ten past four and is due to arrive at Stansted at five past six"

"I've got that. I'll see you at the airport"

"If there's going to be any delays, I'll ring you from Malaga Airport. If you don't hear from me, we should be on time"

"That's okay"

"Thanks Peter, see you tomorrow"

"Cheers"

He then quickly got changed and they both walked out of the back of the hotel onto the beach and took a leisurely walk towards Calahonda. The weather was warm without being too hot and there was a nice gentle breeze which was blowing on their backs. There were very few people about and the only noise they could hear were the waves from the ocean and the sound of their own footsteps. Within half an hour they reached the beach bar and sat at a table outside, there were perhaps another ten people around the bar.

A waiter walked to their table.

"Hello, what would you like to drink?"

David looked at Alisa.

"I think I'll have a bottle of San Miguel, how about you Alisa?"

"I'll have the same please"

"Would you like anything to eat?"

They had not eaten since having a breakfast snack at Alisa's apartment in Seville.

Alisa replied.

"Yes, I think so"

The waiter then handed them both a menu and made his was to the bar to collect the two bottles of San Miguel.

"Should we share a selection of tapas between us, David?"

"Yes, that'll be fine"

They looked at the menu until the waiter came back with the two bottles of beer, which he place on the table with two glasses and some peanuts which were in a small bowl.

"Have you decided?"

Alisa replied by saying.

"Yes, we're going to have as selection of tapas. How about calamare, boquerone, meatballs, chorizo and a piece of tortilla?"

"That's fine by me" said David.

The waiter made a note of the order and collected the two menus from David and Alisa.

David looked at Alisa as well as the view of the ocean.

"This is a wonderful place with the super hotel the views and the pleasant beach bars. It's just lovely to see you again Alisa"

"Thanks David, its nice being with you again. Are you travelling abroad much with work?"

"No, not really, I haven't had to travel anywhere abroad for the past six or nine months. There's too much going on back home, I'm doing quite a bit of travelling around England but not abroad. I'm sure that'll soon change, it usually does"

"How about you? Have you settled in Seville or are there more promotions you could go for?"

"No promotions, I like Seville and I like my job here, it's a lovely city and the surrounding area is nice. Cordoba is not too far away and it's only a couple of hours to Portugal. Parts of the Algarve are very nice"

The waiter arrived with their tapas and they shared the different dishes, looking to catch the eye of the waiter as they emptied their plates.

"Would you like another drink?"

"Coffee for me please" said Alisa.

"I'll have a coffee too please"

The waiter then collected the empty bottles, glasses and dishes.

They sat at the table another half an hour drinking the coffees before David made his way to the bar and settled the bill.

David and Alisa then walked slowly back to the hotel and made their way to the room, where they sat outside on the veranda gazing at the ocean, and enjoying each others company. After a little while, they returned to the bedroom, undressed and lay on the bed before making love again, it was as though they had never been apart. They fell asleep for a little while before getting out of bed, showering and preparing for the evening meal in the hotel.

A table in the water front terrace overlooking the sea was again provided. The hotel advertises the view which takes your breath away and where your meal lasts forever. The Gazpacho Soup and their main meals of Seafood and Meat Paella were typical Spanish cuisine and the House Rioja recommended by the waiter was comparable to many of the more expensive riojas. It was the ideal way to finish the day before they retired to bed shortly after midnight.

The following morning, they had a continental breakfast before enjoying another stroll along the beach, returning to the hotel around eleven o'clock. They said their goodbyes to the staff before taking a steep drive up Mijas and then drove down past Benalmadena Pueblo where they used to live and then yet further down to Arroyo de la Miel. The area between Benalmadena and Arroyo had been built up heavily since David last lived there and had in many ways spoiled the area.

After a short stop in Arroyo de la Miel, they made their way to the hotel where Linda was staying, arriving shortly after two o'clock. As they entered the reception of the hotel, Linda was waiting with her luggage already packed and ready to go.

"Hello David, I've booked out of the hotel. I think its time for me to go home and face the music"

David helped Linda to carry the luggage to the car and when it was all loaded, Alisa drove the half an hour to Malaga Airport. Alisa parked in the car park and they all walked to the Departures at the airport and soon found the queue for the easyJet flight to London, Stansted. David left his luggage with Linda, asking her.

"Will you keep our place and mind the luggage; I need to have a quick word with Alisa?"

"Yes, but the queue is moving fairly quickly"

"That's okay; I'll only be a couple of minutes"

David and Alisa walked a short distance out of the way of the queues.

"It's been lovely seeing you Alisa. I do miss you. I should try to get to see you more often. I'll be in touch soon and that's a promise"

"Thanks David. I think the same. We do need to think about ourselves and where we go from here"

"You're right of course"

He then gave Alisa a passionate kiss before saying.

"Bye for now, speak to you soon"

"Bye Senor Fraudo"

David then walked back to the queue for the easyJet flight and joined Linda Barrett who had been watching David and Alisa.

"What's going on between you and Alisa?"

"Oh, it's a long story"

"It's pretty obvious that you both fancy each other"

"We've known each other a long time"

"Are you both married or is it you that's married?"

"No, neither of us is married"

"Why don't you get together then?"

"As I said, it's a long story"

"Men"

They moved slowly forward before reaching the check-in counter where they provided the flight reference details and handed over their passports, and were then given the passports back together with their boarding cards. There was a slight delay at passport control before they were able to make their way upstairs to the Departure Lounge where they had a quick look in the shops, both buying a couple of litre bottles of Gordon's Gin which were on offer.

They found a couple of seats, but Linda kept getting up and taking the short walk to keep her eye on the screens showing the departure details. As soon as the easyJet details came up confirming that the flight was going to be ten minutes late, she returned to David saying.

"Boarding Gate number eight and the flight is only going to be ten minutes late"

David thought to himself, should he ring Peter Daley but a ten minute delay was not a problem. It was not worth making a phone call. He got up from the seat and they both took their hand luggage and bottles of Gin to the Boarding Gate. After another fifteen minute wait, the air stewardesses arrived and started calling the passengers, starting with the children and any passengers with disabilities. Some had paid the fee for priority boarding and went next, before calling the next sixty passengers. David and Linda were numbered fifty six and fifty seven and were quick to join the queue, where they showed their passports and boarding cards before walking down the stairs to the exit and climbed on the bus that was waiting to take them to the aeroplane. This left within a few minutes and made its way to the easyJet plane where passengers where boarding at both the front and back. David and Linda boarded at the back and soon found two empty seats. The aeroplane was not quite full and nobody sat in the third seat leaving the seat free for David and Linda.

Once the flight was airborne, the steward came down the aisle serving drinks and Linda insisted on buying the drinks

"We'll have two of the miniature bottles of red wine" which were five euros each or two for eight euros.

"Two tortilla wraps" which would also cost Linda another eleven euros.

David did think to himself about being wined and dined on possible fraudulent monies. He would be able to tell this amusing story to Peter Daley and Stuart Bradley the Director of Finance at the hospital.

Linda did not discuss the fraud on the flight home, having been advised by her solicitor and David not to. She did ask David about the next stage.

"When are you going to interview me officially?"

"I'll give you a few days to sort yourself out and I'll have a chat with Peter Daley when we arrive at Stansted. He's going to give you a lift back home to Hackney, and take me to a tube station that will lead me to South Kensington. I'm going to take a few days holiday for the rest of the week, but we'll interview you early next week. I'll also need contact details of your solicitor, have you got them?"

"No, my dad will have all the details"

"What is the best number to contact you on?"

"I'll give you my home phone number in Hackney, it's ex-directory. I won't be using the Spanish mobile number anymore"

Linda handed David a piece of paper showing the phone number and David gave Linda his mobile number and the office number of Peter Daley.

"Where are you going on holiday?"

"I'll be taking a walking holiday in the Lake District"

The rest of the journey was uneventful and Linda managed to get some sleep on the plane journey. The flight arrived in fifteen minutes late at Stansted Airport and after they had been through passport control and collected their luggage, they went through to the terminal and were met by Peter Daley.

"Hi Peter, thanks for coming for us, this is Linda Barrett"

"Hello" Peter said and shook hands with Linda.

"Hello"

"How was the flight?"

"It was okay" said Linda.

"I'm parked in the car park, follow me"

David and Linda then followed Peter through the crowds of people out of Arrivals towards the car park. They soon arrived at Peter's silver Vauxhall Vectra and loaded the luggage into the boot of the car. Peter then left the car park saying.

"I'll get to the M eleven motorway and then head south. When we leave the motorway, Hackney is only about five miles away on the A twelve, where are you staying David?"

"In South Kensington, drop me off at a Tube Station after we've dropped Linda off in Hackney. You live in Edgware, don't you Peter?"

"Yes, I'm trying to think of the easiest way on the Tube"

Linda was listening and then remarked.

"I think I must be a Tube expert, South Kensington is on the Piccadilly line. If you are going towards Edgware, you will probably go somewhere near Caledonian Road, which is on the Piccadilly line"

"I know where the station is, that'll be fine. Thanks"

David then spoke to Peter.

"I've told Linda that we would like to complete the interview early next week. What is your availability?"

"I can't make Monday, but I'll be able to make Tuesday. How will that suit you both?"

"It's okay with me Peter. Is that okay with you, Linda?"

"Yes, providing its okay with the solicitor"

"Linda's parents have arranged a solicitor and he has spoken to Linda on the phone. Linda can't remember the firm, but the solicitor's name is Darren O'Brien. Do you know him?"

"Yes, he works for Howarth and Davies"

Linda suddenly remembered.

"That's right, I remember now you've said the name"

"Do you want me to contact Darren in the morning David and arrange a time?"

"If you would Peter, I'll be getting the train back to Liverpool tomorrow and then I'm going to have a short walking holiday in the Lake District. I'll have my laptop in the cottage and also my mobile"

"I'll send you an email with all the details. Where do you want to hold the interview?"

"We can use the Human Resources Department at the Hospital. Is that okay with you Linda?"

"No, I'd rather not go to the Hospital if possible"

Peter then said.

"We'll be able to use a room where I'm based. It's in offices near Baker Street, is that okay?"

"Fine"

"I'll let Darren O'Brien know the details and I'll send you and him a letter confirming the details"

"Thanks for that Peter. Send me an email with the details and I'll speak to you at the end of this week"

The car journey was over fairly quickly as the traffic was reasonably light, so they arrived at Linda's block of flats at half past seven. David helped Linda with her luggage to the front of the block and then returned to the car before commenting to Peter.

"There was only one set of luggage, I wonder what happened to Keith Simpson's luggage? She must have got rid of it"

"I'm sure she would have taken anything of value but I don't suppose she would have any need for the clothes. She would have dumped them or gave them away"

Peter dropped David off at Caledonian Road Tube Station.

"Thanks Peter, I'll be in touch and we'll meet next week. Don't forget to claim all the expenses for this journey"

"I won't"

He then caught the tube to South Kensington before making his way to the same hotel where he stayed on his last visit to London. He entered the hotel and was recognised by the man on reception.

"Good evening Mr Parish" as he checked the data on the computer.

"Room four, one, three, please complete the registration form"

He was then given the pass card to the room as he filled in the form and made his way to the room on the fourth floor. He left his luggage in the room and then made his way out of the hotel. He walked a little way before he found a Pub and was able to order a Pint of their Best Bitter. He also settled for a Pub meal of Bangers and Mash before returning to the hotel.

The next morning he left the hotel, after settling the bill and made his way on the tube to Euston Station where he caught the 10.15 train which arrived at Liverpool, Lime Street Station at 12.48. He caught a taxi and was in his house by a quarter past one. After an hour in the house, he decided to travel to his cottage in the Lake District that day, rather than wait until the following morning. By the time he had packed all his luggage and equipment it was just before four o'clock and the journey would take between two and two and a half hours.

21

Steve Mitchell was in a room upstairs above a bar he owned in Manchester, with his brother Alan. They were waiting for Ron Thomas to arrive and he said to Alan.

"I saw Sarah walking along Deansgate yesterday; she was hand in hand and very cosy with Phillip Harris, the manager of the Money Transfer Organisation. That's the place which we use to transfer money to Spain, so I chased after them and asked her why she hadn't returned my phone call and she said that she'd forgotten all about it. Anyhow, we ending up going into one of the coffee shops and had a good chat. They've been going out together for about six months and I reckon it's the most serious that she's ever been about any bloke. They knew each other when they were at Liverpool University. When I phoned her, I wanted to know the best way to send money abroad because I thought it was best to send it in small amounts. Last time I sent money to Spain, I spoke to Phillip Harris and one of the girls who worked there, and they reckoned it was better sending one lump sum. Anyhow, I wanted Sarah to check this out and she said it would be better going in one amount. I then quizzed Phillip Harris to see if we would get any discounts because he was going out with my sister. He laughed, but did say they may shave the costs when they were dealing with certain companies and one of those companies was the place Sarah works for. He also said that part of their charges include a nominal transaction charge which meant they would make fifteen charges for fifteen transactions, but only one transaction charge for the combined amount. So, if I get Sarah to make a single transaction, it will save us some money. I don't know how much, but when the time comes I'll find out. He did say that the best way to save some money is in the exchange rate, especially if you are transferring large amounts. That might be negotiable"

"It's nice to know people in the right places, especially if it's our sister and her precious boyfriend"

"Yeah"

They heard the footsteps coming up the stairs and Ron Thomas walked into the room closing the door behind him.

"Hi Steve, hi Alan"

All three sat down around a table where Steve had a folder and a few sheets of paper which had been clipped together. He then started the meeting.

"First of all, Ron, have you told all the crash drivers that we've packed in the car crash business?"

"Yeah, I've told them all and I've paid them what they've been owed. They're okay about it. I did speak to some of them and said that we might be able to use them in any new business we start. A couple of them have proper jobs, one works in a petrol station and another works in a restaurant, which might be useful"

Suddenly a very annoyed Alan broke in.

"What's this other business? You haven't told me anything about it. I'm family, I'm your brother and I want to know what's going on"

"Don't get into a panic, brother. Ron mentioned something to me and I made some enquiries. I then went down to Birmingham to find out if I could have some equipment made, and they're going to charge me a thousand quid per machine but if I buy a few, I'll get some type of discount"

"What type of machines are you talking about, Steve?"

"Skimming machines"

"What the hell is a skimming machine?"

"I've done some research and searched on the internet, and formed some background details on the types of fraud that occur using skimming machines or skimming devices as they're otherwise called. The report shows how frauds occur and what people should do to try and avoid being conned. It was quite easy to get this information which is aimed at stopping skimming, but to be honest, I thought it helped me to understand how skimming works and how to take part. Have a quick look at my report and I'll let you know what I've being doing about it"

Alan and Ron picked up a copy of a report that had been completed by Steve, which read as follows:

THE BACKGROUND TO SKIMMING

Most cases of counterfeit fraud involve skimming, where the genuine data on your card's magnetic stripe is electronically copied onto another card without your knowledge. Read this for further information and tips to prevent yourself from becoming a victim of skimming.

Skimming can occur at retail outlets – particularly bars, restaurants and petrol stations – when a corrupt employee skims your card with a small, hand-held electronic device before handing your card back. Sometimes skimming takes place at cash machines where a skimming device has been fitted to the card slot and a pin-hole camera is fixed above the PIN pad to record the PIN entry. The information is then sold on higher up the criminal ladder, where counterfeit cards are made. Criminals then go shopping with a copy of your credit or debit card while you are unaware of the fraud until a statement arrives showing purchases that you did not make.

WHAT IS BEING DONE ABOUT SKIMMING?

Counterfeit card fraud is regarded as a serious problem in the UK. Skimming is responsible for most of the counterfeit fraud losses but these will be drastically reduced by the introduction of chip and PIN.

The magnetic stripe on plastic cards first appeared in 1972 and has been ensuring cards are genuine since then. However, in recent years, with advances in technology, criminals have developed the means to copy the magnetic stripe and produce a fake card that contains your details.

In the UK cards are now being issued with a microchip that stores the data so securely it cannot feasibly be copied or altered. Already there are more than 76 million chip cards in issue in the UK and by mid-2005 there were over 36 million people with chip and PIN cards.

TIPS TO AVOID BECOMING A VICTIM OF SKIMMING:

Guard your cards – treat them in the same way that you would treat your cash.

Don't let your cards out of your sight when using them to make a transaction. Check your receipts carefully against your statements. If you find an unfamiliar transaction contact your bank or building society immediately.

Report suspected fraudulent use of your card account to your bank or building society immediately. The 24-hour emergency number is on your statement, or call Directory Enquiries for the number.

Various other initiatives are in place to clamp down on the organised criminal gangs who are behind the recent increases in counterfeit card fraud losses:

A specialist police unit was set up in April 2002 to tackle the criminal gangs responsible for counterfeit card fraud. Between then and April 2005 the Dedicated Cheque and Plastic Crime Unit (DCPCU) busted several plastic card counterfeiting "factories" and recovered more than 3,500 counterfeit cards and 40,000 compromised card numbers, resulting in an estimated fraud loss savings of more than £100 million.

The figures produced by Banks indicate that £40 million was lost to ATM fraud in 2004 compared to £8 million in 1998.

Banks, building societies and card schemes are continually increasing the sophistication of intelligent detection systems that can identify fraudulent transactions before you have reported your card's loss or misuse. If unusual spending is detected your card issuer will contact you to check if the transactions are genuine and, if not, an immediate block can be put on your card. The majority of card issuers use these systems with considerable success.

It is reported that many of the Banks have now put in place mechanisms that will show a skimming device has been attached to an ATM, and will trigger an immediate warning to the Bank's Security Controls. The ATM will then be immediately closed down and the police are detached to the location of the ATM within minutes. (This has not been verified as accurate and may be a false warning to try and avoid skimming)

Fraud-prone retailers and geographic areas are identified, and tactical programmes introduced, to increase the likelihood that retail staff will detect the use of counterfeit cards when criminals present them at the sales point.

Alan and Ron completed reading the copies of Steve's report and placed them back down on the table.

Steve then opened the discussion on how to get involved in this type of fraud.

"The report tends to suggest that the Banks have some type of control on preventing skimming appliances. That's a load of rubbish. They are always one step behind. It's not a scheme which we'll do for years, we're not that stupid, we'll do it for a perhaps several months, but less than a year and we'll pack it in at the right time like we did with the car crash scams. I said earlier that you can buy these appliances for a thousand quid but I will put down an order for ten, which I reckon we can get for nine thousand quid. We'll then need some type of computer equipment which will read the data on the cards that have been skimmed to produce cards with the copied information. This will probably cost a few thousand more and we'll need plenty of blank cards, but they'll cost next to nothing. I've made a few notes on what we might expect to make. If we had ten skimming devices in place, which could be in ATMs and it needn't be bank ATMs, there are plenty of supermarkets that have them. Some devices could be used in restaurants, petrol stations or shops and if we took fifty skims and then removed the device, we would end up with copies of five hundred cards. We'll make more money on some cards than we would on others, because it will depend on the persons account and their available funds. I estimate that we would get five hundred pounds from each card, which adds up to two hundred and fifty thousand quid in one days work. We wouldn't do it every day, we'd pick and choose the areas and we might have to get members of our team working in some different places. I know things might go wrong in some cases, but it's an estimate"

Ron then joined in.

"That's sounds a lot of money but it's going to cost us. We're going to need a good team and they'll need good rewards for their performance. They will also have to move pretty fast and get the skimming devices back to us in order that the copy cards can be made as fast as possible. They'll also need to be trained on how to insert the skimming devices"

Alan then said.

"I think Ron's got a point, as some of the people working for us will have a guess on what profits can be made. In fairness, our teams are usually quite loyal and they'll agree a fee before they start. If they tried something on themselves, they know they'd be in for a good thumping"

Steve agreed with both Ron and Alan.

"What do you think of these figures? Ten quid per copy which means they'll get five hundred if they get the fifty skims. We'll then pay them a bonus depending on how much we make on the cards and the bonus could be another five hundred. We'll then have to pay the team members who go out and use the copied cards, it might be the same people but there will probably be some others who'll need to join the team. I reckon they'll be paid ten per cent of what they get. That's ten thousand quid for the team with the devices and twenty five thousand for the others. After expenses, we could clear two hundred thousand pounds for one day's use of the skimming devices"

Alan remarked.

"It sounds possible but we'll have to be on the ball and have some type of timescale for getting the appliances back and using the cards. We might consider giving them a bonus if they return the skimmers within a couple of hours. I wouldn't want them hanging on to the devices for any length of time. It could be risky if they did"

"How about the training?" said Ron.

"I've been told it's a fairly simple thing to operate and install, but they'll show the three of us how when we go and collect the skimming devices and equipment. We'll then leave it to you Ron, to pick the best team. You'll be able to give them some background information and show them what to do. You'll probably know some of the best people already and some of the lads who worked for us on the car crash scams might be okay. Actually, some of the girls were pretty good and it might be worth using some of them in the restaurants, petrol stations or shops"

"I've already made a mental note of the people that I'd like to use but how long will it be before we can get all the equipment?"

"They told me it would only be a couple of days from when I give them a deposit. They'll probably want a quarter before they start the work and the rest when we collect the devices and equipment"

Alan was again a bit cautious.

"How do we know the equipment will work and what happens if it doesn't work?"

"I asked the same question and had to laugh when they gave me the reply. They said that they worked to a high standard and their good name would be damaged if they sold dodgy equipment. If anything failed, they'd provide a replacement, providing it wasn't the fault of the people installing the devices"

Ron then gave his thoughts.

"I think the guys that install the skimming devices will be okay. Some of them are quite high tech and will probably find it easier than us to do, and they'll probably have them fitted much quicker. When are you intending to make the order for the ten devices?"

"I was waiting to talk to you two first, but I'll give them a ring as soon as we've finished talking. I'll take the deposit down later today. We could be ready to start installing the devices within four or five days, but we need to have the team in place and be ready to train them Ron. Is that possible or is it too tight?"

"It should be okay, some of them know that they're on standby for another job already"

"I'll make the phone call now and get some proper dates"

Steve took a slip of paper from his pocket which had the phone number on, and dialled.

"Hello"

"Roy Ironside please?"

"Who's speaking?"

"Steve Mitchell"

"Hang on a sec"

"Hello Steve, this is Roy speaking. What can I do for you?"

"I'd like to buy ten of the skimming devices and the rest of the equipment. If I came down today with the deposit, how long will it be before they're ready to collect?"

"If I know that you're on the way down, I'll get the lads to start the work straight away and they'll be finished by the day after tomorrow. Is that okay?"

"Yeah, you mentioned a discount for buying ten devices. What discount will that be?"

"Ten per cent"

"How about making it twenty per cent?"

"I don't bargain Steve; it's ten per cent or nothing doing"

"No harm in trying, I'd be a bit worried if you did drop the price"

"It was worth a try"

"How many plastic cards do you think I should order?"

"If you're talking about ten devices, I'd say that you were best to remove them after fifty hits, which would work out at five hundred cards. I'd take five thousand to begin with, you can always get some more if things are going well"

"Okay, that's fine by me"

"Make the deposit three thousand quid and we'll sort the rest out when the works been done and you come to collect all the equipment"

"Okay, Roy, I'll leave shortly but it'll probably take me a couple of hours"

"See you later Steve"

Steve then turned to Alan and Ron.

"You'll have heard that I'm going down to Birmingham now

to pay the deposit. The equipment will all be ready by the day after tomorrow"

"That's pretty quick" said Alan.

"Yeah, do you fancy a drive down there Alan?"

"Yeah, are we coming back today?"

"We'll be back by early evening, around six o'clock. Why? Are you seeing the lovely Tanni tonight?"

"Yeah, are you seeing Linzi?"

"No, I gave her the elbow last night. She was getting too serious for me"

"I thought she was a nice girl, she was okay on holiday"

"You can have her if you want to"

"No thanks, I'll stick with Tanni"

"It must be love mustn't it Ron? Will you start the work on the team while we're down in Birmingham"

"Yeah, I'll get on to it straight away"

"Right then, let's get going"

22

David backed his car out of the driveway and drove the three miles to the beginning of the M62 motorway. After ten miles he took a shortcut from the motorway to join the M6 motorway heading north towards the Lake District.

The journey to Tirril is a hundred and ten miles and David left the M6 at Junction 40 taking the A66 and then turning on the A592 at the Discovery Centre towards Pooley Bridge, which runs parallel with the River Eamont. At Pooley Bridge the B road leads to village of Tirril where David has owned a small cottage in the village for some eight years. The traffic had been quite heavy on the journey, which meant that David arrived just before half past six.

As soon as he entered the cottage he picked up the phone and rang the local public house to book a meal for later.

"Hello"

"Hi, it's David Parish, can I book a table for this evening please. It is just for myself, how about eight o'clock?"

"That's fine David, we'll see you then"

"Thanks a lot"

David brought in his luggage and walking equipment from the car and then got ready for the short walk to the Pub for his evening meal. He had a little time to spare so he plugged in his laptop to check on any incoming messages. There were a total of three messages that were of any importance with the first being from Brian Lewis, who assisted David in the Pension fraud in Manchester. Brian had received a message that Carl Sutherland was due to appear in the Local Magistrates Court the following Tuesday, but this would only be an initial hearing and his solicitors would be asking for further time to complete their initial defence preparation. There would be no requirement for either Brian or David to attend the Magistrates Court as there would be two or three appearances before it would be referred to the Crown Court.

The second email referred to a meeting of the Insurance Company Fraud Staff who were involved in the car crash scams, which might involve Steve Mitchell. They were holding two meetings, one taking place in London for the Southern Area and the other in Liverpool for the Northern Area. This last meeting was to be held next Monday which was quite convenient for David as he would be able to attend before going to London the following day.

The third email was from Peter Daley concerning the interview with Linda Barrett. He had spoken to Darren O'Brien, her solicitor, and made arrangements for the taped interview to take place on Tuesday at 11.00 am at Peter's offices near Baker Street. In the email, Peter had mentioned that Darren O'Brien had some concerns that his client, Linda Barrett, had returned from Spain with David, but in fairness, Linda had confirmed to him that nothing had been said concerning the fraud on the journey home. Darren was also aware that Linda had discussed the case in a telephone conversation with David prior to going to Spain, but Peter had assured him that any information provided at that stage would be disclosed at the beginning of the taped interview.

There was not enough time to respond to the emails before dinner so David switched off the laptop and placed it in a cupboard in the lounge. He then left the cottage to make the small journey to the local pub where he would have a pint of one of their speciality bitters with his meal. As soon as he walked into the Pub, he was greeted by one of the ladies serving behind the bar.

"Hi David, haven't seen you for a while, what would you like to drink?"

David looked at the labels on the pumps and noticed one that he had never had before. The Pub often served guest bitters which they would change every couple of months.

"A pint of the new guest beer would be lovely"

"I've booked you the table by the window if that's okay"

She gave him the pint of bitter and the menu and David walked to the table. There were also some specials on the chalk board on the wall and David noticed the Belly Pork. He last had that about a year ago and he thought it was excellent and it was definitely his first choice for a meal this time.

After about five minutes one of the waitresses came over for his order.

"Have you decided what you would like to eat?"

"I think so, is the Belly Pork still on the menu?"

"Yes, it comes with boiled potatoes and vegetables of the day"

"I'll have that please"

"Do you want a starter or anything to drink?"

"No thanks, I'll get another pint when I'm ready"

"That's fine, thanks David"

While he was waiting a couple of his neighbours came into the bar area and nodded their heads as acknowledgement to David.

"When did you arrive, David?" asked one of them.

"Only a couple of hours ago, I've just got unpacked and come straight here for a pint and a something to eat. I've spent too much time lately travelling and then sitting in different offices. I felt I desperately needed some exercise, so I'll be doing some vigorous walking over the next couple of days"

"Where are you thinking of going?"

"I haven't looked at my guide books and maps yet, but I think I'll stay fairly local. I might start by walking around Ullswater Lake"

"All the way round?"

"You must be joking, maybe from this end to the other end and get the boat back"

"That's still a long way. It'll probably take you most of the day"

"I did the same walk about two years ago and left about half past eight in the morning and caught the last boat back to Pooley Bridge which was around four o'clock. I've got the actual times in the cottage, I'll check them when I get back home"

"Yeah, the last boat leaves Glenridding at a quarter past four"

"After that walk, I'll probably call in here tomorrow night for a pint or two"

"You'll need a couple of pints; we might join you here then"

"Great, see you tomorrow"

The waitress arrived with David's meal which she placed on the table.

"Enjoy your meal"

"I certainly will"

The Belly Pork was served in the shape of medallions and did not have any crackling. It had been roasted in juices and was absolutely delicious. The vegetables were cooked to David's taste and came with a dish of small new potatoes.

The meal was soon finished and David went to the bar.

"I'd like another half pint of the bitter please and I'll settle the bill"

He was given the bill and showed his credit card and he was soon given the machine in which to insert the card and key in his pin number. In his role as a Fraud Consultant, he was cautious in handing over his credit card and letting people see him enter his pin number. It was important to him to avoid any problems occurring with credit card copying and identity fraud. He knew that he would be on the receiving end of a great deal of banter if his card was caught in the trap.

Once he had paid the bill, he stayed at the bar to finish his drink and joined in the chit chat. It was around ten o'clock when he finally arrived home at the cottage and opened the laptop to reply to the emails.

He replied to Brian Lewis first thanking him for keeping him updated on the case against Carl Sutherland. Once it got to Crown Court, both he and Brian would receive letters from the Court confirming the dates of the appearances. David would also then hear from the legal team who were completing the work on behalf of David and the Pension Schemes. Normally, when it is being dealt with by the Magistrates there is no need to make an appearance.

The Insurance Companies Fraud representatives were meeting at Liverpool Town Hall at half past ten on Monday morning. David returned the email confirming that he would be attending the meeting which was expected to last a couple of hours.

He then acknowledged the email from Peter Daley advising him that he would be getting the train from Liverpool which is due in London, Euston at about nine o'clock. There would then be the Tube journey and his expected time of arrival at Peter's office would be around ten o'clock. This would then give them time to discuss the interview with Linda Barrett. He also asked Peter to confirm that the Tape Machine was available, otherwise he would bring down his own machine.

Finally up to date, David turned off the laptop and switched on his television to watch the late evening news. Before putting his feet up, he went to the drinks cabinet and poured a glass of cointreau to which he added four ice cubes. What a satisfying way to end a pleasant evening.

The following morning, following a quick breakfast of a piece of toast and a banana, David had a quick look at the walks in the Lake District but decided he preferred taking the walk around Lake Ullswater. He made sandwiches and a flask of coffee, packed his rucksack, and got into his car for the relatively short journey to Pooley Bridge, where he parked and put on his walking boots, shrugging the rucksack onto his back. It was now 8.30 am as he commenced the walk, which was for twelve miles and would take a clockwise journey around the Lake, but the walk would only cover half of the lake. When he reached the southern point of Ullswater, he would head for Glenridding Pier and catch the Lake Steamer back to Pooley Bridge stopping at Howtown.

The first part of the walk took him inland away from the lake and then the biggest climb to the Cockpit Stone Circle before heading back towards Lake Ullswater. Perhaps the first viewing point was Long Crag Cairn which has a tremendous view of the Lake and surrounding area. He then headed towards Howtown and the Pier where the Steamer stops. This part of the walk had taken three and a half hours, but there had been a couple of stops for a drink of coffee from his flask and to take on some water, a necessity when you are walking in warm weather. He had a snack bar to keep him going until lunch time.

It was at these stops that David would often start thinking of solutions to any work problems, the best way forward in some of the fraud investigations and any personal problems. Although the investigations into the pensions scam and the travel fraud were an immediate problem, his thoughts kept moving towards the Mitchell family and perhaps, more important, his relationship with Alisa Garcia. As the walk continued, David thought this was a pleasant way to put the world to rights, but things did not always go to plan. He wanted to see the end of Steve Mitchell, but knew it was going to take a while longer, possibly the first chance being when it was time to make the final payment on the villa in Spain. He knew he would need the help of the police and quite a bit of luck.

The walk was now running parallel with the lake and he passed a group of anglers and a group of people who had set up their small tents near the edge of the lake. Walking was always a social event with regular greetings and little chit chats with all the walkers going in the opposite direction, anti-clockwise around the lake.

He found some boulders at the side of the trail, overlooking the lake and decided to stop for lunch. The sandwiches were unpacked together with the rest of the coffee and David sat on the boulders viewing Lake Ullswater. The contemplation, this time, concerned Alisa Garcia, who loved Spain and her job in the Guardia Civil based in Seville. She also probably loved David Parish but had no intention of leaving Spain. On the other hand, he loved England and his job as a Fraud Consultant, which allowed him freedom within the U.K. and occasionally abroad. He thinks he loves Alisa Garcia and has tried living in Spain but has decided he no longer wants to leave Britain. What is the answer; it is time to carry on with the walk.

He walked across a couple of small rivers, Sandwick Beck and Calehow Beck and he also stopped to read a sign 'Organic Pigs' which then gave their names. There were two pigs in the farm ground, one having a walk and the other lying on the ground having a rest. It must have over indulged with too much organic food.

The ground was quite uneven, at times, with a fair amount of loose rocks and stones and David was quite please to find himself at a farmyard near Patterdale where they served drinks and snacks for the weary walkers. He ordered a mug of tea and sat at one of the benches outside with another dozen walkers. It was now about one mile to Glendenning Pier and the time was half past three which left him three quarters of an hour to catch the Lake Steamer back to Pooley Bridge. The mug of tea was soon finished and David completed the walk to Glendenning Pier, paid for the Lake Trip and boarded the Steamer for the return to Pooley Bridge, which was quite a pleasant way to end the days walk. It was an hours trip, stopping at Howtown, before David disembarked and walked to his car which was parked no more than a hundred yards from the Pier.

The following morning David packed his luggage ready for the journey home but he had decided to stop near Kendal in order to complete another walk. This one was smaller covering only about six miles taking in Scout Scar and Helsington. He did, however, switch on his laptop to check on any messages and take a copy of all his documents onto his memory stick. Knowing he would be leaving the laptop in the boot of his car when he was walking, he wanted any confidential information removed and he had also transferred the information to his desktop computer at home before leaving for the Lake District.

A message had been received from Peter Daley asking David to bring his Tape Machine. Peter worked for an Agency with a couple of other Fraud Specialists and they had pre-booked the two Tape Machines.

David left his cottage in Tirril just after eleven o'clock and made his way to Junction 40 on the M6 where he headed south, leaving at Junction 37 to take the A684 towards Kendal and eventually taking the Underbarrow Road to the Scout Scar Car Park, where he would park the car and start the walk. He managed to miss the car park and had to turn the car round but found it at his second attempt.

The walk lasted about two and a half hours, with David stopping for his lunch at St John's Church, Helsington, where he sat on a bench facing all the gravestones. This was reached after an hour and was half way through the walk.

He eventually got back to his car at the Scout Scar Car Park at two o'clock, and just before it started raining quite heavily.

He changed his boots before getting into the car and making his way to the A591 which eventually led to the M6 at Junction 36, where the traffic was quite light and he arrived home in Liverpool a little before four o'clock.

23

The post had just arrived the following morning and contained nothing of interest when the phone rang. He picked it up.

"Hello"

"Hello David, its Anne Graham from Cheshire Police"

"Oh, Hi Anne"

"I've made some enquiries and I've had an update on Bill Kennedy, who was driving a couple of the cars. There have been no charges made against him and the Insurance Companies are going to pay for the damage done to the cars that he was driving as well as paying him for personal injury. They say that they've phoned the owners of the cars that he was driving who confirmed that they had given Kennedy permission to drive the cars. They've also had the Insurance Claim forms completed by the owners. Apparently Bill Kennedy has his own insurance which is fully comprehensive and allows him to drive other cars, third party, assuming he's got the owners permission. He was driving third party but the accidents aren't being blamed on him. The claims are against the drivers who ran into the back of him. It sounds a bit dodgy and we've got no real evidence that the owners they spoke to are legitimate, but the claims have been paid, so end of story"

"They often pay small amounts because it is easier rather than have the hassle of completing in depth investigations. Their staff costs might end up being higher than the repairs to the cars. I'm at a meeting with the Insurance Company Fraud Investigators next week and I'll bring this up, but I can see their reasoning.

Did you find out anymore about the high number of claims in the Bradford area?"

"I checked the numbers with the Insurance guys and they say the numbers of this type of claim have virtually stopped in the last couple of weeks. It's as though the people running these car crash scams have called a halt and decided enough is enough. I've got nothing that will help you David and we've decided not to approach Steve Mitchell, but we'll still watch him. If he's buying expensive property in Spain, he must have got the money from somewhere"

"Thanks Anne, if I find out anymore, I'll let you know"

"Okay David, I'll speak to you again, no doubt"

Following a weekend of little activity, David had a meeting with the Northern Insurance Companies Fraud Investigators at Liverpool Town Hall. He drove into the town centre and parked in one of the multi-storey car parks, which was only a five minute walk from the Town Hall. One of the main conference rooms had been booked and the signs to the room were quite clearly marked. It must have been about five years since David had last visited the Town Hall. It is an old building but extremely well maintained and has many areas of great historical interest.

Tea or coffee was being served outside the meeting room and he soon linked up with some of the attendees who he had met previously on the odd occasions. He was looking for Tim Evans who had worked with David a few times in the past and was definitely involved in the investigation into the car crash scams. It was his company that had the dealings with Bill Kennedy.

Tim arrived a few minutes later and queued to get a drink before David made his way over.

"Morning Tim, how are you?"

"I'm fine, overworked as usual, but it's not too bad. Why do we have the pleasure of Mr Fraud today?"

"You know me, I like to keep up to date with any frauds that are going on and I often pick up some useful information at these meetings. I know there are a few things on the agenda but I might have an interest in these car crash scams, I'd love to know if you have any names in the frame which might be of interest to some Spanish contacts?"

"Who are you after?"

"I heard that your company were looking at a couple of crashes concerning a bloke called Bill Kennedy who might be involved with somebody called Steve Mitchell"

"Yeah, we didn't have enough to go on and he reckoned that he'd been given permission to drive some friend's cars. One of my colleagues spoke to his so called friends and they supported him, but the size of the claim wasn't that big really to make an issue of it. The police were involved and they knew that Kennedy had worked for Mitchell in the past, but they couldn't prove any connection"

"Do you think they're organised and somebody plans these car crashes?"

"We're absolutely certain as they've been heavily based in a couple of areas. The two main areas have been London and the Bradford, Leeds area of Yorkshire, but they seemed to have stopped recently. We think they'll pick another area which is why it's on the agenda today. If we catch on early, it improves our chances of finding out who's behind these scams. I must be honest and say that the costs of the crashes are not, initially, very high, and we probably haven't looked hard enough, but things will change"

They were all called into the meeting which lasted a couple of hours. A lot of the agenda was not of deep interest to David, but there was a good discussion surrounding the car crash scams. A working group was to be set up, chaired by Tim Evans, which would arrange a monitoring system of this type of scam and, hopefully, create an early warning system which would cause difficulties for the organisers. David had strong doubts that Steve Mitchell would remain involved in these scams; he would

194

probably stop now and look for something different. As they left the meeting David turned to Tim.

"Would you let me know if the name of Steve Mitchell crops up and if any scams start in different areas?"

"No problem, David, I'll see you around"

It was time to travel to London again, and David had arranged for a taxi to take him to the Train Station in order to catch the same early Virgin Express that he had used the previous two occasions. He collected his tickets from the ticket booth at the station and bought a daily newspaper, before making his way to the platform in order to board the train. He found his coach and made his way to the seat, checking the seat numbers to his reservation, in the second class compartment that he had booked. He placed his luggage on top, and took out a folder containing the information he would require in the interview with Linda Barrett. The tape machine was placed next to him but he had not brought the laptop with him on this journey. Surprisingly, the train started and there was no other passenger sitting on the opposite seat to him.

The train journey went quite peacefully, with David studying the folder for about three quarters of an hour before reading the newspaper and having a go at the crossword. Whenever he left his seat he carried the tape machine, not that it is that expensive, but if it was stolen it would create big problems with the forthcoming interview. You are able to take contemporaneous notes of an interview without the tape machine, but this creates so much difficulty, it would be easier to delay the interview until a machine was available.

It was exactly nine o'clock when the train arrived at Euston Station and David was quickly off the train and made his way out of the main station and walked across to Euston Square Tube Station. He then found the Metropolitan line for the short trip to Baker Street.

He then left the Tube Station and walked into Baker Street and turned into the side street and soon found the offices of Marylebone Internal Audit Services, where Peter Daley worked as a Fraud Specialist.

He walked over to reception and spoke to the receptionist.

"My name is David Parish; I have a meeting with Peter Daley"

"I'll give him a ring"

"Hello"

"Hi Peter, I've got David Parish in reception"

"He's on his way"

It was less than a minute when Peter arrived.

"Morning David, did you have a good journey?"

"Yes, it was fine Peter"

"We're in the room on the left and I've arranged for Darren O'Brien and Linda Barrett to be in the room next door. I understand that they are coming together"

David spent a few minutes setting up the tape machine while Peter left to make a couple of cups of coffee and when he returned the machine was ready.

"I think you're fully up to date with this Peter, have you been through the paperwork again?"

"Yes, I think it'll be fairly straightforward and she'll tell us what we need to know. My only thoughts are does she know about Zoe Ferguson and Keith Simpson?"

"I don't know and I'm not going to bring it up until we've got what we want. I might ask for a break towards the end of the interview and ask Linda to leave for a few minutes. I'll then tell Darren O'Brien because he'll find out soon afterwards. Once it starts moving towards Court, he'll be given copies of all the statements including the one from Zoe Ferguson, mentioning her relationship with Keith, which will probably be a bit of a surprise"

"If we don't tell him, he could accuse us of holding back important information, that's if it is relevant"

They had some spare time before Darren and Linda were due to appear and glanced through the documentation once again.

24

It was five past eleven when the receptionist knocked on the door.

"Darren O'Brien and Linda Barrett are next door. I'll bring in a jug of water and four glasses"

"I think we might as well have Darren O'Brien in now, Peter"

Peter knew Darren O'Brien, so he knocked on the door of the room next to theirs and entered.

"Good morning Darren, Good morning Linda"

"Good morning Peter, do you want me to come in first to give me a disclosure pack prior to the interview?"

"Yes please Darren, if you could pop next door now, we'll have a quick chat and give you your copy"

Darren then spoke quietly to Linda Barrett.

"It won't take long. I'll only be a few minutes minutes, wait here till I return"

Darren then followed Peter into the Interview Room next door and Peter introduced him to David,

"David, this is Darren O'Brien"

"Hello Darren, it's good to meet you. We'll show you what we are disclosing at this stage"

Both Peter and Darren then sat down and David handed Darren a file of documents.

"There is not a huge amount of paperwork to show you at this stage. You'll probably be aware that we've spoken to two other people, Zoe Ferguson and Rik Jeffreys. The pack is almost identical to the one we gave to their solicitors. We have enclosed twenty copies of fraudulent travel claim forms, ten of which have been completed by Rik Jeffreys and the other ten by his partner Zoe Ferguson. We also enclose a detailed list of all the travel claims made by them over the period in question which stretches over two and a half years. The total fraud is in excess of two hundred and ninety six thousand pounds and there are just short of fifteen hundred claims, some of which are for two or three journeys. The vast majority of the travel claim forms have been completed by Zoe Ferguson; there are less than a hundred which have been completed by Rik Jeffreys, but all have been authorised by Linda Barrett"

Darren was having a quick look at some of the paperwork and then said.

"This looks quite clear to me. My client wants to be quite open about this fraud. She's clearly upset about the death of Keith Simpson but she appreciates the help that you've given her in getting back from Spain without the police waiting for her. She did say that no questions were asked on the journey home but she did give you some information in a phone call"

"That's correct and I'll bring up what she said early in the interview"

"Okay, I'll spend a little time with Linda, but I won't be too long. One other thing, I have spoken to John Harrison and Anna Young, the solicitors for Rik Jeffreys and Zoe Ferguson. I heard about the relationship between Ferguson and Keith Simpson and thought that my client should be informed. Apparently, Linda had an idea Keith Simpson was seeing somebody but did not know who. John Harrison also told me that he thinks Jeffreys and Ferguson are now back together and all is forgiven"

"I'm glad she knows as it may well have come out sometime today"

They waited about a quarter of an hour before hearing the knock on the door and Darren O'Brien and Linda Barrett entering their Meeting Room. All four then sat around the desk before the interview began under caution.

"I just want to check that you understand what we are going to do. Peter will operate the tape machine and you will hear a loud noise before the start of the interview, this is normal. Has Darren explained what we are going to discuss and the procedures that will take place?"

"Yes, I do understand, thanks"

"Okay, Peter will you start the tape please?"

Peter started the tape and the noise appeared before David started the interview with the opening procedures.

"This Interview is being tape recorded, it is the eighth of May, two thousand and seven and the time by my watch is eleven twenty five a.m. I am David Parish a Fraud Consultant for the National Health Service representing Euston General Hospital. The other officer present is"

"Peter Daley also a Fraud Specialist representing Euston General Hospital"

"I am interviewing, please state your full name, address and date of birth"

"Linda Barrett, Fourteen B, Wellgreen Road, Hackney, London. Date of birth Ninth of September, nineteen seventy eight"

"Also present is"

"Darren O'Brien, Howarth and Davies Solicitors, London"

"We are in the Meeting Room of the Marylebone Internal Audit Services, London. At the end of the interview, I will give you a notice explaining the procedures for the dealing with the tapes and how you can have access to them. Before the interview begins I must caution you."

"You do not have to say anything, but it may harm your defence if you do not mention when questioned something which you later rely on in court, anything you do say may be given in evidence. Do you understand the caution?"

Linda understood this but was clearly quite shaken.

"Yes"

"You are not under arrest and you are free to leave at any time. The reason for this interview is that we are investigating allegations that you were involved in the making of fraudulent travel claims at the Euston General Hospital between October, two thousand and four and April, two thousand and seven knowing the information on the claim forms was false. The total number of travel claims is One thousand, five hundred and twenty-one and the cost of these claims totals two hundred and ninety six thousand and thirty pounds. Do you understand the reason for this interview?"

"Yes"

"If at any time you wish to speak to your solicitor in private or if you wish me to stop the interview for any reason, then tell me and I will stop the interview"

"Okay"

"First of all, I would like to confirm, for the record, some of the information that you gave me in a telephone call on the twenty fourth of April, when I rang you in Spain"

"Okay"

"Zoe Ferguson and Rik Jeffreys were claiming travel expenses and you didn't know that anything was wrong, until Keith Simpson brought it up one evening and told you all about the fraud. Rik had contacted Keith, told him about the fraud and asked if he would speak to you about it. Rik wanted them to be able to carry on claiming travel expenses from the hospital, even though their daughter was no longer a patient, but they asked if you would let them carry on claiming and not to tell anybody. Rik Jeffreys told Keith he would get a share of the money and he could give some to you, but you said that you didn't know how much money Keith had received. Is that correct?"

"Yes, but I definitely didn't know until Keith told me. I don't know how much money they got before then. I wanted to stop after a few weeks but I was too frightened and just carried on pretending that nothing was wrong. I don't know how much money they got although. All together, you're saying it is nearly three hundred thousand pounds"

"We'll come to that later but you're quite happy with what I've mentioned about the telephone conversation?"

"Yes"

"I believe that you were not involved in the fraud until the meeting between Rik Jeffreys and Keith?"

"That's correct"

"We have examined the starting date of the fraud which was October, two thousand and four but tend to think your involvement was not until a couple of months later"

"Yeah, it was just before Christmas"

"In that case your involvement in the fraud will be for a figure around two hundred and seventy thousand pounds"

"I've no idea how much has been claimed, I'll take your word for it"

"I would like you to open the Disclosure Pack and have a look at the first ten travel claim forms which are numbered DP one to DP ten, the first of which was in January, two thousand and five"

Linda opened the folder and looked at the first ten items in the pack.

"They are all travel claim forms which have been completed and signed by Rik Jeffreys. They have then been authorised by you. Do you agree?"

"Yes"

"The address on the claim forms is in Basingstoke but you were informed that they lived in London in December, two thousand and four. You, therefore, knew the address and details were incorrect?"

"Yes"

"You are saying that the address in Basingstoke is incorrect and the information on the travel claim forms is fraudulent?"

"Yes"

"Will you have a look at the next ten travel claims in the pack, which are numbered DP eleven to DP twenty"

Linda again quickly looked through the copies of the travel claims which were in the pack.

"The address on those travel claim forms is also Basingstoke, but they have all been completed and signed by Zoe Ferguson. They have also been authorised by you. Would you agree that they are also fraudulent?"

"Yeah"

"Did you know that Zoe was also completing the travel claim forms incorrectly and that the claim forms were fraudulent?"

"Yes, they were both completing the forms but most of them were completed by Zoe Ferguson. I've no idea how many forms there are, but I know that they are all wrong and they weren't entitled to make the claims"

"Turn to the next page and you will find a summary of all the claims. There are one thousand five hundred and twenty-one listed, and there is a sum of money relating to these fraudulent claim forms which totals two hundred and ninety six thousand and thirty pounds. There is also a sub-total which shows one thousand four hundred and ten claims, with a total of two hundred and sixty nine thousand, nine hundred and eighty five pounds. This does not include the first two months of claims which took place when you had no knowledge of the fraud. Do you agree that these figures are correct?"

"I don't know how much money has been taken or how many claims were made. I am willing to accept that your figures are correct. All I know is that Rik Jeffreys used to meet Keith every few weeks and would give him money. I don't know what Keith did with the money or where he kept it but I've thought about what he gave me. I couldn't have had more than ten thousand pounds but Keith did buy things for the house and I did get a new car. If you're saying the fraud was two hundred and seventy thousand pounds, I don't believe Keith got a third of that. I know he used drugs now and then but he has never bought a load of things. I reckon that Zoe Ferguson has probably got most of the money. You know about Zoe Ferguson and Keith don't you"

Both David and Peter both nodded their heads.

"Maybe she and Keith spent some of the money together, but I don't know. I've searched the flat and checked all Keith's paperwork. There's no sign of any money. Rik knows that Zoe has got the money, he rang me last night"

David and Peter were surprised at this comment, but not as much as Darren O'Brien who was clearly startled, which was noticed by Linda.

"I'm sorry that I didn't tell you Darren, I forgot. He told me that they'd broken up again, I knew they were back together for a few days, but I think he was only after some of the money and didn't get any"

David then looked at Peter.

"I think we have all we need. Is there anything else that we need to discuss Peter?"

"No, I think we have enough"

David then asked a further question to Linda.

"Do you wish to add anything further or clarify any point or anything you have told me?"

"I have told you everything and I can't help you with all the money that has been taken. You will have to ask Zoe. I've lost Keith, I've lost my job and I've got no money and now I'll go to prison.

"I can't make any promises but your full co-operation will be reported when the case gets to court"

"Thanks"

"Here is the notice which explains your entitlement to a copy of the tape used in this interview. This interview is concluded at eleven, forty eight a.m. on the eighth of May, two thousand and seven. Switch off the tape recorder"

In some ways Linda Barrett looked relieved and then spoke to David.

"I know it's your job, but you've also been very helpful to me. How's your girlfriend, Alisa, the Spanish Police Lady?"

"She's fine thanks"

Peter grinned and Darren O'Brien was again puzzled.

Linda and Darren then left the meeting room leaving David and Peter to sort out the tape machine and all the paperwork.

Peter then remarked.

"She may get a shorter sentence than the other two; it may depend on the charges"

"I'll pass it to the legal team acting for the Health Authority and it's up to them to decide the charges. There will be a conspiracy charge as well as other charges for them all. For what it's worth, I don't think she's had that much of the money but that doesn't matter. It's still fraud"

"Hungry, David?"

"Yes, starving"

"Let's go and get a bite to eat. There are quite a few places around here"

"Is it okay if I leave the equipment here for now?"

"Yes, it'll be okay"

They then both left the meeting room together.

25

The skimming devices scam had been in operation for a couple of months when Steve Mitchell called a meeting with his brother Alan and Ron Thomas. In preparation, he had printed out details from his laptop which showed the progress of each individual skimming device and the operators responsible for the device. Any documents printed out for team meetings would be shredded at the end of each meeting.

They had decided to meet at the Mitchell's house in Cheshire and their mother, Paula, had prepared a buffet for the three men so they gathered around the table in the Dining Room before Steve started the meeting.

"I think it's fair to say that our progress in this new scheme has been a success. There were a few problems in the early days and we have lost one of the skimming devices, so now only nine are in operation. Initially, we placed half of the devices in Bank's automated machines, three in cash machines at various supermarkets, one at a petrol station and one in a restaurant. The one we lost was placed in one of the banks. We were a bit unlucky when a member of the bank staff went to draw some cash out one evening and he noticed a difference in the machine. I think he must have been on some type of training course because he recognised the device straightaway. He immediately phoned the police and when they arrived, they took the device out of the cash machine. They also located the camera which showed the people keying their pin number into the machine. Our team member saw what was going on as he was just about

206

to take the device away. Any thoughts on that Ron?"

"No, I think we were just unlucky. My instructions to him were to leave the device in for twelve hours so he put it in at seven in the morning. It was about a quarter to seven in the evening when the police arrived and it was taken out. The only reason our team member saw it was because he arrived to take it out and that's when he recognised the bloke with the police and knew he worked in that branch of the bank. He's the tall fair haired bloke, his name is Rob Wilson"

"You did some of the training on the installations didn't you Alan, anything to report there?"

"In the first week, there were a couple of problems, but we'd given all our team one of the copied cards. They've been told to try it out once the device has been installed and withdraw twenty pounds. If that failed to work, they knew there was something wrong with the device and they soon put it right. We monitor what they withdraw from the machine and it came off their final wage bill"

Steve nodded his head and carried on.

"As you know, we've now reduced the installation in the cash machines located at banks and now have more in the supermarkets and other similar outlets as well as the petrol stations and restaurants. There's no cameras in the petrol stations or the restaurants, but our team have had no problems spotting the punter keying in the pin number and making a note immediately afterwards. They've usually skimmed the card before they get to this stage. Any other thoughts?"

Ron then remarked.

"I think it was a good idea to do the twelve hour installations and have breaks every now and then before we use the devices. We don't want to go over the top and lose some of our controls"

Alan then joined in.

"What have we made so far?"

Steve handed out the sheets of paper showing the breakdown

for each device, which showed the number of cards that had been printed and put into use when drawing cash. It also showed some of the equipment purchased with the cards and the estimated values.

"I know we mentioned maybe making a couple of hundred thousand pounds in a short time, but we've taken the cautious side and the devices have only been used for short periods of time. Also the costs of the cards turned out more expensive than what we thought. I thought they would only cost a few quid but it was a lot more than that. Anyhow, you'll see that we've made a bottom line profit of three hundred thousand quid"

Alan pointed out.

"That's enough for the villa in Spain including what we made with the car crash scams"

"It is, but that'll nearly clean us out. I'd like to carry on for another couple of months, unless we hit any problems. What do you think Ron?"

"I think we're okay for a while longer, but the longer it goes on, the team will tend to make more risks and become a bit sloppy. We'll have to keep a close eye on them"

Steve agreed.

"Yes, I'm aware of that but we'll be careful. We wouldn't be so successful if we weren't"

Both Alan and Ron burst out laughing at that remark. They all finished their buffet meal and made sure that they shredded the documents before leaving the room.

Ron then left the house leaving Steve and Alan to carry on having a chat.

"Do you have any more news on the villa, Steve?"

"Yes, I spoke to Greg Collins in Spain this morning and he reckons that the villa should be complete in two months. He'll want the balance then. I've said that I'll go out in about six weeks to see the progress that they've made and finalise the arrangements. I'll also sort out the legal side and make the payment in one lump sum when I get home"

"Whose name will the villa be in?"

"I don't know, I haven't really thought about it. Probably yours and mine"

"How about Mum and Sarah"

"No, Mum's getting on and Sarah's not interested in our business affairs. We don't see Sarah very often but they'll be able to go out there whenever they want"

"Sarah was here last night with Phillip Harris, he seems a nice bloke. Sarah was introducing him to Mum, so it's got to be pretty serious"

"I didn't know that. Why did nobody tell me?"

"You were out and this is the first time that I've seen you. Mum probably forgot to mention it"

"They're living together in Sarah's flat in Manchester. Her friend Karen moved out a couple of months ago and Phillip moved in then. They were talking about taking a break in Spain and I'd told them they'd get discounts at the hotel on La Grande Club. I gave them some information and they said they'd think about it, but it seemed a good idea"

"I should know about these things as she is my sister"

"I keep an eye on Sarah and check that she's okay and Mum thinks that Phillip is a nice bloke. He did tell us that you'd seen them in Manchester and mentioned saving money and with Sarah being his partner, you can get staff discounts on the exchange rate. You'd have to do the transfer through Sarah's account at his place but there are already accounts in all our names, you, me, Mum and Sarah"

"I've been transferring the money from Bank and Building Society accounts in our names to those accounts with his place and then transferring abroad. It's all perfectly legitimate and he knows the money comes from proper places. It's nothing to do with him how the money got in the Banks and Building

Societies in the first place"

"There's a difference in the buying and selling rates for euros. One rate is around one point forty one and the other is one point forty three, and that makes a difference of fifteen thousand euros when you transfer three quarters of a million pounds. That's where we have to try and negotiate"

"I know all about that but we haven't got to worry about it for a couple of months, when hopefully the villa will be built and ready for us. Did you mention the villa to Sarah?"

"Yeah, it came up and I told them they could go and see how it's getting on. If they needed help in finding it, they should contact Greg Collins in the property office. They said they might do that if they were going to the La Grande Club but they hadn't decided whether they were going or not. That's one of the reasons that I wondered whose name the property was going to be in"

"I'll sort all that out when we get round to actually buying the villa"

Steve kept a watch for a couple of days as the bank staff left the branch. He was able to verify Rob Wilson by his description, and when another staff member had called his name. He followed him to his car, a blue Vauxhall Astra and made a note of the car number. The next day, Steve instructed one of his team to slash all his car tyres and put super glue in the locks. After he finished work that day, Rob returned to his car and struggled to open the door and he then stepped back and saw that the tyres had been slashed. A masked gunman then fired one shot into his leg and Rob fell to the floor, writhing in agony.

Steve Mitchell then said. "That's the punishment for being clever, you've cost us money"

26

The case against Carl Sutherland, who had been receiving his parent's pensions for many years after their deaths, was still continuing, but a final date had now been made for the Crown Court hearing.

Like many other cases, this had been initially dealt with by the Magistrates Court, who had three hearings, one of which was a request for a delay by Carl's solicitors who felt they needed more time to complete their work. Bail had been allowed by the Magistrates and there were no objections by the Prosecution Service.

Brian Lewis, who had worked with David on this case also worked very closely with the Magistrates Court in Manchester. He knew of all the dates and had kept David up to date but there was no requirement to make an appearance at these hearings. David had also kept in touch with the solicitors representing the Pension Agencies who had also informed David that he need not appear. They had also informed David of the charges to be made against Carl Sutherland.

Whilst there had been changes in the Fraud Act which had come into place in January 2007, the offences had started in 1995 and 1997 and the pensions had been stopped by both of the Pension Agencies in January 2007, so it had been decided by the solicitors and the barrister that the previous Theft Act 1968 would be used.

'Dishonestly retaining a wrongful credit'. Section 24A of the

Theft Act makes it an offence for a person if:-
A wrongful credit has been made to an account kept by him/her
or respect of which he/she has a right of interest.
He/she knows or believes that the credit is wrongful.
He/she dishonestly fails to take such steps as are reasonable in
the circumstances to secure that the credit is cancelled.

On the third Magistrates Court appearance, the Magistrates committed the case to trial at the Crown Court because the seriousness of the case was not within their powers. The sentences that may be levied would be in excess of those given to Magistrates. Once again, there was no need for David to attend because it was known that no plea would be heard that day and the Judge would listen to preliminary comments from both solicitors, but would then defer the case and request that a plea is made at the next hearing. It was indicated by both solicitors that a guilty plea would be made and if so, the Judge would allow time for reports on any mitigating circumstances and any reports into Carl Sutherland.

David and Brian Lewis both attended this hearing as they had given Witness Statements but neither expected to be called, as a guilty plea was envisaged. They sat in the public gallery a few spaces away from Carl's sister Rita, with the only other person present being one of the local reporters. Carl was in the box set aside for the defendants and both barristers were prepared when the Clerk of the Courts said.

"Be upstanding for Judge John Bartholomew"

The Judge then sat in his seat and everybody else sat down waiting for the Clerk of the Courts to read out the charges and request a plea. Carl Sutherland remained standing and the Clerk of the Courts then read from his paperwork.

"Carl Sutherland, you are charged with two hundred and thirty six offences under Section Twenty four A of the Theft

Act, Ninety, ninety eight. On the first charge, you dishonestly retained wrongful credits from the North West Transport Pensions Agency for a total of Ninety seven thousand, seven hundred and fifty pounds. How do you plead, Guilty or Not Guilty?"

"Guilty"

"On the second charge, you dishonestly retained wrongful credits from the Local Authority Pensions Agency for a total of Fifty eight thousand, nine hundred pounds. How do you plead, Guilty or Not Guilty?"

"Guilty"

Judge John Bartholomew then spoke to the Prosecution's Barrister.

"Do you have a report?"

"Yes your honour, this is not a one off fraud. A thorough investigation has been made by David Parish, a Fraud Consultant, representing both Pension Agencies. It is a cold calculated fraud that has been in operation since Nineteen, ninety five with respect to the North West Transport Pensions Agency and Nineteen, ninety seven with respect to the Local Authorities Pension Agency. In all this period of time the defendant has had the opportunity to stop the pension credits but refused. When one of the Pension Scheme Administrators telephoned him early in two thousand and seven, querying the death of his parents, he informed him, they were alive and well. He has been in receipt of over One hundred and fifty six thousand pounds which he has used to make his lifestyle more comfortable and allowed him to purchase his own house. There have been no offers to repay any of the money, despite requests from David Parish, the Fraud Consultant, to consider such an action. We find his actions disgraceful, knowing that his parents have died, but continuing to defraud their Pension Agencies, into which they had paid their hard earned monies to give them a more comfortable life in retirement. There are no excuses or mitigating circumstances, and I would like the Court to give him the full custodial punishment allowed by the State"

"Thank you" as Judge Bartholmew turned to the Defence Barrister.

"Your honour. My client is full of remorse for his actions and his health has suffered badly with this whole experience. You will see that he has a clean criminal record with no previous convictions. On the death of his father in nineteen, ninety five, his mother was devastated and completely distraught, as you can imagine"

He then took a drink from his glass of water and David turned to Brian and whispered quietly.

"Here we go again, how many times have we heard this sob story?"

The Defence Barrister continued.

"He was taking care of his mother and completely forgot about his father's pension. It was a few months later when he realised that the pension had continued, but he thought that it was continuing for his mother, who was having financial difficulties. He meant to contact the Pensions Agency but was at first unable to find the contact details and then forgot about it for several months. He then realised that a mistake was being made but decided that his mother needed the pension monies and turned a blind eye to the sorry situation. When his mother died in nineteen, ninety seven, he himself was in a severely distraught state of mind and unable to cope with the financial difficulties. Over the years, he kept worrying about the pension credits, but was fearful of the consequences and neglected to inform the appropriate authorities. He now fully realises his errors and wishes to place himself at the mercy of the court. Sadly, he has neither money nor savings and is unable to make any type of repayment"

"Thank you"

Judge John Bartholomew then looked at Carl Sutherland and addressed him.

"Carl Sutherland, I have listened to both the Prosecution Barrister and your Defence Barrister. I have also examined all the documentation from the investigation that has taken place by the Pension Agencies Fraud Consultant, David Parish. There is no doubt in my mind, that you were always fully aware of the fraud that you were committing, and continued with the frauds for a period of twelve years, which has allowed you to purchase your own house. I also note that you have made no attempt to return any of the fraudulent gains to the respective bodies. I am also aware that the solicitors acting on behalf of the Pension Agencies are considering civil action to recover the funds. The value of the house will go some way to repaying this fraud and it is a course of action that has my full approval. I am sentencing you to eighteen months imprisonment. Take him down"

As they left the Crown Court, Brian spoke to David.

"I think that's the best that we could hope for. I would have expected two years imprisonment but the Judge has hinted at a civil action, and I'm sure we'll go down that road"

"Yes, you're right Brian. Now for the next case"

27

The bitterness between Zoe Ferguson, Rik Jeffreys and Linda Barrett had not helped their solicitors in the preparation for the Fraud Case, which was now due to appear in the Crown Court in London. The normal channels of law had been undertaken with the passage through the Magistrates Court and the initial hearings in the Crown Court. It had now reached the stage where they were going to plead guilty and the Judge would be passing sentence.

John Harrison was the solicitor acting for Rik Jeffreys and his partner, Anna Young was the solicitor for Zoe Ferguson. On the advice of John and Anna, it had been agreed that there would be the one Barrister acting for them. Darren O'Brien who was the solicitor acting for Linda had appointed a different Barrister. They had all been charged with the same offence and were being prosecuted at the same hearing.

The fraud had started three years ago and they were being charged under the Theft Act 1968 and the Fraud Act 2006 as well as a charge of conspiracy.

False Accounting is covered by Section 17 (1) (a) of the Theft Act 1968 which make it an offence for a person to dishonestly and with a view to gain for him/herself or another or with intent to cause loss to another, to destroy, deface, conceal or falsify any account or any record or document made or required for any accounting purpose'

Section 2 of the Fraud Act 2006 covers Fraud by false representation.

Zoe was standing in the waiting area with her solicitor Anna Young and Rik was talking to John Harrison and his Barrister, Howard Douglas, who had just finished talking to Zoe and Anna. It was just after ten o'clock and they should have been in Court already.

A little further along, there was a heated discussion taking place between Darren O'Brien and the Barrister for Linda Barrett, Katherine Walton. David Parish and Peter Daley, who assisted David in this case, had now been asked to join the discussion by Darren O'Brien.

Darren spoke to David and Peter.

"David, Linda Barrett has not turned up to Court. I have tried ringing her at home and there is no answer to my call. I've also tried ringing her on her mobile, but that is switched off. We've told the Usher and he's gone off to have a word with the Judge. He's going to blow his top but will probably allow a few hours delay, would you two go over to Linda Barrett's flat to see if you can find anything out. She might have disappeared but she has always attended the previous hearings without any problem. I know she'll listen to you and I've arranged for one of my colleagues to meet you outside her flat. I've got your mobile number and I think you've got mine. Let me know what's going on when you get to her flat"

"Okay, Darren, we'll jump a cab to Hackney"

"I'd better let John Harrison know what's going on. The Usher will be back in a few minutes"

David and Peter left the Crown Court to catch a taxi and Darren followed Katherine Walton over to the other groups.

Katherine spoke to Howard Douglas.

"There's a problem, Howard. Linda Barrett has not turned up. We've told the Usher and he's gone to see the Judge. Darren has sent one of his colleagues to her flat and they're going to meet up with David Parish and Peter Daley. Hopefully, we'll be able to sort it out, but she might have disappeared. Darren has tried contacting her without success"

Zoe Ferguson who had been listening was clearly annoyed.

"What does this mean, it looks as though she's done a runner and gone back to Spain?"

Anna tried to calm her down.

"We don't know what's going to happen but we'll soon find out. Here comes the Court Usher"

The Usher approached.

"I have spoken to Judge Lawson. He is extremely annoyed but has deferred the start of the case until two o'clock this afternoon. I hope, for your sakes, that you get Barrett here by that time"

David and Peter Daley were in the taxi heading for Linda Barrett's flat in Hackney when Peter remarked.

"I wonder what's gone wrong with Linda Barrett. I was chatting to Darren earlier and he said that he had spoken to her yesterday, she was just checking what she needed to bring with her today. She was convinced that she was going to prison for a long time and had told the landlord of the flat she was expecting to move out"

"If she was going to disappear and not turn up for court, I'm sure she would've done it before now and not let Darren down. I know she's guilty of fraud but I find it a bit strange and a bit worrying because I thought that she'd face up to what's she's done and take the consequences"

They arrived at the block of flats where Linda lived and David quickly paid the taxi driver. The colleague of Darren's was waiting outside the flats and was immediately recognised as Michael Downing by Peter.

Peter shook Michael's hand saying.

"Hi Michael, good to see you again. We've been to this block of flats before when we dropped Linda Barrett when she returned from Spain. We know the number but don't know which flat it is, do you know?"

"Yes, it's the one on the left on the first floor. The curtains are drawn"

Peter and David both looked up at the flat and could see all the curtains closed although it was eleven o'clock in the morning. They entered the block of flats and made their way to the first floor flat and David rang the doorbell. He could hear the chimes of the bell so knew that it was working. When they received no answer, he tried again. There was still no answer so David looked through the letter box.

"I can't see anybody but all the lights are on. We need to get into the flat but let's check with the neighbours first in case they've seen anything or they may have a spare set of keys"

There were three other flats on the same floor and they all tried one of the flats each. David and Michael got no answer at their flats but a girl in her early twenties opened the door for Peter.

"Hello, we're Linda Barrett's solicitors and we're concerned for her safety. The curtains are drawn and the lights are on. Have you seen her recently?"

"Erm, I saw her yesterday about six o'clock when she was going into the flat, but I haven't seen her since"

"Do you know if anybody would have spare keys for her flat?"

"I don't know, but she's quite friendly with the old dear downstairs. The flat on the left as you come through the front door"

"Thanks for your help"

Peter stayed upstairs while David and Michael went down and rang the doorbell of the ladies flat. It was opened fairly quickly be an elderly lady.

David spoke to the lady.

"We are trying to contact Linda Barrett who lives upstairs and have tried her door bell but received no answer. We understand that she is friendly with you, have you seen her? We were due to meet up with her today"

"Who are you?"

"This gentleman is from her solicitors and I'm a business colleague"

"If you're her solicitor, you should know where she is today" Michael replied.

"She should be in Crown Court, but she hasn't turned up. Her curtains are drawn in the flat and the lights are on. Do you have a spare set of keys for the flat; we want to make sure that she's okay"

"Yes, I've got a spare set, hang on a minute"

She went away, coming back quickly and handed the keys over to David.

"I'll come up with you in case I can help"

They all climbed the stairs and David opened the door of the flat but then spoke to the elderly lady.

"Please wait here for a minute while we check the flat to see if everything's okay"

They entered the flat and went into the different rooms with David going into the lounge. As soon as he entered he saw Linda lying on the settee. There were tablets lying on the table by the settee and empty containers.

"In here" he yelled.

Peter and Michael arrived as David was feeling for a pulse.

"She's dead; I would think she has been for a few hours at least. Ring for the Police and Ambulance and check that our friend is okay outside"

Michael headed outside to talk to the elderly lady and Peter phoned 999 on his mobile giving full details to the operator. David looked at the table with the tablets and saw that there was also a note left on the table. He did not need to touch the note but knelt down and read it.

Dear Darren,

I am sorry that I did not come to the Crown Court today. I knew that I was going to go to prison and deserved to be sent to prison, but my life was over anyway. I have lost Keith and lost my job and I cannot face the thought of prison. That would be worse than what I have done now. You have been kind to me as well as David Parish and his Spanish Police Lady girlfriend, Alisa Garcia. Thank them for the help they gave me. I hope Zoe and Rik go to prison for many years because this was their fault. They got Keith and me involved and now we are both dead. I have not got any of the money and neither has Keith. I think Zoe has got it all. Fraud - why did they do it?

Linda

Peter returned to the room.

"The Ambulance and Police are on their way. Michael is downstairs with the lady"

"There's a suicide note on the table. Don't touch it but you can have a read"

Peter read the note.

"It's sad really and she was certainly annoyed with Ferguson and Jeffreys"

"I'd better ring Darren and let him know"

David took his mobile out of his pocket to ring Darren.

"Hello"

"Hi Darren, its David here. Bad news I'm afraid, we've found Linda, but she's committed suicide. It looks like a drugs overdose and there is a suicide note addressed to you. We can't touch it but I've read it and it apologises to you for the trouble she's caused. The Police and Ambulance are just arriving, I'd better go and see them and let you deal with the Judge and the others"

"Oh, the little fool, what a waste. Thanks David, I'll speak to you later"

Darren walked over to the two Barristers, Katherine Walton and Howard Douglas who were deep in discussion and waved over John Harrison and Anna Young.

"I've just been informed that Linda Barrett is dead, it would appear that she committed suicide last night. She had left a suicide note. I think we'd better go and inform the Court Usher and let him find out what the Judge has got to say"

Darren and the two Barristers walked towards the Ushers room and John Harrison and Anna went to see Zoe and Rik who were looking rather bewildered.

John then said to Rik and Zoe.

"I've just heard that Linda is dead. It would appear that she's committed suicide. Darren has gone to tell the Usher"

Zoe looked in control but Rik looked utterly shaken.

"That's the two of them dead now. What have we caused?"

Zoe quickly replied.

"Oh shut up, that has got nothing to do with us"

Darren and the Barristers went into the Usher's room who immediately asked.

"What news have you got for me?"

Darren spoke quietly.

"Linda Barrett is dead, it would appear she committed suicide last night and she has left a suicide note"

"Thank you. I'll go and have a word with Judge Lawson. Wait here"

The Usher returned ten minutes later.

"The case is deferred for a week. He will then continue with the other two and he will pass sentence assuming they retain the guilty plea. Ten o'clock next Tuesday"

"They'll still be pleading guilty" replied Howard Douglas.

Rik and Zoe stood up while the charges were read to them in the Crown Court. It had been agreed by both parties that the conspiracy charge would not be used.

"Zoe Ferguson, you are charged with one thousand, five hundred and twenty one offences of False Accounting under the Theft Act, Nineteen, sixty eight and Fraud by False Representation under the Fraud Act, Two thousand and six, in that you obtained by deception the sum of Two hundred and ninety six thousand and thirty pounds from the Euston General Hospital. Do you plead guilty or not guilty?"

"Guilty"

"Rik Jeffreys, you are charged with one thousand, five hundred and twenty one offences of False Accounting under the Theft Act, Nineteen, sixty eight and Fraud by False Representation under the Fraud Act, Two thousand and six, in that you obtained by deception the sum of Two hundred and ninety six thousand and thirty pounds from the Euston General Hospital. Do you plead guilty or not guilty?"

"Guilty"

Judge William Lawson looked at the Prosecution Counsel, Stephen Donald.

"Mr Donald"

"Thank you your honour. This is a case of fraud covering over two and a half years in which the defendants continually obtained false travel claims. We are not talking about a small number of claims but a total in excess of one thousand five hundred, in which the National Health Service lost nearly three hundred thousand pounds. This money could have been used to help sick people including children and it was while their own daughter was in hospital that they decided to undertake this fraud. They decided to continue with this fraud and it was only when an elderly lady overheard Zoe Ferguson speaking, that the fraud was stopped by the authorities. A sum of twenty thousand pounds was returned by Zoe Ferguson but she had promised to repay fifty thousand pounds when she was interviewed by David Parish, the Fraud Consultant for the National Health Service. The rest of the money has never been recovered and any civil action taken by the Hospital may be faced with difficulties. Sadly, their greed involved recruiting two other people into their scheme, Keith Simpson and Linda Barrett. Both of them are now deceased and whilst no direct blame is placed on Rik Jeffreys and Zoe Ferguson, it does show what may occur when people continue to defraud for a period of time. For the fraud offences we are looking for a long custodial sentence"

Judge William Lawson then looked at the Defence Counsel, Howard Douglas.

"Mr Douglas"

"Your honour, I do not intend to go into a long closing defence argument. My clients have admitted the offences which started when they were in great financial difficulties. Once this scheme had been in operation for several months, they had great concerns on what they were doing but regrettably, they became a little greedy. They are now full of remorse and are extremely worried about their daughter if they were to go to prison. The Prosecution Counsel mentioned the promise by Zoe Ferguson to return fifty thousand pounds but when she went to check this cash, she found there was only twenty thousand pounds. Both my clients have no knowledge of the monies that have been taken and assume it has all been used or possibly lost or stolen. My clients are now at the mercy of the Court"

Judge William Lawson then addressed Rik and Zoe.

"I have, in this role, come across many different crimes but this continual fraud against our National Health Service is perhaps one of the most disturbing that I have listened to. You continued with this fraud without any concerns to people requiring hospital treatment. In your greed, you recruited two other people, Keith Simpson and Linda Barrett, who have now lost their lives. My sentence does not take their deaths into account but I would have expected more remorse from you. After all, they were fellow conspirators and part of your team. I do not believe that all the proceeds of this crime have been used and I believe that one of you knows where the money is, and how much money is still available to satisfy your greed. The Proceeds of Crime Act, two thousand and two introduced the Assets Recovery Agency. I will instruct them to make a search for the missing monies but I will now give you the opportunity to repay some of the proceeds of your criminal activities. I am sentencing you both to two years imprisonment but you must repay the sum of one hundred thousand pounds within three months. If you do not repay this money, a further twelve months will be added to your sentence"

As Zoe and Rik were being escorted out of Court, Rik yelled at Zoe.

"Give them the money, I haven't got any. You're hiding it and I don't want to serve another year because you're so selfish and greedy. Give them the money, Zoe"

28

Whilst the relationship between Sarah Mitchell and her brother, Steve, was virtually non-existent, she had started to get a little friendlier with her younger brother, Alan, when she had been meeting her mother, at the families Cheshire home.

Alan had mentioned the villa that was being built at La Grande Club and the visits with their girlfriends to the luxury hotel on the complex. He also offered to get Sarah and Phillip discounted rates at the hotel if they ever wanted to pay a visit. They decided that they would like a break for a few days and they checked the internet and obtained a couple of seats on the plane. As promised, Alan had contacted Greg Collins in the Estates Office, who obtained the cheap rates for Sarah and Phillip.

They caught the morning flight to Murcia which arrived mid afternoon and they then arranged a car-hire in order to drive to the La Grande Club complex and the hotel. As they arrived Sarah remarked.

"This is a lovely place and the hotel looks super"

They parked outside the hotel and collected their luggage from the car and went into the hotel reception.

Phillip spoke to the receptionist at the desk.

"My name is Phillip Harris and this is my girlfriend, Sarah Mitchell, we have a room booked for four nights"

The receptionist looked at the computer screen and said.

"Yes, Greg Collins has booked the room, it is room two, one three on the second floor. May I have your passports please?"

Phillip handed over the two passports and his credit card in order that any purchases would be set against their room bill, rather than keep paying with cash.

Sarah was curious to see the villa being built for Steve and said.

"Where will we find Greg Collins?"

"He's probably in the Estate Office. It's only a short walk to the left as you go out. You will see a sign as you leave the hotel"

"Thank you"

The receptionist returned the passports and Phillip's credit card together with the door entry cards.

"Greg has also arranged a free meal at the hotel restaurant this evening as part of the package. Enjoy your stay"

Sarah quickly replied.

"Oh, we will thanks"

They then made the way to the hotel room and Phillip turned to Sarah.

"Why did you want to know about Greg Collins?"

"I want to be nosy and have a look at the villa. He'll be able to tell us all about it. I don't suppose that we'll ever use it much, it'll be Steve's big toy. He did tell Mum that she could use it, but she's not that keen to come to Spain, with what happened to Dad. We'll go round there tomorrow morning"

The hotel room was lovely and once they had unpacked, they spent an hour walking around the site before returning to the hotel. They then decided to have a dip and sit around the swimming pool for a couple of hours before getting changed for the evening meal. The waiter caught the attention of Phillip who turned to Sarah.

"What do you fancy to drink?"

"How about a small jug of sangria?"

"Good idea"

The waiter smiled and went to get the sangria.

The following morning, Sarah and Phillip had breakfast in the hotel and then went to find Greg Collins. They soon located the Estates Office and went inside where a man was sitting at the desk and said.

"Good morning, can I help you?"

Sarah replied.

"I hope so, are you Greg Collins?"

"Yes, I'm afraid so"

"My name is Sarah Mitchell and this is my boyfriend, Phillip Harris"

Greg stood up and shook hands.

"Your brother Alan contacted me and asked me to book you a room at the hotel. I hope that it's okay"

"Oh, it's lovely, thank you" said Sarah.

"Did you get your free meal?"

"Yes thanks. I'm being a bit curious really. My other brother, Steve, is having a villa built here, and we wouldn't mind having a look at it while we're here. Is that okay?"

"No problem, do you know where it is?"

"No, I've got no idea"

"I've got to go near there in about half an hour; I'm meeting the family who are buying a villa nearby. I've got to sort some paperwork first, but if you give me ten minutes I'll give you a lift"

Sarah replied.

"That's super. Thank you"

Greg drove them to the villa and opened the front door. He showed them part of the villa which looked virtually completed before saying.

"I've got to go to this meeting. It will only be for about half an hour, feel free to look around and I'll pick you up on the way back if you like?"

Phillip turned to Greg.

"You sure it's not a problem, we'll walk back if it's easier?"

"No problem at all, I'll see you in about half an hour"

Sarah and Phillip started to walk round the villa, having a good look in each room before Phillip remarked.

"This is a super villa, it's so spacious and it's an ideal place to live in, never mind just for holidays. Pity you're not too friendly with Steve, he might have let you use it"

"I'd rather not use it and be friendly with him. It is lovely though, too good for him"

They unlocked the back patio door leading towards the swimming pool and went outside. The gardens had been virtually completed and the swimming pool was finished apart from having no water inside.

Sarah was having a good look around.

"This will be finished in a couple of weeks and then all the furniture can be brought in. I think Steve will be coming out shortly to finalise all the details and make the final payment"

Greg Collins pulled up outside the villa as Sarah and Phillip were walking round the front of the villa. He got out of the car and spoke to Sarah.

"What do you think about the villa?"

"It's lovely"

"I suppose you'll be coming out quite often?"

"No, I don't get on with Steve. Alan spoke about it and I was just curious. We wanted a few days break and the hotel and complex were tempting from what Alan had said, so we thought we'd come here for a holiday and have a look at the villa at the same time. It looks nearly finished to me"

"It is almost finished. I've got a meeting with the builder and surveyor later today. If they give the okay, I'll be giving Steve a ring, telling him it's nearly ready and he should be coming out to finalise the purchase and check the villa over. We'll have to sort the furniture out with him, but we have most of the details"

"Are you going to speak to him?"

"No"

Greg then drove them back towards the hotel but Sarah saw the shops and turned to Greg.

"Drop us off here Greg, we'll have a look at the shops"

"Get your credit card ready Phillip, you might need it"

They all laughed as they got out of the car.

There was a ladies clothing shop just after they had passed the Banco de Murcia and Sarah quickly entered. She was having a good look at the clothing and shoes but was only half way round the shop and Phillip was trying hard not too look bored but Sarah could tell by his face that he was.

"Go back to the hotel, Phil and I'll follow you when I've finished having a browse"

"You don't mind?"

"No, push off"

Steve smiled as he left the shop saying.

"See you later; I'll be having a beer by the pool"

Sarah had a look around the shop but only purchased a pair of sandals. She then called into the Banco de Murcia before returning to the hotel and finding Phillip drinking a beer by the pool.

Greg Collins had a meeting with the builder and the surveyor later that day, and was given the all clear to contact Steve Mitchell in order to complete the purchase. He phoned Steve on his mobile.

"Hello"

"Is that Steve Mitchell?"

"Yeah, who's this?"

"It's Greg Collins from Le Grande Club"

"Oh, Hi Greg"

"The villa's virtually finished, Steve. It's time for you to come out, get your surveyor to have a look and make arrangements for the final payment. When can you come out?"

"I'll come out early next week, I'll let you know what day once I've booked the flight"

"Do you want a room in the hotel?"

"Yeah, I'll probably come out on my own"

"Okay, I'll sort a room for you. I met your sister today; she's out here with her boyfriend, Phillip. They've had a look at the villa"

"Sarah's in Spain at Le Grande Club?"

"Yes, you didn't mind her seeing the villa did you?"

"No, I didn't know she was interested"

"Yeah, I think she rather liked it anyway. Bye Steve, I'll see you next week"

29

The scheme using the skimming devices has been the most successful fraud that Steve Mitchell has undertaken. The use of the false cards with the copied strips had been beneficial in obtaining cash from the ATMs and the purchase of goods, which were easily disposable. The total funds received were in excess of that required by Steve to buy the villa in Spain, but it also allowed him to place extra money in his own little nest egg.

The members of the team would always check the skimming device by making a small withdrawal, using cards that he had provided. Ron Thomas was able to gain access to the Banking systems for these cards and he checked to make sure the team were only withdrawing the nominal amounts, usually twenty pounds. He soon became aware that one of the team was cheating on them, and had withdrawn in excess of a thousand pounds without informing him.

Ron called round to see Steve and told him.

"Steve, one of the team has been withdrawing excessive funds from one of our test cards. Up to now it's over a thousand pounds and it's possible he may be using some of the false cards to get even more extra money. I can't tell with those, but his overall returns are less than everybody else"

"Who is it?"

"Derek Lipton"

Steve was a bit taken back by this name.

"He worked for us on the car crash business, didn't he? I

thought he was one of our best team members"

"Yeah, he only got married about six months ago. I don't know if that's got anything to do with it. Do you want me to have a word?"

"No Ron, I'll deal with it. I've got his address and personal details"

"Okay boss"

"Apart from that, this has been a good business for us Ron. You've done a good job, here's your reward. There's fifty thousand pounds in there"

He then handed Ron a package containing the cash.

"Thanks Steve, should we carry on with this or scrap it while we're doing well"

"Give it a bit longer, maybe a month. I've got to go out and check the villa next week. I think it's nearly complete and we'll have a chat when I get back and decide then"

A couple of days later, Steve took the place of Ron, and collected the money the team had obtained with the false cards. It was collected at a warehouse that Steve used for some of his legitimate enterprises and generally took place in early evening, when the warehouse was empty and the site was fairly quiet. If any members of the team queried his appearance and not Ron's, he told them Ron was away for a couple of days. The team were always given set times to arrive and Derek Lipton was the last on the list.

When he arrived he was surprised.

"Hi Steve, where's Ron?"

"I've given him a few days off, there were some things he wanted to do"

Derek handed over the proceeds from his day's work which was checked by Steve and placed with the rest of the cash.

Steve then spoke to Derek.

"You've done work for us in the past, haven't you? You

were involved with the car crashes and now, these skimming devices"

"Yeah"

"I want to pick your brains; I've got something to show you. Let's go to the back"

Derek followed Steve through the warehouse and outside through the back door. Steve then confronted Derek.

"Do you think you've been well paid for the work that you've done so far?"

"Yeah"

"You know that you're supposed to withdraw twenty quid on a test card as soon as you've inserted the device?"

"Yeah, that's what I've been doing"

"You're a liar. We've got access to the bank accounts for the test cards and you've been drawing more money than you're supposed to and keeping it for yourself"

The colour drained from Derek's face.

"I didn't do it very often. I've only just got married and I bought the wife a few things and it's been costly setting up our house. I'm sorry Steve; I'll pay you the money back"

"How much more have you pinched besides the test card money"

"Not much"

"Not much is too much. Nobody does the dirty on Steve Mitchell and lives to tell the tale"

He then took the handgun from inside his jacket pocket and fired the one shot, which was enough to kill Derek Lipton and make his new wife a widow. Ron Thomas then came out of the warehouse to help Steve get rid of the body and clear up any mess. The body was taken away late that night and left at the entrance to a small wood a few miles away. It was discovered the next day as Steve had wanted; he didn't want a big search being made in a few days time, when his wife would have reported him missing.

The body of Derek Lipton had been found by a man taking his dog for a walk in the Cheshire countryside. Chief Inspector Anne Graham had overall responsibility for the murder enquiry. Several days had passed and the police were struggling with their enquiries and Lucy Lipton, Derek's wife had been unable to provide any assistance. She was clearly distraught, but there was a feeling that she had something to tell the police, but was reluctant to say anything against Derek.

The bullet that had killed Derek had been sent to forensics and was being examined by Michael Rogers. He was looking closely, through the microscope, to see if there were any markings such as grooves which might prove which gun had been used. He then sat up and went to one of the evidence cabinets and took out a second bullet which he examined closely. He was in no doubt that the two bullets had been fired by the same gun. The first bullet had been taken from the leg of Rob Wilson, a bank teller, some days before.

Michael picked up the phone and dialled the number for Cheshire Police.

"Hello, Cheshire Police"

"I'd like to speak to Chief Inspector Anne Graham please"

"Who is it speaking?"

"Michael Rogers from Forensics"

"Hello Michael, have you got anything for me?"

"I've checked the bullet taken from Derek Lipton and it matches with another bullet, which has been fired by the same gun. The bullet was taken from the leg of a bank employee, Rob Wilson. I know that's not your case but I know a bit about it. He was shot by a masked gunman who said to Rob, That's the punishment for being clever, you've cost us money. Apparently, Rob had discovered a skimming device in one of the Banks cash machines and the shooting was his punishment for being clever.

He was clearly out of favour with the gang running this scam. Hope that helps you"

"Thanks Michael, I know who's in charge of that investigation and I've already been passed some information"

Anne sat back and thought about the information that she had been given and then walked out of her office and went to see Detective Sergeant Trevor Cochrane.

"Trevor, I'd like to go and see Lucy Lipton, will you come with me?"

"Sure"

"I've just had Michael Rogers from Forensics on the phone. The bullet that killed Derek Lipton came from the same gun that was used to shoot Rob Wilson, a bank employee who found a skimming machine in the banks cash machine. I'm sure there's going to be some connection and it wouldn't surprise me if Derek was involved in the scam. Maybe he got greedy and received the ultimate punishment"

Trevor drove the car and they soon arrived at the house of the Lipton's. Lucy answered the door and Anne said.

"We need your help Lucy, can we have a word?"

Lucy led them into the lounge and they all sat down before she asked.

"Have you caught the person who killed Derek?"

Anne replied.

"Not yet Lucy, but we have some more information. The bullet that killed Derek came from the same gun that was used to injure a bank employee. He was shot in the leg because he discovered a skimming machine in the bank's cash machine. We think he was punished for stopping this scam at his branch of the bank"

Lucy broke into tears.

"Derek only did it to raise some extra money for our house"

"What did he do Lucy?"

"He wouldn't tell me all the details or who he was working for, but he did tell me he was involved in fixing these devices to cash machines. That's all I know but he's worked for these people before"

"What work was that?"

"He didn't tell me much, but he was involved in car crashes. He would be given a car and was told to drive in front of another vehicle and then brake hard, causing somebody to crash into the back of his car. They would then claim the insurance money. He only told me because he suffered a bad neck on a couple of occasions and I asked him what had caused it. I don't know any more. I never wanted you to know what Derek had done"

"He never mentioned who he was working for?"

"No, he was too frightened to say anything else"

"Thanks Lucy, you've been very helpful"

"I hope you catch who killed Derek"

"We will"

As they drove away, Anne said to Trevor.

"We had somebody in concerning a car crash scam and we weren't able to find out who was behind it, but we did know that he had worked for Steve Mitchell. I wouldn't be surprised if Mitchell was behind the car crash scam and the skimming devices. I did speak to David Parish, Mr Fraud, and he had found out that Mitchell was buying property in Spain and was trying to raise a million pounds. The Spanish Police are also interested in Steve Mitchell because of a bank robbery several years ago, when a bank employee was shot and Mitchell's father took the blame, but they were sure that the father didn't fire the gun"

Trevor thought about this.

"I remember the shooting in Spain, Frank Mitchell went to jail and died of cancer. The bank employee had relatives in the Spanish Police"

"That's right; I'll have a word with David Parish to found out where Steve Mitchell is up to with the property in Spain. He's got a contact in the Spanish Police and he'll probably find out quicker than going through the official channels."

30

Steve Mitchell had been making arrangements to transfer the balance of over eight hundred thousand pounds from various accounts to the Money Transfer Organisation in Manchester. He had taken a quick trip to Spain and decided to make some minor changes to the villa and had agreed the type of furniture which was to be purchased. There had been a slight delay with the completion of the property in the Le Grande Club complex and the delivery of the furniture took a further two weeks.

He telephoned Greg Collins to check on the up to date situation.

"Hola"

"Hi Greg, its Steve Mitchell. Is everything finished with the villa?"

"Yes Steve. The builders have now left the site and all the furniture was delivered yesterday. All we need now is the money and then we'll complete all the legal work with your solicitor, Pepe Fernandez"

"Okay, I'll arrange for the money to be sent to Pepe Fernandez at the Banco de Murcia"

"I'll speak to you in a few days when the money has arrived"

"Cheers"

Greg then opened his phone directory and looked up the phone number of Inspector Felipe Garcia. He then dialled him.

"Hola, La Policia"

"My name is Greg Collins from La Grande Club; may I speak

to Inspector Felipe Garcia?"

"One moment, I'll put you through to him"

"Hola Greg. How are you?"

"I'm fine. I just thought that I'd let you know that I've spoken to Steve Mitchell today. The villa is now complete and he is going to transfer the balance of one million, two hundred thousand euros within the next few days. He'll send it to Pepe Fernandez at the Banco de Murcia"

"Thanks Greg, I'll speak to my contacts in England"

Felipe immediately phoned David on his mobile.

"Hello"

"Hola David, its Felipe"

"Hola Felipe"

"I've just heard that Steve Mitchell is going to send out the balance of the euros required to pay for the villa. It's one million, two hundred thousand euros and will be sent to the Banco de Murcia for the account of Pepe Fernandez. He'll then finalise the purchase"

"Thanks a lot Felipe. I'll contact Chief Inspector Anne Graham at Cheshire Police and then we'll contact the Investigator at the Revenue and Customs. They'll be interested in where he's raising the money and if it's legitimate, has he declared it and paid his tax. I doubt it. I'll let you know if anything's happening"

"Thank you David"

As soon as David had finished the phone call, his mobile rang again.

"Hello"

"Hello David, its Anne Graham"

"I was just about to ring you. Felipe Garcia has just rang and told me Steve Mitchell is going to send out one million, two hundred thousand euros to Spain to buy the villa. That's just over eight hundred thousand pounds. It should interest Revenue and Customs"

"I'll have a word with them. I've rang you because there's been a killing and a punishment shooting. We know that's it's something to do with a skimming device scam on cash machines and there's a strong possibility that it's down to Steve Mitchell. Maybe that's how he's raised the money for the villa"

Steve had transferred money from various sources to the Money Transfer Organisation and a total of eight hundred and thirty thousand pounds had been placed in the name of Sarah Mitchell. He then phoned Sarah.

"Hello"

"Ho Sarah, its Steve. I've put the money in Phillip's place. You've got to go in and make the transfer to Spain. You've got the details haven't you?"

"The Banco de Murcia, account of Pepe Fernandez. I've got all the account details. I'll go over at lunch time"

"Thanks Sarah, I'll see you around"

Sarah walked over to the Money Transfer Organisation and spoke to Jenny Percival because Philip had gone out for lunch.

"Hi Jenny, I'd like to transfer the money from this account to Spain. It's going to the Banco de Murcia and must be sent in euros. Phillip has agreed with my brother Steve that we'll get a favourable rate. It'll probably be staff rate because I'm Phillips partner. Here are the details of the bank account"

"Thanks Sarah, Phillip did mention you'd be transferring some money. It works out at one million, nine hundred and ninety eight thousand euros"

"How long does it take?"

"You're best to allow three days. I'll send it now but the Spanish end may be a bit slower"

"Thanks Jenny"

Sarah left the office and returned to work and phoned Steve.

"Hi, the money's has been transferred to the Banco de Murcia.

241

It worked out at one million, nine hundred and ninety eight thousand euros. It'll take a few days to arrive"

"Why?"

"Oh, it can be slow at the Spanish end"

"Thanks Sarah"

Three days later, Steve phoned Greg Collins at La Grande Club.

"Hola"

"Hi Greg, its Steve Mitchell. Has the money arrived yet?"

"I haven't heard from Pepe Fernadez. When did you send the money?"

"Three days ago"

"It should arrive at anytime. There can be delays because your money will be sent from Manchester to London. It is then sent to the Head Office of the Banco de Murcia who then sends it down to the branch. They'll credit the account and let Pepe Fernandez know. I've known the branch to write to the account holder and that takes a couple of extra days. If you like, I'll give Pepe a ring and ask him to chase it"

"Okay, will you give me a ring back?"

"Sure, it's Friday today, so it'll probably be Monday"

Greg was going out and decided he would call at the office of Pepe Fernandez whilst he was on his travels. Later that afternoon he walked into the Pepe's office and spoke to the receptionist who he knew quite well.

"Is Pepe available for a couple of minutes?"

"I think so, I'll tell him you're here"

She returned, having spoken to Pepe.

"He'll only be a couple of minutes"

Pepe's voice soon boomed out.

"Greg, come in"

"Hola Pepe. Have you received the money from Steve Mitchell for the purchase of the property at La Grande Club?"

"No. He rang me three days ago to tell me he had sent the money. I hadn't heard anything this morning, so I rang the Banco de Murcia. They said they'd received nothing for me and contacted their Head Office and they've told the branch they've had no transfer from England for my account. They should've had the transfer two days ago. They don't think it's been sent"

"I wonder what's going on. I said I'd ring him on Monday"

"I'll check with the Banco de Murcia on Monday morning and let you know"

"Thanks Pepe"

Pepe rang Greg on Monday morning.

"Hola"

"Hola Greg, its Pepe. No money has arrived at my account with the Banco de Murcia, and they've checked with their Head Office. I'd better ring Mitchell as he is my client"

"Thanks Pepe"

The phone in Greg's office rang half an hour after he had spoken to Pepe.

"Hola"

"It's Steve Mitchell. I've just had Pepe Fernandez on the phone and he's saying that my money hasn't arrived, I don't know if I believe him, maybe he's on the fiddle"

"I'm sure he isn't Steve. You should start by checking at your end and get them to trace the money transfer"

"When's the final date you'll allow for completion of the villa?"

"It should be the end of this week, but I'll give you an extra few days if there's a problem"

"Thanks"

Steve quickly travelled to Manchester and walked into the offices of the Money Transfer Organisation and spoke to Jenny Percival.

"Is Phillip Harris in?"

"No, he's on holiday"

"I deposited eight hundred and thirty thousand pounds into my sister's account last week and it was being transferred to the Banco de Murcia, but they've told me it hasn't arrived"

"I did the transfer last week for Sarah and it was sent to the Banco de Murcia"

Steve then got out a piece of paper and handed it to Jenny.

"Here are the account details of my solicitor in Spain, Pepe Fernandez. Are they correct on your transfer?"

Jenny looked at the details on the money transfer to the Banco de Murcia and turned to Steve.

"No, they're not. The money has gone to the correct branch of the Banco de Murcia but not the account of Pepe Fernandez"

"Whose account has it gone into?"

"Sarah Mitchell"

Steve stormed out of the office and phoned Sarah at home on his mobile and got the answering machine. He then rang her at work and was told she had gone on holiday for a few days. The door to Sarah's flat was easy unlocked by Steve and he had a quick look around to see if he could find any evidence of where she had gone. There was nothing to be found so he started Sarah's computer to check out the emails and whilst there were no messages in the open files, she had not removed the deleted emails from the system. A flight had been booked for the previous evening, but only for Sarah and no return flight had been booked.

31

Steve returned to his own office where Alan and Ron Thomas were waiting. The look on his face told them that all was not well.

"We've got a problem. The money to pay for the villa, over eight hundred thousand pounds has not arrived at my solicitor's bank in Spain. It was sent last week by Sarah, but it didn't go to the account of Pepe Fernandez. It went to an account in the name of Sarah Mitchell and she's now gone to Spain, probably with her boyfriend Harris"

Alan intervened.

"There must be some mistake, Sarah wouldn't take the money, and she's never been involved in anything dodgy all her life. Anyhow, why did you get Sarah to send the money?"

"I got a better exchange rate"

"Is that all?"

"Yeah, why?"

"If the police made a check on the transfer of money abroad, Sarah's name would be in the frame"

"That's her hard luck, I'm not going to take the wrap"

"She's your sister Steve, she's family. We don't do the dirty on family"

"She's done it on me. Nobody does the dirty on Steve Mitchell and lives to tell the tale"

"What the hell do you mean?"

"I thought I made myself clear. She is dead and so is her boyfriend Phillip Harris. I'll take care of them myself"

"You can't, I won't let you. I'll do everything I can to stop you. She's our sister. Why can't you get the money back and leave it at that?"

"Nobody does the dirty on Steve Mitchell and lives to tell the tale"

Alan stormed out of the office and Ron turned round to Steve.

"I can guess how you feel but have a think about this before you do any more. This could split your family and Alan will not be on your side. Don't forget, he knows what's gone on over the years and could bring us all down"

"If he's not careful, he'll go the same way as Sarah and her boyfriend"

Alan returned to the family home in Cheshire and spoke to his mother, Paula.

"Mum, there's a problem. Steve asked Sarah to send the money to Spain to pay for the villa. It was supposed to go to Steve's solicitor but it looks as though Sarah sent it to her own personal account at a bank in Spain. Now, Sarah and her boyfriend have gone to Spain and Steve's going crazy. He's threatening to go to Spain and kill both of them"

"He's going to murder his own sister?"

"I've tried to reason with him but he won't listen. He got Sarah to send the money in case there was a comeback and the police found out. He would've then put the blame on Sarah"

"When's he coming home?"

"He didn't say, but I don't think it will be too long"

"I'll speak to him. He'd never get away with harming my daughter. Family is family, his father stuck up for him years ago and he should do the same now, no matter what Sarah has done. He might think I don't know what's been going on over the years but I know a lot more than he thinks"

Steve arrived home later that evening to find both Alan his mother waiting for him. Alan immediately said.

"I've told Mum about the money and what you're planning to do to Sarah"

"It's got nothing to do with you. Keep out of it for your own sake"

"Are you threatening me as well?"

"If you like. You shouldn't bring Mum into this; we keep Mum out of all our businesses"

Paula then screamed at Steve.

"I'm threatening you now, Steve. If anything happens to my daughter or to Alan, I'll make sure you suffer. I'm warning you, leave my family alone. If you harm them, you're no longer a member of my family"

"Idle threats. I'm going to pack my bags, I'll stay somewhere else tonight"

Steve then went upstairs and was down within fifteen minutes carrying a bag which he could use for hand luggage on a plane. He shouted at Paula and Alan.

"Keep out of my business. Nobody does the dirty on Steve Mitchell and lives to tell the tale"

Paula was in tears as she heard the front door slam.

"When's he going to Spain?"

"I don't know, I'll give Ron Thomas a ring, he might know"

Alan rang Ron on his mobile.

"Hello"

"Hi Ron, its Alan. Steve's just stormed out of the house. He's had a big row with me and Mum. Do you know when he's going to Spain?"

"You know that I'd never grass on Steve, but I think he's going over the top. I didn't tell you but he's going tomorrow morning from Manchester Airport. He's got a gun hidden in Spain, probably the same one he used years ago"

"Thanks Ron"

He then tried to ring Sarah on her mobile but the line was dead.

Alan turned to speak to his mother.

"He's going to Spain tomorrow morning. It'll be the same flight that we went on last time. It leaves around eleven o'clock and gets into Murcia about three in the afternoon. I'll see what other flights are available"

He went to the computer and looked at flights before returning to speak to his mother.

"I've booked a flight leaving Liverpool at half past nine tomorrow morning. It's going to Alicante but hopefully, I'll be in Murcia before Steve. I'll then try and find Sarah and Phillip"

"Be careful"

Alan left early the next morning to make his way to Liverpool Airport and Paula waited nearly all day before making a phone call.

"Hello"

"Is that David Parish?"

"Yes, who is this speaking?"

"My name is Paula Mitchell, I'm sure you've heard of my son Steve Mitchell. Don't ask me how I got your phone number, but I don't want to talk to the police"

"That's no problem Paula, go ahead"

"I know you have contacts with the Spanish Police and I think I may need their assistance. I don't know if you're aware that Steve is buying a villa in Murcia?"

"Yes, I do know"

"He got my daughter to send the money to Spain from her boyfriend's Money Exchange place but she didn't send the money to his solicitor. She sent it to an account in her name in Spain. I don't know why and I haven't been able to speak to

Sarah or her boyfriend Phillip. I presume she's with him now. Anyhow, Steve is going mad, as you'd expect, and he's gone to Spain today saying he's going to kill Sarah and Phillip. His flight arrived in Murcia around three o'clock and my other son Alan has gone out to try and stop him. He flew from Liverpool to Alicante but should have arrived before Steve"

"I understand what you're saying Paula, but the Spanish Police won't be able to hold him and I doubt if our Police have anything to go on"

"I thought you might say that, but I know where there is plenty of evidence. Have you heard about these devices that can go on cash machines which copy the details and let people steal from their accounts?"

"Yes, there are some of those scams going on at the moment"

"Steve has been running one of those scams and has recorded all the information on his laptop computer. He's also got information about car crashes on the same laptop"

"Where's the laptop?"

"It's hidden in the house but I know where it is and I've checked that it's still there. I also know where there's a gun which was used to kill somebody and injure a bank employee"

"This needs a police search and warrant. I can't do that, I'll need to involve the police"

"That's okay but I haven't told the police and I won't admit to this phone call"

"That's fine Paula. I'll ring our police now and then I'll ring the Spanish Police unofficially. It'll give them time before they hear through the official channels. You'll be having a visit from our police fairly quickly and hopefully the Spanish Police will get to Steve before he gets to Sarah"

"Thank you. Oh, there's something else. He's got a gun hidden in Spain. It's the same gun that he used to shoot the man in the Spanish bank robbery a few years ago"

David immediately rang Chief Inspector Anne Graham on her direct line.

"Hello, Anne Graham"

"Hello Anne, its David Parish, I've got something for you and you've got to move quick"

"Go on"

"I've just had a phone call from Paula Mitchell, Steve Mitchell's mother. Apparently, her daughter Sarah was told to send the money for the purchase of the villa to Steve's solicitor. She sent it to Spain but into an account in her own name and she's in Spain now, probably moving the money elsewhere. Steve has found out and has just arrived in Spain and he's going to kill his sister and her boyfriend. I understand that he still has the same gun that was used in the bank robbery on the Costa del Sol years ago. Paula wants to save her daughter and will implicate Steve in the skimming device scam and the car crash scam. All the information is on his laptop which you can go and collect from her house. She will also show you the gun that's been used to kill Derek Lipton and shoot Rob Wilson. I said you might need a warrant but you'd be there quickly. I'll give Felipe Garcia and Alisa a ring in Spain but can you go through the proper channels. Alan Mitchell has also gone to Spain to try and stop Steve"

"We'll be at Paula's house within the hour and I'll sort out the warrant. Once we've got something, we'll tell the Spanish Police but we'll also tell them that you've told Felipe Garcia. I'll speak to you later"

David then rang Felipe Garcia.

"Hola David, have you got some news?"

"Oh yes. The British Police are raiding his house anytime now and should have the evidence to charge him with murder, attempted murder and several cases of fraud. They will then issue a warrant for his arrest and you should hear about this through the official channels within the next couple of hours. The problem is Steve Mitchell is in Spain, at a guess, somewhere near the La Grande Club complex. To cut a story short, it seems that his sister Sarah has taken the money being used to buy the villa. It was sent to Spain but not to the account of Pepe Fernandez; instead it went to a personal account of Sarah Mitchell. I understand she is also in Spain with her boyfriend Phillip Harris and Steve has gone out to kill them both. I've also been told he will use the same gun that crippled Luiz. Steve's brother Alan has also gone out to Spain to try and stop Steve. Steve arrived about three o'clock at Murcia Airport and Alan arrived earlier at Alicante Airport. We want to try and stop these murders but, obviously, need your help"

"Thanks David. I don't need to wait for the official request, I'll get a team together immediately and we'll go after Steve Mitchell"

"Good luck, I'll update Alisa"

"No need, she's here in Murcia on the Guardia Civil business. I'll tell her and let her know you'll speak to her later"

Anne Graham arrived at the Mitchell house accompanied by a team of police officers. Paula Mitchell opened the door and without a word being spoken she led them through the house towards Steve's office. She collected a key from a drawer and handed it to Anne saying.

"Open the wooden door in the cupboard and then slide up the rear panel"

Anne did as she was asked and as the rear panel was lifted there was a door to a safe. She put on gloves and opened the safe door then removing a lap top computer and a handgun.

Paula said to Anne.

"You will need a password to gain access to the computer. Try the word Superman"

"Thank you. We'll let you know when we have some news"

"Okay"

Anne had already discussed the situation with her boss and decided no action would be taken against Paula.

Once they reached the Police Headquarters, the computer was passed to the experts and the gun to Forensics. Within the hour, it had been confirmed that it was the gun that had been used to kill Derek Lipton and injure Rob Wilson. A search on the computer showed immense detail into the frauds relating to the skimming devices and the car crashes. There was enough evidence to charge Steve Mitchell with several fraud offences and conspiracy.

Contact was made with the Spanish Police but they advised Anne Graham that the matter was already in hand, and an armed team had been set up headed by Felipe Garcia. All their police officers had been informed to keep a look out for Steve, Alan, Sarah and Phillip.

32

There was intense activity by La Policia Murcia the following morning. They had discovered details of the cars hired by Steve at Murcia Airport and by Alan at Alicante Airport. Steve was driving a grey Ford Mondeo and Alan had a red Vauxhall Astra. A couple of officers had been sent to La Grande Club to check if anybody had registered at the hotel but they had drawn a blank.

The same two officers, who were English speaking, then called to see Greg Collins.

"Hola. We have been sent by Inspector Felipe Garcia to check if you have seen Steve Mitchell since yesterday?"

"No"

"Have you seen Alan Mitchell?"

"No"

"Have you seen Sarah Mitchell or Phillip Harris?"

"Yes, I was driving past and saw Sarah and Phillip going into the Banco de Murcia about an hour ago"

"Have you seen them since then?"

"No, it's worth trying the Bank"

"Yes, thank you, we're going there immediately. If you see any of the four people, please ring us immediately"

The officers called at the Bank and then rang Felipe Garcia.

"Hola Felipe. There is no sign of Steve and Alan Mitchell but Sarah and Phillip Harris were in the Banco de Murcia just over an hour ago. Greg Collins saw them as he drove past and the Bank Manager confirmed they had called in to the branch.

He wouldn't give us the full details of why they were there, but he did say all they did was transfer money from one account to another. They told him they were staying locally and he saw them drive away in a small blue Peugeot"

La Policia arranged visits to local hotels and soon found where Sarah and Phillip had registered. They were not in the hotel but their clothes were still in their room and they were not due to leave until the following day, when according to the manager, they were flying back to England.

Greg Collins was leaving work at seven o'clock in the evening when he saw Alan pass driving a red Astra, so immediately phoned Felipe.

"Hi Felipe, its Greg. I've just seen Alan Mitchell drive past in the red Astra. He looks as though he's heading towards the villa that they're buying. There's nobody up there at this time of the day, it'll be fairly quiet. Do you know where the villa is situated?"

"Yes Greg. We did check it earlier today but there was no sign of activity. Keep out of the way, we'll go up there again"

Alan drove up to the villa and saw Steve walking around the side. There were two cars parked outside, a grey Ford Mondeo and a blue Peugeot. He parked the car and got out and then followed the trail taken by Steve around the villa. The glass sliding doors were open and Alan went inside where he heard Sarah screaming and yelling at Steve, and as he entered the lounge he was confronted with Steve pointing a gun at Sarah and Phillip.

Steve turned to Alan.

"What the hell are you doing here?"

"I've come to stop you making an idiot of yourself by killing Sarah and Phillip. Put the gun down"

"Don't try and be clever. You know my rules. Nobody does

the dirty on Steve Mitchell and lives to tell the tale and that includes you as well as these two"

Sarah then screamed.

"I haven't got the money. I've already told Steve"

Alan was quite calm and spoke to Sarah.

"What's happened to the money Sarah?"

Sarah was sobbing as she replied.

"I opened an account with the Banco de Murcia when I was last in Spain. Phillip didn't know anything about it and when I was told to transfer the money, I didn't send it to his solicitor, I sent it to my account. I then booked a single flight to Spain so that I could move the money somewhere else and that's when I phoned Phillip and told him what I'd done. He told me I was stupid and booked a flight himself so he could come with me. When we arrived he told me to give the money back and we went to the Banco de Murcia this morning. I then transferred the money from my account to the account of Pepe Fernandez, his solicitor so he can now buy the villa. I've already told him all about this but he's not even listening"

"What made you take the money?"

"I suddenly realized that by using my name to move the money out of the country, I would be taking the blame if the police found out. He was using me and it was nothing to do with getting a better exchange rate from Phillip"

"Is that right Steve?"

"Any good criminal always covers his tracks. I'm the expert and I don't make mistakes or leave somebody behind who'll grass on me. Get over there Alan"

"Don't be such a bloody idiot Steve. You've got your money back and you can now buy this villa here in Spain. Sarah is your sister, okay she made a mistake but she's given you your money back. Mum's told me Sarah, you're having a baby and it'll be her first grandchild. I told Mum that I'd make sure you were okay, you're not going to kill the baby and Sarah are you Steve?

Give me the gun and let them get out of here"

"How many times do I have to tell you? Nobody does the dirty on Steve Mitchell and lives to tell the tale. That includes brothers, sisters, boyfriends and their babies"

Alan walked towards Steve hiding his view of Sarah and Phillip. The first of three shots were then fired and Alan fell to the floor. Phillip tried to grab hold of Sarah and turn her out of the way, when the second shot was fired and Phillip slumped to the floor leaving Sarah screaming wildly.

"Phillip, Phillip. Why have you done this to him, he's done nothing wrong. He saved your money"

Sarah then bent down to hold Phillip when the third shot was fired.

After a few seconds, Sarah looked up and saw three armed policemen. The one in front had fired the shot that killed her bother Steve. He then turned to Sarah as the other two checked Steve, Alan and Phillip.

"I'm Inspector Felipe Garcia. Are you okay?"

"No he's shot my brother and my boyfriend"

Felipe then knelt down to have a look at Phillip.

"He's still alive, get an ambulance quickly"

One of the policemen called the ambulance which arrived within ten minutes. Felipe had staunched the flow of blood before Phillip was taken into the ambulance with Sarah. The two brothers Alan and Steve were dead.

33

Alisa Garcia phoned David the following morning.

"Hello"

"Hola Senor Fraudo"

"Hola Alisa my love, how are you?"

"I'm fine, which is more than I can say for Steve Mitchell"

"What's happened?"

"He caught up with Sarah and Phillip and was about to kill them when his brother Alan arrived on the scene. Steve ended up shooting Alan dead and shooting Phillip, but he hasn't died. Felipe arrived just after the first two shots were fired and shot Steve Mitchell dead before he could turn the gun on Sarah. They operated on Phillip last night and he's regained consciousness this morning. Sarah is with him and he'll be okay and will be able to return home within a couple of weeks. Nobody has been informed about the death of the Mitchell brothers yet, not even their mother. I don't know if you want to leave it until we tell your police or do you want to start the arrangements?"

"I'll have a word with Anne Graham from Cheshire Police and see what she thinks"

"Would you like a visitor?"

"I hope you're talking about yourself?"

"Of course, I wouldn't mind having a week's holiday in your Lake District"

"You're more than welcome"

"I've got to go back to Seville today but I'll be able to come out in three or four days time. Is that a problem?"

"Nothing's a problem for you Alisa, I'll see you then. Let me know details of when you're arriving and I'll pick you up"

"Bye Senor Fraudo"

Anne Graham and David called to see Paula Mitchell but before they could ring the door bell, Paula answered the door.

"What's happened?"

"Can we come in?"

Paula didn't need to be told to sit down and you could tell from her face that she knew there was going to be bad news.

"You've got bad news, haven't you?"

Anne said.

"I'm sorry to have to tell you that your two sons have been killed in Spain"

"What about Sarah?"

"She's okay but Phillip was shot, but thankfully, he'll be okay. He's in hospital and will be home in a couple of weeks"

"What happened? You tell me"

Paula looked at David.

"I'm sorry but Steve shot Alan and Phillip. He was then shot dead by Spanish Police"

"Why would he kill Alan? I thought you might catch up with Steve"

"Alan died saving the life of Sarah"

"He was a good boy, he was led by Steve and did everything he told him. I'll go to Spain to see Sarah and Phillip. Is that okay?"

"Yes, but you should know that Phillip's parents are going to Spain today"

"That's okay, I'll go out in a couple of days after I've spoken to Sarah. Did the laptop help you?"

"Yes, we've got lots of details of the fraudulent activities but there are no names of those involved"

"Ron Thomas is the man you need to speak to. He knew what went on"

"Thank you Mrs Mitchell. You have my phone number if you need me"

"I'll ring you in a couple of days. Goodbye"

"Bye"

David and Anne left Paula Mitchell in her grief.

David's mobile rang two days later.

"Hello"

"It's Paula Mitchell"

"Hello Mrs Mitchell"

"I'm going to Spain later today and I'd like you try and arrange a deal with the police and all the companies involved in Steve's criminal activities. I want no action to be taken against Sarah or me and I'll return the million pounds, which was going to be used for the purchase of the villa. I know you'll probably take legal action to get this money but I'll save you the problem. I've already agreed with La Grande that they'll refund the money after taking out a cut for their expenses. I've heard that you've arrested Ron Thomas and he's admitted some part in the scams"

"I can't make any promises but I'll speak to the police and they'll talk to the banks and insurance companies"

"Thanks"

Anne Graham was not available when David rang the police and he, therefore, sent her an email message and received a reply later that day. Discussions had already taken place with the Crown Prosecution Service and the banks and insurance companies. They were going to start proceedings to obtain the monies that had been sent abroad, but, apart from Ron Thomas, no further prosecutions were being brought by the police. It was not considered to be in the public interest to make charges against Sarah and Paula Mitchell, with the deaths of the two Mitchell brothers, and there was insufficient evidence against anybody taking part in the skimming device and car crash scams. If Paula Mitchell was going to repay the million pounds, this would be the end of the matter even though it was felt that the frauds were much more than a million pounds. Anne also informed David that she would be visiting Paula Mitchell to discuss the repayment.

In the next few days, David was updated on the current situations with regard to Zoe Ferguson, Rik Jeffreys and Carl Sutherland. Zoe had agreed to make a repayment of one hundred thousand pounds. She had been escorted from the prison by the police, and taken to a location where she had hidden the money. She then handed over a hundred thousand pounds in cash. It meant she and Rik would not have to serve an extra year in prison. Carl Sutherland had given the authority for his house to be sold and the profit of eighty six thousand pounds was returned to the Pension Agencies.

A year later, Sarah Mitchell had married Phillip Harris and had a baby son, who they called Alan. Paula had bought them a house in Manchester as a wedding present. It had cost five hundred and fifty thousand pounds and was paid with Steve Mitchell's little nest egg. She had never told Sarah and Phillip where the money came from although they had their suspicions.

A few months later, Zoe and Rik had been released from prison and decided to make up their differences and get together again. They moved out of London and went to live in Basingstoke, near Zoe's mother and where Alice had been staying, whilst they were in prison. They both got jobs and were able to make a deposit of forty two thousand pounds on a new house.

David had been called in to investigate a dentist, who had fraudulently claimed hundreds of thousands of pounds over six years. The claims were for work completed on deceased patients, patients who had been living abroad for years, fictitious patients and work that had never been competed at all. They were examining all the claim forms that were held centrally when he was informed that the dentist had fled to Spain. It was time to talk to Alisa again and he returned to his Liverpool home that evening, where his Spanish long time partner Alisa was busy cooking the evening meal of Paella. Alisa was on a long term secondment, acting as a Liaison Officer for both the British Police and the Spanish Police, currently looking at extradition issues between the two countries. She had been living with David for the past six months. He hugged Alisa as he went into the kitchen before saying.

"My fraudulent dentist has gone to Spain and we think he's staying in Murcia. It must be time to visit Felipe. I'll have to report this fraud to the Spanish Liaison Officer in the British Police. Her name is Alisa Parish."

Alisa gave David Parish a playful punch on the arm.